# The
# H.A.L.
# Experiment

# The H.A.L. Experiment

## James Williams

*Nature vs. Nurture*
*with a twist*

iUniverse, Inc.
Bloomington

# The H.A.L. Experiment

iUniverse books may be ordered through booksellers or by contacting:

iUniverse
1663 Liberty Drive
Bloomington, IN 47403
www.iuniverse.com
1-800-Authors (1-800-288-4677)

ISBN: 978-1-4620-2283-0 (pbk)
ISBN: 978-1-4620-2284-7 (ebk)

Printed in the United States of America

iUniverse rev. date: 05/24/2011

For information about James's upcoming presentations and work, visit www.jamesmw.com

# CONTENTS

Chapter 1 .................................................................. 1
Chapter 2 ................................................................ 11
Chapter 3 ................................................................ 21
Chapter 4 ................................................................ 32
Chapter 5 ................................................................ 40
Chapter 6 ................................................................ 45
Chapter 7 ................................................................ 60
Chapter 8 ................................................................ 67
Chapter 9 ................................................................ 84
Chapter 10 .............................................................. 95
Chapter 11 ............................................................ 103
Chapter 12 ............................................................ 113
Chapter 13 ............................................................ 123
Chapter 14 ............................................................ 130
Chapter 15 ............................................................ 137
Chapter 16 ............................................................ 143
Chapter 17 ............................................................ 155
Chapter 18 ............................................................ 160
Chapter 19 ............................................................ 168
Chapter 20 ............................................................ 175
Chapter 21 ............................................................ 182
Chapter 22 ............................................................ 191
Chapter 23 ............................................................ 201
Chapter 24 ............................................................ 211

Chapter 25 ..................................................................... 217
Chapter 26 ..................................................................... 222
Chapter 27 ..................................................................... 230
Chapter 28 ..................................................................... 240
Epilogue ......................................................................... 245

To Nikki

*My best friend in the fifth grade*

There is nothing either good or bad but thinking makes it so.
                                                  —*William Shakespeare*

# Chapter 1

*March 17, 2010—2 p.m.*
*Buffett Elementary School, Main Hallway*

Ten-year-old Lenny was struggling in the fourth grade, both academically and socially. He didn't fit in with the other students in his class, who declared him an outcast. He had trouble taking notes in school, misunderstood most of what his teacher, Mrs. Redbear, said, and when he asked her to repeat what she'd just told the class, she'd reply, "Why should I? Everyone else understood me!" When Lenny complained that he did not get it, instead of helping him, the teacher told him that since he spoke English like everyone else, there was no excuse for why he couldn't understand her.

One of the saddest things about school, however, was that whenever he tried to tell people that kids were bullying him, instead of feeling sorry for him, they would say things like, *"That's a normal part of childhood," "Why haven't you extended the hand of friendship yet,"* or *"It's just your misperception, those kids are trying to be nice."*

Since no one in the adult world listened to him, no one knew what he was going through, no one cared about his suffering, and no one understood him ("Why should it hurt you? It doesn't hurt me!") or even tried to. Everywhere he felt

1

alone, even in a group of kids who were supposed to be his "peers."

Each morning, he woke up exhausted because of his chronic sleeping trouble, which no one would fix because, according to the adult world, "Children don't have sleeping problems," only to be fed what he perceived to be smelly white vomit for breakfast. Sometimes he would fall asleep in school, only to get punished as if he had done it on purpose, even though he could not really wake up until 11:00 a.m.

The "vomit" actually consisted of Cream of Rice, but it seemed like vomit to him, it smelled like vomit, and felt as slimy as vomit. He hated Cream of Rice, but no matter how much he complained, his parents would still feed it to him, and eventually they punished him for his complaints.

Then he went to school, which was a worthless waste since he spent more time afraid of being bullied than actually learning anything. In the winter months he was late for class each day because he had so much trouble tying the laces on his shoes when he had to change from boots to shoes. He hated shoelaces, and no matter how much he tried, he was unable to tie them tightly enough, and they automatically untied themselves five seconds after he started walking to his classroom.

Even though people had begun to invent devices to replace the laces on shoes, his mother would not buy them for him. So there he was in March, four days after spring break ended, walking down the school hallway as his shoelaces untied themselves, thinking that there were three more days to go until a promised weekend, three more months until the promised summer vacation, eight more years until the promised end of school when he was eighteen.

After a horrible day at school, he could not even relax as he had to cope with the homework that he struggled with each night. His mother was tired of helping him, causing him to fail his assignments and most subjects in school. At least she did make sure to remind him each morning if he had his homework with him before going to school.

The only bearable times in his life were the designated breaks from school and weekends, when he could just stay home, be himself, and possibly read his favorite comic books, such as *Chloe and Allie*. One good thing about Mrs. Redbear was that although she assigned difficult homework each school night, she did not assign homework on Fridays or weekends, viewing weekends as a time of rest. For Lenny, they truly were.

But often he thought: Why? Why did he have to suffer like this? Did other children feel this way? What had he done to deserve his life? In his mind, he acted the same way every other child in the world acted. And he wondered something else: He saw numerous advertisements for products that made people live longer. But why would anyone want to live longer? Given how miserable life is, wouldn't they be happy when it was over?

He also thought: Why was he never able to understand others? Why was he never able to figure things out the way other people could? And if he was the same as other children, why did he *feel* so different? Why did certain things hurt him when they did not hurt others?

Lenny was not autistic, or rather, he had never been diagnosed that way. Nor did he know about this disorder until he saw a famous autistic cattle woman on TV talking about how difficult it was for her to understand other people and the world.

*This is what I have*, Lenny thought, but he kept his conclusion to himself in case his mother found out and punished him for it.

However, on this morning, he wasn't thinking about autism or his mother, but rather, about how to avoid the bullies as he walked from his classroom to the office of the social worker, Mrs. Melanie Ting-Pot, or "Mel" for short, for his weekly visit. He hoped that she said something besides, "You *have* to play with other children. It says so in your IEP."

He was out of luck, however, for when he turned the corner, three school bullies—Othello, Macbeth, and Hector—were walking toward him. All were in the fifth grade, they always seemed to be together, and they would make fun of Lenny whenever they saw him.

"Hey," Othello called out, "why should a Nazi have the right to be in an American school?"

The bullies stopped and surrounded him.

"I—I am not a Nazi," Lenny stuttered in reply.

"Sure ya are," Macbeth taunted him. "Your name is Führer, and the Führer was the head of the Nazi party."

"It's Fahrer, not Führer," Lenny corrected him. Bullies are not known for their linguistic prowess.

"Close enough," Hector chimed in. "We're going to beat you up, *kraut*."

"I am not a Nazi," Lenny cried in despair. "I am an American." He covered his head with his arms and closed his eyes.

"Hey, what are you afraid of? Are you a chicken, too?" asked Othello.

"Yeah, he's chicken," Hector agreed. "Buck buck buck buck bu-gawk!"

Then all three bullies started dancing around him, flapping their bent arms like chickens. Most kids would laugh at this ridiculous behavior, but Lenny was terrified.

"Chic-ken chic-ken, Len-ny's a chic-ken!" they all chanted in unison.

"All right, all right, I'm a chicken," Lenny said with his eyes still closed, "but I'm not a Nazi."

"Of course you are! *Jawohl, mein Führer!*" Hector said. He was the worst one.

"Stop it!" Lenny cried, putting his hands over his ears.

"Are you s-s-scared of us?" said Macbeth. "Is that your problem, Nazi?"

Lenny realized it was hopeless to reason with these idiots so he pushed his way out of the circle of bullies, went into a corner in the hallway, sat down heavily on the carpet, and pulled the plug. He huddled into himself, his head down, and he stayed there. In the autistic world, this is called "cocooning," or "playing frozen."

"Hey, you *are* a chicken," said Hector. "A big fat chicken sitting on your nest."

Abruptly, Macbeth said, "Well, we gotta go, birdbrain. But when we come back, we better not see you here."

"Or else," said Othello.

Lenny looked up. "Or else what?" he said in terror.

"Or else you're gonna be dead meat that we feed to the cannibals."

"Cannibals?" Now Lenny was really confused. "Are there cannibals in Illinois?" He didn't know that some people ate other people in his home state.

"Of course there are, dummy," said Hector. "They have red faces and dress up in clothes made from human skins and they build their houses out of human leg bones and they chop off people's heads, scoop out the brains, and use their skulls as soup bowls. They eat the brains as a juicy appetizer. But you won't care 'cause you'll be dead."

"Stop it!"

Lenny looked around and immediately sighed in relief. Alice Meacham had come to the rescue. She happened to be going to the bathroom too.

Alice represented the one exception to all of the people who misunderstood him in his miserable life. She was his true friend, a girl who had been nice to him since the beginning of the year. They were in the same class together, and she defended him when others made fun of him. While he was rejected by the rest of his class, Alice would come over to Lenny's house, and they would have fun together. She, too, liked the same comic strip—*Chloe and Allie*—that he liked.

Alice accepted Lenny; however, Alice's friends did not. Lenny once tried to hang out with Alice and her friends Claire and Tammy, and Alice tried to get her friends to tolerate him, but they didn't. So Alice and Lenny made a deal that whenever she hung out with them, he would let them hang out together and she would pretend that she didn't know him. During lunch and recess, Alice hung out with them, and Lenny agreed to leave them alone. But whenever Lenny found Alice by herself, then she and Lenny would hang out together. This was also helpful for him, too, as he had a hard time hanging out with more than one person at a time.

Lenny felt that Alice understood him in ways others didn't. They did things that other ten-year-olds would consider weird. For example, they both loved to reenact scenes from *Chloe and Allie*, watch TV shows and movies they liked such as *Looney Tunes: Back in Action*, and just talk about their thoughts and feelings—something few fourth graders would ever do with a member of the opposite sex. Alice planned to come over to Lenny's house this weekend, and he looked forward to it all week.

"He's my friend, and he's not a cannibal!" Alice declared, looking the bullies directly in the eye, which would have been impossible for Lenny.

"Oh, so this is that girl you have a crush on!" Hector taunted Lenny. "You have a nice girlfriend there."

"We're just friends, so be quiet!" Alice exclaimed.

"I bet you two are in love. That's what you do over the weekend. Share your love together," sneered Hector.

"No, we don't. We just play games together. It's none of your business anyway."

Lenny yelled, "Yeah, shut up!" Then immediately he became afraid and put his head back down in his lap.

"You know what? I'm gonna beat you up if you don't admit you have a crush on Alice," warned Macbeth.

"Lenny and Alice sitting in a tree, K-I-S-S . . .," Othello sang, then paused. "K-I-S-S . . . um, E?"

Lenny's head was still in his lap, but he rolled his eyes in secret at such as imbecile.

"Stop it and go away!" shouted Alice.

Macbeth looked down the hall, nudged Othello, who nudged Hector, then they all just sauntered away.

"Thanks, Alice," said Lenny, looking up and making brief eye contact, as much as he could manage.

"It's fine. Don't let those morons bother you," said Alice.

"Lenny!" the stern voice of a middle-aged woman echoed through the hall. Lenny looked up and saw Mrs. Mel Ting-Pot coming toward him. That was obviously why the bullies had moved along.

They never teased other kids in front of adults, which was why the adults at Lenny's school denied that the bullying that Hector, Macbeth, and Othello did even existed.

"Hector," Mrs. Ting-Pot said as the three bullies passed her. "Have you seen Lenny Fahrer? He's supposed to come to his weekly visit with me."

"Yes, ma'am," Hector said politely. "He's right over there."

Spotting Lenny on the floor, Mrs. Ting-Pot shook her head. "I hope he did what he was supposed to do last week. Did he extend the hand of friendship to any of you last week? That's one of his IEP goals."

"No, ma'am," replied Macbeth.

"Well, have a nice day," Mrs. Ting-Pot said, nodding to the three boys. Then she walked over to Lenny and looked down at him. "Get up and come with me," she said curtly. "And remember what I told you? Don't spend all of your time with Alice. You need to make other friends as well—friends who are *boys*."

Obediently Lenny got to his feet, and Alice went into the bathroom. Inside, Alice noticed that paint had been peeled from the walls. She hoped that she didn't get in trouble or anything as she did what she needed to do and left.

As they went down the hall, Mrs. Ting-Pot continued, "I'm very disappointed in you, Lenny. I've told you over and over that you just have to extend the hand of friendship to the children around you. Why weren't you nice to those three boys? They just want to be your friends."

"They're bullies."

Mrs. Ting-Pot stopped walking and looked Lenny straight in the eye, which made him feel as if she were shooting him with arrows. "Bullies? No, no. They're nice boys. And we don't allow name calling in our school. Anyway, we are not here to discuss them, but rather you—why you refuse to make friends. They're only extending the hand of friendship to you, but you have misperceived their overtures, as usual. You can't spend all of your time hanging out with Alice. I know she's your friend, but you need other friends as well—friends who are *boys*." Every week it was the same thing.

"But they threatened to chop me up and feed me to the cannibals."

Mrs. Ting-Pot glared at him sternly. "I've heard many lies in my life," she said, "but none as bad as that. Now come to my office."

They resumed their progress toward the department named SPECIAL SERVICES, which was where all the kids who didn't fit in were supposed to learn how to do so.

"I'm not lying," said Lenny. "I can't do it. Whenever I try to lie, I feel so bad that I have to tell the truth. It burns a hole in my brain."

"But I've heard you before. Numerous times you have blamed Hector, Macbeth, and Othello for hitting you when all they did was extend the hand of friendship. That's what friends do."

*But that isn't what friends do,* Lenny thought. How many guys shook hands when they ran into their friends?

"Why don't you ever understand my point of view?" Lenny asked.

She replied, "Because your point of view differs from the average person's! And in this country, the rights of minorities do not prevail."

"But—but they called me a Nazi because of my name."

Mrs. Ting-Pot opened the door to her office and motioned for Lenny to come inside then sit at the small round table. When she was seated herself, she said, "Now, Lenny, kids say that kind of thing as a sign that they like you. Jokes are a sign of friendship. You had no reason to sit in the corner like that."

Lenny looked down at his hands. She acted like this every week. He felt like Mrs. Ting-Pot was not there to help him or learn about his thoughts and feelings but merely to have someone agree with everything she said.

"Yes, ma'am," he said mechanically. "Sorry, ma'am."

Mrs. Ting-Pot looked shocked. "Why, Lenny, that was wonderful," she said. "Your IEP says you are to learn to respond properly to adults in four out of five attempts with eighty percent accuracy. You were polite just now in your first attempt, with one hundred percent accuracy! I can check the box that says 'Sufficient progress' on your next status report! I'm so proud of you!"

"Yes, ma'am," said Lenny.

"That's two!" she exclaimed.

Lenny cringed, until he reminded himself that she was counting *up*, not counting him down for a punishment.

"Yes, ma'am."

"Would you like to see your IEP, Lenny?"

"Yes, ma'am."

"Why, that's three," she said, getting up and walking over to her file cabinet, where she looked through a drawer of IEP files until she found Lenny's. She got it out, opened it up, and then took it to Lenny. "I'm going to show you one goal you don't seem to be progressing toward."

She opened a page of Lenny's IEP, which showed some of his goals. He noticed one of them that said: *Lenny will become and remain friends with Othello, Macbeth, and Hector in four out of five attempts with 80% accuracy.*

"You see, Lenny? Your IEP says that you are to become friends with them. Your assignment this week is to extend the hand of friendship to Hector, Macbeth, and Othello, since they are hall monitors and thus models of good behavior," Mrs. Ting-Pot instructed Lenny.

"Yes, ma'am," Lenny repeated, although he no longer understood a word she was saying.

# Chapter 2

*March 17, 2010—3 p.m.*
*The Fahrer Residence*

Meanwhile, Christina Fahrer, Lenny's mother, was in her kitchen washing dishes when she looked at the time. Seeing that it was already three o'clock, she gasped and then felt the usual dread. In fifteen minutes, she would have to pick her weird son up from school.

At least today she would have a break from his standard complaints about bullies and teachers who talked too fast. Today she had an appointment with a local psychiatrist, Dr. John Griffiths.

As usual, when she got to his school, Lenny was sitting on the ground behind a tree while other kids tried in vain to talk to him. Christine shook her head as she saw her son bury his face in his lap, rejecting every overture of friendship.

"Lenny!" she called out her window, and immediately he jumped to his feet and ran to her car.

As he got into the back seat, he was happy and relieved that his ordeal was over for the day. But when his mother asked, "What happened at school today?" Lenny burst into tears.

"I was bullied by Othello, Macbeth, and Hector on the way to Mrs. Ting-Pot's office, and she yelled at me for not extending the hand of friendship to them."

Sighing her usual sigh, Christina said, "Lenny, I'm glad she did that. You know you have to make five friends by the time you graduate from the fifth grade. It says so in your IEP."

"But they're bullies!" Lenny sobbed. "Weren't you ever bullied in school?"

"Of course. Everyone is bullied. But I never complained about it. I always accepted it as a part of life. In fact, when I did complain, my father belted me for telling, and I never did it again. It was legal to hit your kids in those days. Not like today. It's a shame, too, kids having all these rights nowadays. All it's done is allowed children to think. That's your problem, Lenny. You think too much."

"I must clarify that," Lenny said, feeling better now that he had a philosophical topic to focus on. "The only people who think are the ones who are hurt. You are not hurt all day long, so that is why you do *not* think."

"LENNY!" his mother screamed. "I can't take this anymore! We are going to see Dr. Griffiths right now. Maybe he can figure out what's wrong with you."

Lenny did not know who Dr. Griffiths was, but he assumed that this doctor would be angry at him the way everyone else was.

When they got home, Lenny immediately started to take his shoes off, as his mother had taught him to do.

Christina went to check on the roast simmering in the slow cooker, then called out, "Keep your shoes on, put down your backpack, and get back in the car."

Lenny kept taking his shoes off, as he'd been programmed to do after being reprimanded for weeks.

Christina walked back out of the kitchen, then said sternly, "Lenny, I told you to keep your shoes on, put your backpack down, and get back in the car."

The tone of her voice caused Lenny to freeze. He knew now that he was doing something wrong. It took him a moment to process three commands in a row, but finally he retied his shoes as best he could and followed his mother out to the car.

Lenny climbed into the back seat, and his mother got into the driver's seat. They drove west on Westleigh Road to Green Bay Road, which they took north to Rockland Road, which became Scranton Avenue, where the doctor's office was located.

When they got to the doctor's office, the mom parked, and they got out of the car and entered the office building.

### 3:30 p.m.
### Dr. Griffiths's Office

Dr. Griffiths had a very small office, but he owned the entire building. He rented out the larger offices to other doctors so he could make enough money to survive.

Even though the waiting room was tiny, it was filled with chairs, a lot more than most of the other waiting rooms that Lenny had waited in. He was tired, so he lay down across a row of three padded chairs.

"Lenny, get up!" his mother ordered. "Other people need to sit in those chairs!"

Lenny looked around. No one else was in the room. The receptionist was on the phone and ignoring them, but Lenny recognized that his mother was embarrassed. He tried to lie down in every waiting room, and every time, his mother was embarrassed. Lenny, however, could not understand what she was feeling. Although he got angry and frustrated and confused, he had never been embarrassed, and did not know what it felt like.

"Lenny, get up!" his mother repeated, and he realized that he was still lying down. "You're ten years old! You should know better than to lie down in public!"

Lenny sat up, even though he felt uncomfortable doing so. He felt off-balance, and his back hurt. He was afraid of falling over unless he concentrated very hard on remaining seated.

The receptionist got off the phone, and said, "May I help you?"

The mother got up and walked toward the desk. Since her attention was turned away, Lenny immediately lay back down again.

"We have an appointment at four o'clock."

"Here are some forms to fill out," the receptionist said, handing them to the mom. When Christina turned back, Lenny immediately bolted upright before she could catch him.

For ten minutes, the mom scribbled answers on the forms, while Lenny looked forward to being in the doctor's office so he could lie down on the couch. That's what people always did when they went to a psychiatrist in the movies.

Finally, a bearded, white-haired man walked into the room and said, "Lenny? I'm ready for you."

Lenny and his mother followed the man into the therapy room. Lenny happily saw the couch and went over to lie down on it. That seemed okay with the bearded man.

"Lenny," he said gently, "my name is Dr. Jonathan Griffiths, and I will be your doctor today. Would you like to tell me why you're here?"

Lenny closed his eyes, but the question caused something in Lenny's mother to burst, and she sobbed and started her long, sad story.

"Lenny is . . . such a . . . difficult child. He always has been. He cries when no one else does, feels pains that no one else does, hears . . . noises that no one else does . . . and every day he complains about the kids in school. But it's not just school." She sighed, then her voice broke on another sob. "When he was only two years old, he tried to push visitors out of our house. Whenever I ask him to be nice to someone else, he clams up and won't talk. I know it's my fault. Oh, if I'd only been stricter with him . . ."

"Calm down, Mrs. Fahrer," the doctor said in a soft, kindly voice, which got Lenny's attention because it didn't hurt his ears. "It's not your fault. He could have a developmental disability . . . such as attention deficit disorder . . . or autism."

Now *that* got Lenny's attention. If he hadn't been so comfortable lying down, he might have sat up in surprise.

"Autism?" his mother gasped. "My child has . . . autism? Don't autistic children bang their heads and recite batting averages all day long? Lenny hates baseball."

"They don't always."

"And—oh, no—don't autistic people end up *killing* themselves?"

"Mrs. Fahrer," the doctor said with a hint of sternness in his voice, which even Lenny could detect. "If your child has autism, then *you* are the person who is most essential in making sure that he does *not* kill himself."

Lenny's mother started wringing her hands and rocking back and forth in an autistic manner herself. "He's my only child," she cried. "My little Lenny."

"Now remain calm, Mrs. Fahrer. I'd like you to tell me how Lenny behaved as a baby, whether you noticed anything different about how he acted when compared to other babies."

"Well . . ." The mom licked her lips and thought for a moment. "Because he is my only child, I can't really compare him to a normal baby. I do remember that he had an extreme startle reflex, and that when he was frightened and crying, picking him up and holding him made it much worse, as if he were afraid I would eat him or something. He reminded me of a cat, who was always trying to wiggle away when he could, or become completely still when he realized he could not get away. The only thing that would calm him down would be to sit by himself in his stroller facing the wall."

"I see. And do you recall how he behaved when he was eighteen months old? That's when these disorders often show up."

The mom thought. "Well, now that you mention it, I signed him up for a toddler swimming class, and your child had to be eighteen months old on the first day of class. He was exactly two weeks too young, so I falsified his birthday, moving it back two weeks. The first two sessions, he was a daredevil, jumping into the pool and giggling and trying to swim and splash. Another parent commented about how fearless he was, and I could tell that she was jealous because *her* child wouldn't even put his toe in the water, he just sat at the edge and cried. But on the third session, which would have been right when he really turned eighteen months, Lenny took one look at the pool and started screaming. He refused to go into the water, and he ran back into the locker room holding his ears. When I carried him back to the pool, he threw himself on the floor and started banging his ear against the tile."

"Hmm," Dr. Griffiths commented. "Now that's a significant indicator." He scribbled something into his notebook. "What did you do?"

"Well, I didn't know what to do at first. But then that other parent gave me this triumphant look, because now *her* precious angel was swimming just fine, and I"—she shook her head—"I just couldn't stand the embarrassment. The humiliation. So I picked Lenny up and threw him in the water. You know, sink or swim?"

Dr. Griffiths glanced over at the Lenny to judge his reaction to the story. Lenny continued to rest, although the memory of that torture was as immediate as if it were yesterday.

"So what happened?" the doctor asked.

"He sank."

Again, Dr. Griffiths looked over at Lenny to see if there was any reaction.

"He sank?"

"Yes. He dropped like a stone to the bottom of the pool. I saw his hair waving around like seaweed on the bottom. He actually sank and just sat down on the bottom of the pool. He didn't struggle or try to come up." She exhaled as if irritated by the memory. "I was so embarrassed when I had to jump in and pull him out. My hair was ruined. But little did I know that this was just the beginning. There were seven more weeks to the class, and I had to hold Lenny in the water the entire time. You really would have thought he was a cat, kicking and shrieking and clawing me for the entire half-hour that I held him there. I just couldn't look that other parent in the eye."

"I can understand how painful the entire experience must have been for you."

*Painful for her?* Lenny thought. *What about me?* He replayed the doctor's statement in his mind a few times. The other important word was "understand." Dr. Griffiths understood Lenny's mother. Therefore, it would be impossible for this guy to understand Lenny. Well, at least his couch was comfortable.

"Yes, yes, it has been," the mother replied, grateful that someone could, at last, sympathize with her plight.

"What about his language development? Could I ask Lenny some questions?"

"Oh, he was a late talker, but he's just fine now. He talks too much, in fact."

"Lenny?" the doctor asked.

"Lenny!" his mother commanded him sternly. "The doctor is speaking to you."

Lenny lifted his arm and started writing the alphabet in the air. This was something he did to calm himself down during moments of extreme stress.

"Lenny," the doctor repeated softly. "I'd like to ask you some questions."

Lenny remained silent.

The mother leapt to her feet. "I am SICK of this!" she screamed, then marched over to Lenny's side. "You answer Dr. Griffiths . . . or else."

"Shh," said the doctor. "Please be patient. Lenny is scared."

Now the mother was furious. "I DON'T CARE IF HE'S SCARED!" she roared. "WHEN SOMEONE ASKS HIM A QUESTION, HE HAS TO ANSWER!"

"Yes, that's true, but it's wrong to yell at him."

"WHO ARE YOU TO TELL ME NOT TO YELL! I'VE HAD TO ENDURE YEARS OF THIS!"

Lenny's eyes popped open, and he struggled to sit up. "Or else what?" he asked, his comprehension having gotten stuck on what his mother had said five statements ago.

The doctor turned his attention to Lenny. "I'd like to ask you some questions, Lenny, and I want you to tell me the answer that is in your mind, not what you think I want to hear."

"Or else what?" Lenny repeated.

"Lenny, there are no consequences for not speaking. But I'm hoping to get to know you better."

The doctor waited for Lenny to process this while the mother huffed and looked away.

"Now, Lenny," the doctor resumed, "do you have trouble understanding people?"

"Yes."

"Why? Do they talk too fast?"

The mom interrupted, "Don't put words into his mouth."

The doctor nodded as if he had heard that one before, then clarified, "That's good advice for a normal child, who needs to find his own way in the world. But for an autistic child who doesn't have the words to say what is in his mind, then by all means, we *need* to put words in his mouth, words that he can then use for himself . . . So Lenny, why can't you understand other people?"

Lenny looked down at his hands, as if he were afraid of what his mother might do to him. "Well . . ." he said softly. "They, um, they talk too fast."

"It must be horrible. I understand. And do you ever feel as if you do not know what is going on around you?"

Lenny looked quickly at this mother, then whispered, "Yes."

"Do you feel as if you are in danger, that any moment you might be murdered?"

"Yes! How do *you* know?"

The doctor smiled. "There are actually a lot of boys and girls just like you, and they feel just as confused. What do you do to comfort yourself?"

"I, uh, I . . ."

"Do you sit in a corner, roll into a ball, and get into your cocoon?"

Lenny's eyes lit up. "Yes. Yes! That's it!" Then his face fell. "Is that wrong? Are you going to punish me, too?"

"Who else has been punishing you?"

The mother raised her hands. "Don't look at me. I don't see him all day."

"Do you have any friends?"

"Yes, he has one friend," Christine blurted out. "A girl named Alice," the mom went on. "But she isn't a real friend. They just read comic books together."

"How do you feel about that, Lenny?" the doctor asked. "Do you want to have more friends?"

"No. Kids are mean."

"Well, then, would you be happier if you didn't go to school?"

"Yes."

"Maybe that will be possible."

The mother gasped. "What did you say? He has an IEP that says he has to—"

"Yes, yes, I know. Almost every child who walks into this office has an IEP, all written up in absurd scientific language as if they were a pigeon in a lab."

Lenny giggled, imagining himself to be a pigeon pecking Hector's eyes out.

"Lenny!" his mother admonished him. "It's rude to laugh."

"That's all right," the doctor reassured her. "Well, Lenny, I'd like you to take a short test. It's called the Barrington Autism

Diagnostic Test for Educational Staff and Teachers. It will take about thirty minutes, and there are no wrong answers."

Lenny laughed harder at that one. He couldn't stop laughing even when his mother gave him a stern look that warned of dire consequences when they got home.

# Chapter 3

Dr. Griffiths turned to Lenny's mother, who was about to reprimand Lenny for being rude. "Your son is quite perceptive. He's figured out the acronym for this test."

The mother thought over the words, then smiled a brief and unenthusiastic smile.

"BAD TEST," she mumbled.

"Before we begin, Mrs. Fahrer, I'd like you to leave the room. I think Lenny will feel more comfortable if he's not searching for the answer that you consider to be 'right.'"

"Leave the room? Why do I have to leave the room? I'm paying for this visit, aren't I?"

"Well, yes, but—"

"Then I get to watch."

"But that—"

"Otherwise we leave."

"That's not in Lenny's best interest. I promise, he won't feel a thing."

The doctor waited for someone to laugh at this attempt at humor. When no one did, he continued, "Your presence may distract him."

The mother exhaled wearily. She did that many times every day. "Very well, I'll leave." Secretly she was happy to get away from Lenny for a time and think only about herself.

After she left, Lenny said, "What are you really going to do to me? Are you going to hit me?"

"No, no, Lenny," the doctor reassured him. He stood up and got a book off his shelf. *Administering the Barrington Autism Diagnostic Test for Educational Staff and Teachers.*

He showed the cover to Lenny, then waited for the boy to laugh.

Lenny chuckled at the addition of "A" to "BAD TEST," then grew silent, waiting for the Bad Test to begin.

"The first part of the test involves some simple questions. First question: Two is to four as three is to . . ."

Lenny thought for a moment, then said, "Five."

"Why?"

"Because two was added to two to make four, so I added two to three, to make five. The rule is add two to the first number."

"I'll accept that. Second question: Which one doesn't belong: knife, fork, spoon, and broken glass."

"Spoon."

"Why?"

"Because it's the only thing that isn't sharp."

"I accept that. Now do you know the characters Bert and Ernie on *Sesame Street*?"

"Yes."

"Well, one day, Bert makes a peanut butter sandwich for himself and seals it in a dark container marked BERT so that Ernie can't find it. Then Bert walks away to do some work. Ernie comes into the kitchen, finds the peanut butter sandwich, decides he wants to save it for later, so he hides it to a dark container marked ERNIE. Then he also leaves. When Bert returns, in which container does he look *first* for the sandwich?"

"The container marked ERNIE."

"Why?"

"Because that's where it is."

"But why do you think Bert would know that?"

"I can't tell you that because I am not Bert."

"But can you imagine being Bert?"

Lenny thought for a moment, then said, "No."

"I'll accept that," said Dr. Griffiths. "Let's continue. I'm going to tell you a short story, and I want you to tell me what's wrong with it: A woman had the flu twice. The first time it killed her, but the second time she had a mild case."

"I . . . I don't get it," Lenny said, flinching, expecting the doctor to yell or punish him.

"Think harder. What happens when you get killed?"

"You die. What does that have to do with anything?"

"When you die, can you get sick again?"

"I don't know! I've never been dead! When you die, you go to heaven. So if she had the flu twice, the second time she was in heaven."

"I accept that answer," Dr. Griffiths said, although he was concluding that Lenny had the thought patterns of an autistic child. Then he decided to try something else. "Now I am going to say some numbers, and I want you to repeat them back to me: 1 5 3 8 6 9 5 4 8."

"1 5 3 8 6 9 5 4 8."

"Excellent! You're the first nine-year-old in this office who's been able to remember those numbers after hearing them just once."

"8 4 5 9 6 8 3 5 1."

Dr. Griffiths looked down at his book. "Why, Lenny, you recited them backwards. How did you do that?"

Lenny could do that because whenever he heard words, he typed them on the computer screen in his mind, then read them off the screen. It was easy to read those numbers backwards when they were typed on a screen.

"Now, Lenny, I would like you to arrange some blocks for me." He showed Lenny a series of arrangements made out of children's blocks, and he copied them all perfectly.

"Great. Now I want to show you some pictures." He showed Lenny a picture of a man and a woman. They both had short hair and were wearing jeans. "This is a picture of Robert and Mary. Point to Mary."

Lenny looked at the haircuts. No clue there. He looked at the jeans. No clue there. He looked at the eyelashes. They looked the same. He guessed and pointed to Robert.

The doctor showed Lenny a series of pictures, and each time he gave the wrong answer when asked to identify the women in the photo, since they all had short hair.

"Now, Lenny, I'm going to show you a series of pictures, and I want you to put them in the proper order and then tell me a story that illustrates the pictures."

Here is what Lenny saw:

Picture 1: Girl 1 is taking a piece of chalk from Girl 2.

Picture 2: Girl 2 is drawing on the sidewalk while Girl 1 is standing next to her.

Picture 3: Girl 2 is offering a piece of chalk to Girl 1.

Picture 4: Both girls are sitting on the sidewalk drawing with chalk.

Lenny looked at the pictures, confused about 1 and 3. They looked identical to him.

"Well," Lenny said, "I think the order is: 4, 1, 3, 2."

"Hmm," Dr. Griffiths said, not expecting that order. "Tell me the story."

Since Lenny had watched hundreds of movies in this life, he was good at dialogue.

"In the first picture, the two girls are drawing pictures on the sidewalk. Then one girl says, 'Can we trade chalk? Friends share with each other.' So the girls trade.

"The other girl doesn't like the new piece of chalk so she says, 'You tricked me. You gave me a bad piece of chalk. You're a bully.' She hands her piece of chalk back.

"The first girl says, 'Gee, you're weird. I'm not playing with you.' So she jumps up and just watches."

Dr. Griffiths wrote something on his sheet of paper.

Then he said, "I'll show you four more pictures. Put them in order, then tell me the story."

Here is what Lenny saw:

Picture 1: A teacher is in front of a class, saying, "Good morning, class!"

Picture 2: The teacher says, "We're going to have a test."

Picture 3: The teacher looks at one student and says, "John, are you paying attention?"

Picture 4: The students are busily writing on their papers.

Here is what Lenny said: "The correct order is 4, 3, 2, and 1."

"Hmm," said Dr. Griffiths. "I don't know how you got that sequence. Should the teacher say 'Good morning,' before she talks about a test?"

Lenny thought about this. He was usually confused by what other people said, and he couldn't remember what his teacher said first in the morning.

"Yes," Lenny said, because he had learned through experience that when he didn't know the answer to a question, saying "yes" often worked.

"Now, Lenny, here is the final sequence, which is also the final question on the test."

This made Lenny happy because it meant he could soon go home.

Here is what Lenny saw:

Picture 1: A boy and a girl are playing chess in a backyard.

Picture 2: A boy and a girl are leaving their house.

Picture 3: A man is saying, "You should go outside and get some fresh air!"

Picture 4: A boy and a girl are playing chess inside a room. A man is saying: "Are you going to sit inside all day?"

Lenny thought about this, or rather, he tried to think, but all he could focus on was the fact that he was going to be released soon.

Finally, Lenny said: "The correct order is 1, 2, 3, 4."

Dr. Griffiths knew then that Lenny had stopped processing information, so he said kindly, "We're all finished, Lenny. You did a great job." Even though this was one of those lies that normal people tell to disguise an uncomfortable truth. "Now I would like you to sit in the waiting room while I talk to your mother."

"Did I pass the test?" Lenny asked anxiously.

"There are no right answers," the doctor said, "but do you ever feel confused or alone even when you are in a group of people, or different from the kids around you?"

"Yes, all the time."

"Well, you are correct in your feeling. You *are* different."

"Am I sick?" Lenny cried.

"No, no, you're quite well. But let me talk to your mother first."

Lenny left, and the doctor called Lenny's mother into the office. She looked like she was ready to burst into tears.

"Is my son going to be all right?" she asked.

"Do you want to hear the good news or the bad news first?"

"What bad news? Oh, Doctor, what's wrong with him?"

"Well, I have to tabulate the results, but from Lenny's unconventional answers, I would say that he has high-functioning autism."

Christine gasped. "Oh, no! Lenny is going to become the next Rain Man?"

"No, Mrs. Fahrer, Lenny is much more high-functioning than that. In fact, the good news is that Lenny has a much higher chance of succeeding in life than Rain Man. You should be thankful for that. But the person who has the most control over Lenny's future is . . . you."

"Me?" Christine exclaimed. "What do I have to do with this? I didn't make him autistic! What is high-functioning autism anyway?"

"Before I tell you the official answer to that question, I want you to know that what we call 'autism' and the symptoms of autism are not the condition itself. What we call 'autism' is actually the behaviors of all human beings who are the victims of stress and discrimination. Have you ever read about how black people acted when they were enslaved? And do you remember how Gandhi taught his fellow Indians to defend themselves against the British? He told them to freeze and become inert because they couldn't fight back with weapons or force. Autistic people employ the same method of resistance."

Christine nodded. Lenny did freeze up a lot.

"It is my belief that autism is a small neurological disorder that causes big problems. Although some of those problems are unavoidable, most of them stem from the age-old instinct that people have to exterminate those who are different."

"But I've always tried my best to take care of Lenny and to give him what he needs."

The doctor nodded. "I am sure that you tried. Unfortunately, what you have tried to do has probably made his autism worse."

"How can that be?"

"Lenny, as his test results will show, does not think or reason the way you and I do. He does not understand the flow of normal events, and as a result, he feels that his life is unpredictable and, therefore, he experiences a constant sense of danger. He is like a preyed-upon wild animal, never sure when a predator is going to pounce on him from behind a bush. Because of this, his five senses have become overdeveloped, as if they are constantly looking out for danger. He perceives things at an extreme level, which keeps his nervous system in a constant state of stress. For example, when the bell goes off for a normal fire drill in school, an ordinary child is startled but he knows and can reason that the bell is harmless and he is in no danger. His nervous system calms down after a few minutes. But an autistic person cannot calm himself down. And he cannot reason that the bell is harmless. To him, the bell could be signaling the end of the world.

"Another example is change. When your schedule changes, you can reason that everything will still be okay. But the autistic person cannot predict that everything will be okay, so he becomes panicked that the new schedule, which he is not familiar with, might expose him to some new danger. Autistic people do not understand a lot of what is going on around them and why people do the things they do. An autistic person relies on experiences, not predictions or reasoning, to feel safe. So when something changes, he can no longer feel safe, because he has no idea what the change may mean."

"Oh, my poor Lenny!" Mrs. Fahrer wailed. "What can we do to treat him?"

"Autism itself is an untreatable condition. It lasts a lifetime."

"Oh no!"

"However, there are ways to reduce or eliminate the symptoms of autism, which are causing the problems. It is up to you now to help Lenny become functional as an autistic person."

"What can I do? Is it expensive?"

"Well, first, you must reduce the stress and unpredictability in his life. Stress will eventually ruin his health, and I have even known autistic individuals who committed suicide rather than try to live in a world that was not set up for them."

"But the world is what it is. How can I change it?"

"There are many things you can do. First, you must stop trying to change him, stop yelling at him, and start listening to him. You have to honor what he says, respect his wishes, and accept him as he is right now. You should reward him for the good things he does, for autistic people are some of the most kindhearted and moral individuals I have ever known. Next, I would greatly recommend that you pull Lenny out of school and homeschool him."

"HOMESCHOOL HIM?" Christine screamed, so loudly that Lenny heard her in the waiting room. Instantly he jumped up and went to the door so he could eavesdrop on the conversation. He was liking this Dr. Griffiths more and more.

"Yes," the doctor said firmly, "and I think you will see big changes in him. For one thing, it is torture for an autistic child to have to sit still at a desk all day. They simply cannot do it. They also feel trapped and tortured because they are confined in a noisy building with horribly loud bells blasting their ears all day long. Also, they are subjected to the wrong kind of socializing. You see, most children hate being confined to a classroom with people they have not chosen to befriend, so they take their anger out on the weaker children, like Lenny, who do not know how to fight back."

"But homeschooling . . ." she protested, thinking about how she would endure Lenny's presence all day long.

"It's your choice. But if you can't do it yourself, there are professionals who understand autistic people, and they can do it for you. There are no rules governing homeschooling in Illinois, as long as Illinois history is taught at some time. There haven't been any restrictions since 1950."

Christine was silent for a moment. Lenny pressed his ear to the door more firmly so he wouldn't miss a word.

Finally she said, "I'm not sure I can do this. But I might be willing to let someone else try."

Lenny sighed in relief, smiled to himself, then walked back to the empty row of chairs and lay down. Maybe there was hope for him after all.

From the moment they left the doctor's office, Lenny's mother was so scared and sad that she now thought her life was hopeless. Her son was autistic. It was just too much for her. She cried and cried, and whenever Lenny tried to comfort her, she would yell at him. After all, it was his fault that he was causing her to cry. *He* had autism.

## 5 p.m.
## The Fahrer Residence

When they got home, she asked Lenny to go up to his room and remain there. She wanted to be alone. Lenny did, and his mother spent the rest of the afternoon calling all her friends and drowning them in her sorrows. She even called the school and made an appointment to discuss this tragic thing that her son now had.

Lenny decided to start on his homework. He had been assigned two math worksheets and had to do his 20 pages of reading. He decided to do the reading first, as that was easiest for him before doing the math, which he knew he would struggle with.

Lenny listened to each conversation through the floor while doing his reading, and then as he struggled with his math, and he, too, felt a horrible sadness come over him. It *was* his fault. *He* was responsible for making his mother cry.

The phone calls went on for hours. Lenny finally finished all his homework, but still the wailing and the tears continued. When Lenny's father, Marty, came home at seven, the crying still had not stopped. Marty asked what was going on, and between sobs and "Hang on, Judy, I'll be right back," Christine explained that their son had a hopeless condition called autism and that their lives were now ruined.

"But autism should not—" Marty began.

"Hang on, Judy," Christine said into the phone again, then turned her attention to her husband.

"Autism should not be seen as a death sentence," Marty explained calmly, always taking the other side of any position. "It's not Lenny's fault that he has a disability."

"Whatever," Christine replied, then turned her attention back to her phone call.

"Is there any dinner?" Marty asked hopefully.

Christine shook her head as she walked over to a chair and threw herself into it.

The crying continued well into the night. Marty heated up some leftover pizza, and he and Lenny ate in silence. Lenny didn't say anything for the rest of the day, for he knew that, just like in a courtroom, anything he said could and would be used against him. No matter what his father said to comfort, or argue with, his mother, it did not work. The crying continued.

It continued far into the night. The noise was so loud that Lenny could not sleep. He didn't remember when he fell asleep, but when he woke up, it was morning, and the crying had stopped.

That made Lenny happy. What also made him happier was the anticipation of his playdate with Alice, when he looked forward to telling her all about his new diagnosis.

# Chapter 4

*March 18, 2010—12 p.m.*
*Buffett Elementary School Cafeteria*

The next day at lunch, Alice sat with her friends Claire and Tammy, as always. Although Buffett Elementary had a hot lunch program, Alice's mother made a lunch for Alice every day.

"Peanut butter and jelly again," complained Alice. "My mom always gives it to me."

"Yeah, we know," said Claire. "Hey, Alice, want to see the new silly bands I got?"

Alice politely nodded. She wasn't that interested in silly bands, but still was willing to listen to Claire in order to maintain their friendship. Friendship to her often meant listening and hearing things she really couldn't understand. However, the motivation to remain friends was strong enough so that she would listen to them politely.

"This weekend Liz showed me the ones she got at Disney World," said Tammy.

This did interest Alice, who enjoyed watching Disney Princess movies, although Liz was one of Tammy's friends that didn't get along well with Alice. Just as Lenny didn't play with Claire and Tammy, Alice never played with Liz.

"What Disney Princess bands did she get?" Alice asked politely.

"Snow White, Cinderella, Belle, Ariel, and Jasmine."

"Okay, so I traded my two red car bands for two turtle bands. I love turtles," said Claire. She took a yellow band off her right arm to show that it was shaped like a turtle.

"Did you trade any with Liz?" asked Alice.

"Oh, no, she wouldn't do that," said Claire. "She wanted to keep them."

"So have you bought any more silly bands, Alice?" asked Tammy.

"Oh yeah," Alice lied. In reality, she hadn't bought any and had no interest in buying them. "Got a kitchen pack. With knives and forks and stuff."

"Can we see them?" asked Claire.

"No, sorry. My mom doesn't let me bring them to school," Alice replied, continuing her lie.

"Your mom is crazy," said Claire. "Really. You should be allowed to bring them. Even Dr. Wikedda says it's okay to bring them to school."

"So what colors of Princess bands did Liz get?" asked Tammy.

"Blue, green, red, and yellow."

"How is your book report going, Claire?" asked Alice, hoping she could change the subject from silly bands.

"Good," said Tammy. "I'm now reading the second Harry Potter book."

"Is that hard to read?" asked Alice. She liked the movies but had not read the books.

"Not really," said Claire. "Besides, I only have to read one book this month because of Mrs. Elderton's rule."

"What's that rule?" asked Tammy. "I thought you had to read two books a month."

"Yes, but Ms. Elderton lets us read only one book if it's over three hundred pages. And the Harry Potter book's longer than that."

"So are the books like the movies?" asked Alice.

"They're different, and a lot more detailed. The movies cut out a lot from the books," said Claire.

"Like what?"

"Well, in the second book, there's a ghost party that Harry goes to. But in the movie, the party doesn't take place."

"A party? What happens there?" asked Alice.

"It's the celebration of Nearly Headless Nick's five hundredth deathday."

"Wow, I didn't know that was there," said Alice.

"Yep," said Claire. "And it's funny, too. The ghosts all celebrate, and Peeves makes his usual insult."

"Who's Peeves?"

"Oh, he's not in the movie. Peeves is a poltergeist, a ghost that makes trouble for others."

"What does he do?" asked Alice.

"Oh, he causes trouble and says crazy things. At the deathday party, he makes fun of Moaning Myrtle," said Claire.

"So where are you now in the book?"

"At the part where Harry is hearing voices in the walls."

"At Lockhart's office?" asked Alice. "Or when the writing is on the wall? Is it as scary as in the movie?"

"Yep," said Claire.

"Not again," Tammy groaned. She didn't share their interest in Harry Potter, but she had to put up with it, at least for a while. "Do you like my new earrings?"

"I didn't see them," said Alice, leaning over.

"See?" Tammy pulled back her hair to show Alice.

"What are they?"

"They're crystal heart earrings. I like the crystal lining on the hearts."

"Where did you buy them?" asked Claire.

"I bought them at Claire's. Just like your name," said Tammy, giggling.

"I love Claire's. Did you see those pillows they have?" asked Claire.

"No," said Alice.

"Well, you might like them," said Claire.

"What?" Alice was no longer paying attention.

"They have these special pillows for each letter of the alphabet," said Claire. "I'd buy a C for myself, a T for you, Tammy, and an A for Alice."

"Does it hurt to get your ears pierced?" asked Alice. She had not gotten her ears pierced.

"It does, but it's worth it," said Tammy. "You should get your ears pierced. You're the only girl I know who hasn't done it. I couldn't wait until I was eight and my mom let me get them pierced."

"Yeah, you should. I love my earrings," said Claire.

"I just don't know. I never really liked earrings," said Alice. The thought of having needles pushed into her earlobes was making her queasy, and she couldn't concentrate on anything besides that.

"Meanwhile, that gross boy Todd has done it again," Tammy said. "Today he interrupted the teacher *again*, and didn't raise his hand. He just blurted something out."

"And he hums in class all the time," said Claire. "I wonder how anyone could be his friend."

"Boys act gross anyway," said Tammy.

"I don't know how you stand Lenny," Claire said to Alice. "I could *never* be friends with a boy."

"He's not my friend," said Alice, following the social rules of girl groups.

"I see you talking to him," Tammy persisted.

"Tammy, I've told you before. He's just a boy in my class."

"Are you sure he's not your friend?"

"Yes!"

"Well, anyway, Todd is just crazy. I see him do so many gross things."

"What has he done now?" asked Claire.

"Well, not only does he interrupt, but he wears these weird clothes. He always comes in these black sweatpants, and these shirts with crazy sayings."

"Like what?"

"Like, 'I have twelve toes. Do you?' Or, 'I wanna love you.' Like anyone would love *him*."

"That is crazy," Claire agreed.

"Well, what can I say? Boys are just weird."

"I agree," said Alice. "Three boys that I think are crazy are Hector, Macbeth, and Othello. You know them?"

"Oh, those hall monitors! They think they're *so* important," said Claire.

"They're horrible," said Alice. "They make fun of me all the time."

"They're just weird boys," said Claire. "But then, that's how all boys are."

"Yep. I wonder why they even exist," said Tammy. "Girls act so much better and so much more nicer."

"Of course, there is one boy who is not gross," said Claire.

"Who's that?"

"You know," said Claire. "Justin Bieber." She sighed dramatically.

Alice was silent. She didn't like Justin Bieber, but her friends obsessed over him. Alice didn't understand the paradox—why was it that they felt that boys were gross, yet they acted madly in love with Justin Bieber, a boy that, ironically, none of them would probably ever get to talk to.

"He's so *cute*," Tammy sighed.

"And I can't wait until I get a copy of Justin Bieber's new CD?" asked Claire.

"Your mom's going to buy that for you?" asked Tammy.

"Yep," said Claire. "Next week, it's finally coming out. *My World 2*.0. I've been waiting for it now for a whole month. I'm looking forward to being able to listen to it on my iPod, and to just own his music."

"So would you like to be a hall monitor?" asked Alice, hoping to change the subject. She couldn't care less about Justin Bieber or facts about his life.

"Alice!"

The three girls looked up to see Dr. Wikedda's secretary at their table.

"Alice, please come with me to the principal's office."

"What's wrong?" asked Alice.

"Dr. Wikedda wants to see you."

Alice shoved the rest of her lunch into her lunch bag, got up, and followed the secretary, who led her to the principal's office. On the one hand, she felt scared, not knowing how she had gotten into trouble. On the other hand, she felt happy that she didn't have to continue listening about silly bands, earrings, Todd, or Justin Bieber.

In the office, the principal, Dr. Wikedda, asked Alice to sit down in one of the chairs. Alice did not come alone—two other girls, Mary and Lori, also came to the office. Alice did not know either of them.

"Girls, sit down."

"Yes," said Alice.

"Alice Meacham, Mary Bettendorf, and Lori Roselle. You are called in here today because in recent weeks, the girls' bathroom in the center hallway has been defaced."

"What do you mean?" asked Mary.

"Someone has been peeling the paint off the walls of the girls' bathroom," said Dr. Wikedda. "Have you noticed that there have been holes in the paint on the stall doors and other walls? The custodian just painted all the bathrooms, and he's very upset."

"Yeah," said Mary.

"Well, a girl whose name I will not say told me that you three peeled all of that paint."

"I didn't peel a single piece of paint off a wall," said Lori.

"Neither did I," said Mary.

"Me neither," said Alice.

"Well, the truth is, I already had someone willing to tell me that you girls peeled the paint. And even worse, I was told that Alice here was in charge of your group, and told you, Lori and Mary, to peel the paint."

"What?" cried Alice, completely confused.

"And the hall monitors *saw* you walk into the vandalized bathroom yesterday. I asked them if they had seen anybody right after discovering the paint had been peeled. And they told me they saw you, right after you talked back to them while they were trying to comfort that boy . . . what's his name again? Your friend?"

"Lenny?" Alice said in a daze.

"You see, you *do* know what I'm talking about. They reported seeing you going into that bathroom right before the vandalism was discovered. Until I can find someone else to admit that they peeled the paint, all three of you will suffer the consequences. You will all have to stay in for recess, starting next Monday. Although Alice may have decided to peel the paint, I will punish you all equally. After lunch, starting on Monday, and for the rest of the week, you will report to the principal's office."

"This is so unfair. Who told you that we peeled any paint, or that Alice told us to, someone I don't even know?" cried Lori.

"That I will not tell you," said Dr. Wikedda.

"Why?" asked Alice.

"Because, Alice, if I told you, you could use that information to try to make yourself innocent," said Dr. Wikedda. "The fact is, you will be staying in for recess for a week, and if you don't, you will get detention."

"But what if you find out that we didn't peel the paint, like we tell you," said Lori. "Then what?"

"Okay," said Dr. Wikedda. "If I do find out that someone else did peel the paint, by Monday, you will not have to stay in for recess. But since there are four witnesses, Alice, it looks like you're the guilty party. You girls may go back to recess now for today and then, back to class, but report here after lunch on Monday."

# Chapter 5

*March 18, 2010—12:45 p.m.*
*Buffett Elementary School, Mrs. Redbear's Classroom*

Lenny was not the same boy that he was the day before. Now Lenny was a boy with autism. Lenny had a condition that marked him as different. Unfortunately that knowledge didn't change the way the world treated him, and it didn't change his life. He still sat at his desk in school that afternoon, after lunch and recess was over, unable to understand what his teacher was reading to the class for their daily Social Studies lesson.

"Today we are going to learn about Frederick Douglass," said Mrs. Redbear, Lenny and Alice's teacher, then she began to read from their textbook. "'Frederick Douglass was an abolitionist who was born in 1817. He . . .'"

Although Lenny knew that she was introducing somebody, he did not know what "abolitionist" meant. He tried and tried to think about what that could mean and where he had seen the word before. He still struggled to remember where he had seen that word when his teacher had already finished the first paragraph and was on to the next one. Lenny wondered why teachers spoke and read so quickly, unaware that some of their students could not keep up. He turned his attention away from the teacher's voice and started to think again: Had he ever heard the word "abolitionist" before? He had heard about slavery, but this had been the first time he had heard the word "abolitionist." He was so determined to find out what the word meant that he raised his hand in despair.

"Do you need any help, Lenny?" Alice whispered to him from two seats away, still upset from what happened to her over lunch. Alice would often ask if he needed help in class, but Lenny was too scared to say yes for fear he would get in trouble.

"No," whispered Lenny.

Mrs. Redbear stopped reading and said impatiently, "Yes, Lenny? I see you've interrupted me again. I've told you many times you're not supposed to do that."

"Uh," he began, "what's an abolitionist?"

The rest of the class erupted in laughter.

"Does Lenny need the paragraph repeated because he wasn't paying attention or didn't understand . . . again?" She seemed to be addressing everyone except Lenny.

"And Alice," she said, this time looking straight at her, "don't think I didn't hear you offering Lenny help. You know that would be cheating. You offer help again and I'm sending you to the principal's office."

Mrs. Redbear was unaware that Alice had already been to the principal's office earlier that day for lunch.

Realizing that he could not tell the truth without being made fun of, Lenny lied and said, "No, I don't. It's just that I, uh, I have to go to the bathroom," which, in fact, was true because he had been holding it in, afraid that he would get teased for having to ask.

Mrs. Redbear sighed. "Very well, if he needs to go, he may," she said, again seeming to address the rest of the class instead of Lenny.

So Lenny left the room, hoping that he would not be teased by the bullies, and walked toward the bathroom.

But out of sheer bad luck, Othello, Macbeth, and Hector happened to be walking down another hall, coming toward him. He also saw his mother walking down the hallway. This shocked him, but he decided not to say hello out of fear he'd get the bullies' attention. And then, he noticed that Maddie was also in the hallway. She was the worst girl bully in the school, and she made fun of everyone. Sometimes she even made fun of Hector.

Lenny looked for somewhere to hide. To his left was the boys' bathroom. If he went in right now, the bullies might not see him.

As he heard their voices, he ducked into the bathroom and hid behind the door. He sighed in relief as they walked on by.

Peeking from behind the door, Lenny saw their backs disappearing in the distance, and he raced into one of the stalls.

Lenny pulled down his jeans and tried to relax. However, he heard the murmur of voices, coming nearer. He always used the stalls—never the urinals, because he lacked the motor skills to unzip his zipper, and used to get made fun of for having his pants fall down to his ankles. The stalls were a lot safer.

"Stop. Wasn't Lenny just here?" asked Hector in the hallway.

"He went in there," Lenny heard Maddie say. "You can ambush him—I can't, I'm a girl."

Then Lenny heard the bathroom door burst open and the sounds of heavy shuffling footsteps echoing in the tiled room.

"Well, if he's here, I'll call him a turkey to get him out of where he's hiding. I have to pee," Hector announced.

"Hurry up," Macbeth said impatiently.

Quickly Lenny sat down on the seat, pulled his legs up against his chest, and held his breath as he heard approaching footsteps. Then BANG! went the door to his stall. In his haste and fear, Lenny had forgotten to slide the lock.

Hector looked at Lenny, then at the jeans wrapped around his ankles.

"Why are you in here?"

"I'm here to use the bathroom," said Lenny.

"Liar. You came in to hide from us, turkey."

"I came to go to the bathroom," Lenny insisted.

"You're lying so we won't make fun of you, or beat you up! You better answer me . . . why are you in here?"

"It's . . . it's . . . none of your business," Lenny declared.

With one hand, Hector grabbed him by the collar and pulled him to his feet. With his other hand, the bully made the universal sign for a gun, with thumb upraised and index finger pointing straight out at Lenny's forehead.

"Say that to me again," Hector snarled, pointing his index finger into Lenny's face, "and I'll kill you."

Lenny's defiance died.

Hector dropped Lenny roughly back on the toilet seat and quickly left the stall. Lenny pulled up his pants and ran out of the bathroom.

To his surprise, his mother was still in the distance, standing in the hallway. What was she doing at school? He hoped she wouldn't see him—so he flattened himself against the wall. As soon as the three bullies pushed their way through the door, Lenny slipped back into the bathroom.

As Mrs. Fahrer spotted the boys and started walking their way, they quickly put phony smiles on their faces. Maddie went into the girls' bathroom since she wasn't in the mood to be phony.

"Why, Hector," Mrs. Fahrer exclaimed. "And Macbeth and Othello. How nice to see you again."

"Thank you, ma'am," Hector replied with his best fake voice.

"I heard you all have become hall monitors. I certainly wish that my Lenny would be as successful in school as you all are."

"Thank you," said Othello with his own false voice.

Mrs. Fahrer said to Hector, "When my son extends the hand of friendship to you, dear, as he's been told, please say yes."

"Why, of course, Mrs. Fahrer," Hector crooned.

As she walked away, the three bullies kept their phony smiles in place until she turned the corner and disappeared down the hall. Then their lips dropped into their normal sinister and threatening snarls.

Hector pulled open the bathroom door and taunted, "Did you hear what your mother said, turkey? You have to 'extend the hand of friendship.' Give me your hand so I can break it off and watch you gobble."

Suddenly someone else called out, "Lenny? Is Lenny Fahrer in there?"

Mrs. Redbear came into view, and the three bullies immediately smiled again.

"Oh, Lenny," Macbeth said sweetly through the open door, "your teacher's looking for you."

"I'm here," Lenny said meekly, walking out of the bathroom.

"Come back to class now. You're taking too long," she chided him.

"Okay," he said.

And so Lenny returned to class, having been unable to go to the bathroom.

# Chapter 6

*March 18, 2010—1:00 p.m.*
*Buffett Elementary School, Dr. Wikedda's Office*

Meanwhile, as Lenny was trying to hold it in back in class, other matters concerning him were taking place in the principal's office.

Just like Lenny, I'm sure you're wondering why Lenny's mother was inside the school that day. Remember that she was still in denial about her son's diagnosis, so she made an appointment with the school principal to discuss what Dr. Griffiths had said. And as Lenny was walking uncomfortably back to class, his mother was walking to the principal's office for the meeting. She waited in the waiting room for Dr. Wikedda, who was late.

"I'm sorry to keep you waiting, Mrs. Fahrer," the principal said as she hurried into the room. "I had to meet with the custodian about repainting one of the bathrooms. We caught three girls who were peeling the paint off the walls."

Mrs. Fahrer thought, *Huh. And they think my son is autistic! What about those girls?*

The principal sat down at her desk and said, "So what seems to be the problem?"

"From the moment my son entered this school five years ago, he has complained about being teased and having no friends at all even though he refuses to try to make them. He thinks nice children such as that Hector are bullies when it's Lenny who refuses to extend the hand of friendship."

The principal nodded her head sympathetically.

Mrs. Fahrer continued, "Finally, I snapped, and last week I couldn't take his complaints anymore. I took him to see Dr. Griffiths, a psychologist in Highland Park. He gave Lenny something he called the BADTEST. Are you familiar with it?"

"Yes, I am. It's used to diagnose autism, I believe."

"You're right, it's . . ." Then her eyes once again filled with tears, which began to run down her cheeks and smear her makeup. "It's a test to determine whether a child has autism. And that's what Dr. Griffiths said! My poor Lenny has autism! How can that be? No one else in our family has that horrid condition."

"Autism is on the increase, Mrs. Fahrer, although we still don't know why."

"And the worst thing," Christine wailed, "is that Dr. Griffiths said I should take Lenny out of school and . . . and homeschool him! Can you imagine?"

Since Dr. Wikedda was the principal of a public educational institution and her salary depended on having students in her building, no, she could not imagine homeschooling any child.

"Why did he say that, I wonder, after only a single assessment. Before you do anything, you should be certain of the diagnosis. Many children who are diagnosed with autism on the basis of a test really do not have the condition at all. Also, since it is a disorder involving socially unacceptable responses to the environment, adapting that environment to fit the child is . . ."

Dr. Wikedda paused. She was about to state a case in favor of homeschooling.

"But how can I disprove a standardized test?" Christine asked.

"Although standardized tests are accepted in the field of psychology, we educators do not automatically trust them," Dr. Wikedda replied.

"But last year at the parent meeting, when we were complaining about all the standardized tests our kids had to take, you said they were the most efficient measurement available today."

"I said that? Oh, yes, well," Dr. Wikedda sputtered, realizing she had contradicted herself. "What I mean is that you cannot trust standardized tests to diagnose autism."

"Then how *do* you diagnose it?"

"Well, you look at a child's behavior. How he moves, whether he makes eye contact with you when he speaks. And come to think of it, Lenny does behave like an autistic child. I haven't seen many in my day, but the numbers keep increasing."

"He acts just fine at home," Christine countered. She knew that wasn't quite true, but her Lenny was just shy, certainly not seriously impaired.

Dr. Wikedda found herself in a state of conflict. On the one hand, as the principal, she was obligated to toe the party line and insist that public school was the best place for all children. But as a doctor, even a lowly Ed.D., she had to support the opinions of a fellow doctor. On the other hand, Dr. Wikedda was actually a sincere person, who did not live up to her name. She had her own opinions about disorders such as autism.

"That could be true," Dr. Wikedda said finally. "And maybe a change of environment is what he needs to help him make friends and feel more comfortable. You have the legal right to educate him at home, where you say he feels comfortable and doesn't give you trouble."

"But how can I do that?" Christine wailed. "I do not know how to teach."

"I think I might have a solution for you. I know a woman who wants to start a charter school for autistic kids, based on what we've just talked about—that changing an autistic person's environment can change his autistic behavior. She hasn't gotten her project off the ground yet, so I'll bet she'd consider tutoring Lenny for a brief period of time—say, two months. That should give us time to see whether environment is really a factor in his behavior. We'll still let him associate with that girl Alice Meacham, and modify his IEP a bit to say that interacting with Alice indicates 'satisfactory progress' toward his IEP goal of making friends. He's lucky that he's growing up in today's world. Back in my day, boys and girls were never allowed to be just friends."

Suddenly Christine saw an opportunity to rid herself of her difficult son, at least for a little while.

"Do you think . . ." she began, then hesitated.

Dr. Wikedda waited, then said, "Yes, go on."

"Since Lenny needs a change of environment, do you think she would consider having him come to live at her house—kind of like a boarding school except in a private home?"

"I'll talk to her, and see if she's interested. By the way, I have been curious about environmental changes having a negative impact on a normal child. Although this school has not had many autistic children, we have seen lots of spoiled, privileged, overindulged children. Sometimes I wonder what would happen if we took someone normal and nice, such as that Hector Fairfield, whom you mentioned, and subject him to the treatment that we give our special-needs children—you know, feed them awful, tasteless, therapeutic food, then punish them when they complain or get sick. Make them earn every single privilege with points and stickers and take away a sticker every time they make the tiniest mistake or for the tiniest infraction of rules they do not understand or agree with. Yell at them a hundred times a day, criticize everything they do with comments such as, 'How could you be so stupid?'"

Christine looked away for a moment. That certainly sounded like her home.

Dr. Wikedda continued: "If we subjected a normal child to the indignities that autistic kids are subjected to in the name of therapy, 'for their own good,' I predict that normal child would start acting autistic within a month. However, if we start respecting Lenny, letting him eat what he wants, socialize or be alone as much as he wants, and treat him with kindness and respect, I also predict that he'll start acting more normally, even at school."

"But you can't do that, can you?" Christine asked. "You couldn't really do something like that to a normal child, could you?"

"No. That is, not without an IEP."

"Oh."

"I'll see if my friend, Patricia, is willing to educate Lenny for two to three months, using unqualified acceptance and respect as her educational principles. I'll make the arrangements, then get back to you."

"Thank you, Dr. Wikedda." Mrs. Fahrer rose to leave.

The principal smiled politely as she watched Lenny's mother exit her office. Then her smile turned smug and somewhat sinister. She was hatching a plan in her mind—could she pull it off? What if Lenny was treated with kindness and respect, and became normal? On the other hand, what if she somehow managed to hatch a plot against that bully Hector, and treat him like an autistic kid—would he start acting autistic? And what of Alice? Was she really capable of peeling paint off bathroom walls? Perhaps she was autistic herself, and that's why she and Lenny got along. Alice could prove useful in ways yet to be determined. Perhaps as Lenny recovered from his autism, he would recognize the disorder in Alice and consequently reject her, as any normal child would.

Dr. Wikedda would have to work out the details, but she might just make a name for herself in the professional world—and get rid of three problem children in the process. Hector, Alice, and Lenny . . . Codename: H.A.L.

From now on, she would think of them as the three subjects of the H.A.L. Experiment.

## 8 p.m.
## Patricia's Apartment

Dr. Wikedda had just finished getting ready to go to Patricia's house to explain her experiment. In her attaché case, she had stowed four thousand dollars in cash as payment for services rendered. She'd deduct it from her income as a business expense, and besides, if she won the Nobel Prize later on, this modest investment would be worth it.

Patricia was waiting outside her apartment building when Dr. Wikedda arrived.

"Hi, Dawn," Patricia said.

"Hi, Patricia. Could we step inside?" She pointed to her attaché case.

"Sure thing."

When they got into Patricia's apartment, they both sat down in chairs.

"So," Patricia said, "what can I do for you?"

"Well, I have a business proposition for you. There is a child in my school named Lenny Fahrer, who was just diagnosed with autism. He has acted strangely since the first day he arrived, but his mother is skeptical about the diagnosis, and frankly, so am I. Personally I believe that autism is caused by a mismatch between an individual and his environment."

Furtively she looked around the room, as if there were a possibility that someone could overhear. "Now you're not to repeat this to anyone. Promise?"

"I promise."

"I don't believe that the school environment is appropriate for Lenny."

Patricia's eyes grew wider. Even though she believed that the public school environment was problematic for all children, it was heresy for a school principal to say so. She was skeptical. Perhaps Dr. Wikedda was just saying that to get her to be more willing to participate in the experiment.

"Did you tell Lenny's mother that?"

"No, thank God I didn't have to. Lenny's doctor told her that. He told her to homeschool him as a treatment for his autism, and because she says she has no idea how to do this, I'm wondering if you could be his teacher. In fact, I'm hoping that he can actually live with you for at least two months, so that you can totally control his environment and his social experiences. You would become his tutor, his friend, and his temporary parent."

Patricia thought it over, then finally shook her head. "I can't."

"Why not?"

"I don't think I'm qualified. Having a strange child move in with me is a risk. What if we don't get along? No . . . no, I can't."

"I'll pay you, of course."

"No, I can't."

Dr. Wikedda opened the attaché case.

Patricia's eyes grew wide. "Well, now, I just might consider it. How much?"

"There's four thousand here. With more to come once the experiment is completed."

"All right, I'll do it," Patricia agreed, since she could really use the money. "I haven't been able to find a teaching job. Not with my educational beliefs anyway. I also would like to gain some experience with autistic kids before I start my charter school." Patricia did not believe in standardized tests, which made her virtually unemployable in the teaching profession. "Plus, this money will compensate me as I won't be able to work as much. Just because I don't go to an office each day like you doesn't mean I don't work, Dawn. I'm a copyeditor.

I edit books at home, and if Lenny's here, I won't be able to work full-time on my assignments."

"Good. The H.A.L. Experiment will begin next Tuesday, March twenty-third, and end on Tuesday, May twenty-fifth. You are to pick Lenny up from school and bring him here. Tell him that his parents are going on a two-month vacation, and that you are his babysitter. He is going to have a meltdown most likely, because he hates change, but you are to be unconditionally accepting and sympathetic. You are going to let him do whatever he wants in your house—"

"Whatever he wants? But what if he tries to set the place on fire?"

"He won't. If you treat him with kindness and respect, listen to him, and treat him the way a normal child should be treated, I predict that he won't cause you any trouble, and furthermore, that his autism will gradually diminish. Even though you will probably get angry at him a lot, you must never yell at him. If he makes social mistakes, you can discuss what happened, but you must never tease him or make fun of him or say, 'How could you be so stupid?'"

"Is that what his parents do now?" Patricia was starting to feel real sympathy for this young man she had yet to meet.

"I'm sure they do. You must also tell him that you believe homeschooling is best for him, and you are trying it out. If it works, you'll ask his mother to continue."

"That should motivate him."

"Indeed. And while you are teaching him for the next two months, you are to honor him as a worthy person."

"Okay, I'll do it," Patricia said, nodding. "It sounds like it could be fun."

Dr. Wikedda went home, excited that her plan was taking shape. One half of the experiment had been set into action. Now she needed to organize the other half—which involved taking a normal boy and altering his environment so that he experienced firsthand what an autistic child went through. All day long, seven days a week, he'd be reprimanded, yelled at, criticized, corrected, teased, and forced to do things that were scary or painful. His life would be controlled by points and star charts, and nothing he did would be considered right and acceptable.

This was the tricky part of the experiment, for although homeschooling Lenny was absolutely legal with both his parents' consent—which wouldn't be hard to obtain since his mother and father were always trying to find ways to get rid of him—bullying his counterpart was definitely not.

To pull it off, Dr. Wikedda would have to create an air-tight consent form, and get the parents to administer the abuse. She also decided that she would not tell them that this experiment also involved Lenny. In addition, to minimize the possibility of the parents discovering Lenny's side of the experiment, she decided to stagger the starting date. Lenny's experiment would start on Tuesday, but Hector's would start on Wednesday.

### March 19, 2010—9 a.m.
### Buffett Elementary School, Dr. Wikedda's Office

The next morning, in her office, she called Hector's parents, Mr. and Mrs. Fairfield, to schedule a meeting. Then she set up a second meeting with Hector's homeroom teacher (Mrs. Jill Appell), the social worker (Mrs. Mel Ting-Pot), the gym teacher (Mr. Sirius Lee O'Beas), the lunch and recess supervisor (Mrs. Terry Palmer), and the music teacher (Mr. John Birdson).

When the Fairfields entered the school building, Mrs. Fairfield had a sinking feeling. She was afraid her son had committed a horrible act or was in some kind of very bad trouble.

Dr. Wikedda greeted them at the door to her office.

"Is our son in some kind of trouble?" Mr. Fairfield asked right away.

"No," the principal reassured him. "Although he does need some special help."

"In what way?" Mrs. Fairfield asked.

Dr. Wikedda took a breath. How she spun her answer would determine whether these two parents would fall for her idea.

"Well, I'll be frank. Hector suffers from an environmental disease."

"What?" both parents cried in unison.

"Hector is a spoiled child."

"Now see here—" Mr. Fairfield complained.

"It's not his fault," the principal interjected. "He got that way because of the environment in this city and this school. We would like to conduct a brief experiment to see whether changing his environment can make him less spoiled. It's based on the old 'nature versus nurture' debate in psychology."

Mr. and Mrs. Fairfield thought this over.

To Mrs. Fairfield, Dr. Wikedda asked, "Have you noticed that your child is spoiled at home?"

"Well, to be honest, he does seem a bit spoiled. But all modern children are that way, as you know."

"Oh, yes, I know," the principal replied, nodding. "But does his behavior bother you?"

"I'll admit, he always does seem to ask for too many things for Christmas, and he becomes a raging monster if he doesn't get everything that he wanted, and he'll often throw presents over his shoulder he doesn't like instead of politely saying thank you. I have also heard that he teases other children, although that doesn't bother us since all children tease each other."

Dr. Wikedda refrained from commenting about that misconception. "Go on," she said instead.

"And, well, what really angers me is that he never seems to be grateful for anything that he has. He always seems to want more and more and more."

"And does this make you feel anger toward him?"

"Well, now that you mention it, yes, yes, I do feel angry."

"All the time?" Dr. Wikedda put her best sympathetic shrink expression on her face.

Mr. Fairfield piped up, "Yes, all the time."

"Now, dear . . ." his wife countered.

"Well, you do. And—and so do I. That kid drives us crazy!"

Dr. Wikedda smiled. She knew just how to spin her proposal.

"How would you like to get rid of that anger, and help make Hector more grateful? This will help him later on in life."

Mr. and Mrs. Fairfield looked at one another.

"Sure," Mrs. Fairfield said.

"I'd like your family to participate in an experiment. First, it will help you get rid of all the rage you're feeling against your son. And second, it will help him become less spoiled and more able to face life's challenges."

"That sounds interesting," Mr. Fairfield commented.

"This technique was originally devised by Dr. Ivar Lovaas, and it involves breaking a child out of his old patterns so he can develop new, healthier ones. At home, I want you to watch everything that Hector does, and I want you to reprimand him for every mistake he makes. Yell at him if you have to. Put him to work every waking minute, and don't allow him to play or have any free choice. If he shows any free thinking, I want you to punish him. If he complains, I want you to punish him even more."

"Hmm, this sounds brutal," Mrs. Fairfield said.

"But it is necessary, to break the old patterns. You must take away the child's ability to think for himself so that you can rebuild him the way you want. He'll thank you in the end."

Dr. Wikedda didn't really believe this, but after all, as a school principal, she often had to assert things she didn't believe in. She was actually hoping that by treating Hector the way autistic children were treated, he would, in fact, begin to act autistic. Since Hector was a bully and a nuisance, she didn't really feel guilty about messing up his life. And after all, she was only recommending what Dr. Ivar Lovaas actually did to autistic children, without the electric shocks, cattle prods, and other physical tortures that Dr. Lovaas employed.

She pulled out her carefully written consent forms.

"Now, do I have your consent?"

"Okay," Mr. Fairfield said, nodding.

"Please sign these standard consent forms. After all, Hector is a nice young man, and you want what's best for him."

Both parents signed.

As they stood up, Dr. Wikedda handed them an instruction sheet. "Now here is a summary of what we discussed. I'm going to give you some time so you can prepare. Begin the morning of next Wednesday, and I'll be checking in with you for the next two months. If you have any questions, feel free to call my cell phone anytime of the day or night."

"Thank you," said Mrs. Fairfield.

"And the main thing, as Coach O'Beas always says, is to go out there and have fun!"

## 12 p.m.
## Buffett Elementary School, Dr. Wikedda's Office

During the lunch hour, five staff members reported to the principal's office, as instructed.

"What do you want from us?" asked Mr. John Birdson, the music teacher.

"I'd like to tell you all about an experiment that we will be conducting in our school. It's being funded by a—by an independent source, and if successful, it could revolutionize how special education students are treated in our schools."

"That would be nice," quipped Mr. O'Beas. "They're a real pain in the butt in gym class."

"The experiment will involve three students—Lenny Fahrer and Alice Meacham . . . Do you all know them?"

"Of course I know him," said Mrs. Ting-Pot. "He's that troublesome kid who's been refusing to socialize with his peers since the day he entered this school. And she's that meddlesome friend of his."

"He was just given a diagnosis of autism," Dr. Wikedda continued.

"Oh, no," Mrs. Ting-Pot said. "Does that mean he's entitled to more services?"

Dr. Wikedda thought about that for a moment, and it gave her an idea.

"Well, yes, in a way. This experiment is part of the additional services for Lenny, and also for another troublemaker in our school, Hector Fairfield."

"The bully?" Mrs. Appell asked. "He's in my class."

"Yes, one of our new hall monitors."

"Is he entitled to special ed services?" Mrs. Ting-Pot asked.

"Does he have an IEP?" Mr. O'Beas wondered.

"No," the principal replied. "Bullying is not considered a disability."

"So what's involved with this experiment?" Mrs. Appell said.

"It is my—I mean, it is the belief of the research organization that what we regard as a disability, such as autism, is actually a logical reaction to the wrong environment. Lenny overreacts to everything in the school environment because it is the wrong one for him. Therefore, he has been granted a two-month leave of absence, during which time he will be homeschooled by someone who is familiar with autism and who can adjust Lenny's environment to make him comfortable. She will treat him with unconditional kindness and respect, which I'm sure he has almost never experienced in his short life. The goal of his part of the experiment is to see whether improving the way we treat an autistic child will improve the outcome."

Mrs. Ting-Pot shook her head. "I doubt it," she said. "That kid's hopeless."

"That's what we want to find out. And conversely, we want to find out whether changing Hector's environment will affect his behavior also. If we treat him the way we currently treat Lenny, will Hector become autistic?" Meanwhile, I want to see if Alice stays friends with Lenny if he changes due to being homeschooled.

Five pairs of eyes looked at the principal.

Mrs. Appell finally spoke. "But isn't autism a neurological condition? Isn't someone born with it?"

"Yes, but perhaps the behaviors associated with autism are not predetermined. That's what we aim to find out. That's where you come in. For the next two months, I want you to treat Hector the way you currently treat Lenny. I want you to criticize everything he does. I want you to make up illogical rules and punish Hector for not following them. I want you to single him out for ridicule in front of your classes. I want you to insist that he associate with students whom he does not know or dislikes. And I want you to forbid him from associating with those other two bullies—those Shakespearean kids. What are their names?"

"Othello and Macbeth," Mrs. Ting-Pot supplied. "Their mothers were taking a Shakespeare class at the community college when they were both pregnant."

"Sirius, I want you to pay careful attention to everything Hector does. Make sure you ridicule him for every mistake, and talk loud enough so the other kids can hear you."

"But Dawn, I cannot treat Hector like an animal! It's barbaric!" Mr. O'Beas protested.

"Sirius, during gym class, how do you treat Lenny Fahrer?" Dr. Wikedda asked.

"That's different. He behaves so badly and does so many things wrong that I have to treat him that way. No matter how much I punish him, he still misbehaves."

"Does he intentionally misbehave?"

"I think he does. But he always claims that he didn't understand a rule or didn't know it existed."

"Precisely," said the principal. "You are going to put Hector in the same situation. Punish him for rules that he doesn't know exist. Invent something that makes no sense. Then he'll be able to experience what Lenny goes through every day."

"But Hector is a model student! How can I treat him that way?"

"If you can treat Lenny that way, you can treat Hector the same," the principal argued.

"It will only be for two months," Mrs. Appell chimed in. "And besides, you won't have Lenny Fahrer to kick around anymore—at least till the end of this school year. Then who knows? Maybe Lenny will like homeschooling so much that he'll never return!"

Everyone burst out laughing.

"Okay," Sirius said finally. "I'll do it for the greater good."

Everyone laughed again.

# Chapter 7

*March 20, 2010—8:45 a.m.*
*The Fahrer Residence*

Two days ago, Lenny finally got to use the bathroom when his class went to gym. But that was just a distant memory today. Today was Saturday, and this was the day Alice was coming over.

Although he had been friends with her since the beginning of the school year, he still could not fully trust her. Having been rejected by so many kids in his life, he always felt like he had to have his guard up whenever he talked to anyone. He never knew when he was going to get rejected again, and he felt that if he emotionally prepared for it, he wouldn't feel as hurt whenever someone did push him away.

His mother's ritual of forcing him to eat slimy food didn't seem to bother him as much today, because what mattered was that he was going to play with Alice. He thought to himself, *When should I tell Alice that I have autism? When's the right time? Or do I even have to tell her at all?*

After swallowing a few spoonfuls of his smelly vomit breakfast, it was around nine and Lenny had an hour until his friend came over. Alice was coming at ten o'clock, so Lenny decided to prepare for her arrival. Alice and Lenny loved to reenact skits from their favorite comic book series, *Chloe and Allie*. It was a comic strip about two friends, a boy and girl, who were in the second grade, the girl's stuffed alligator, and their misadventures as well as their own hatred of school. Lenny and Alice enjoyed this series as they felt they could relate well to the characters, being good friends themselves. Lenny would play Timothy, and Alice would play Chloe and Allie. Issues from gender superiority, to philosophy, to making fun of teachers were all discussed in the strip. It was actually this common interest—*Chloe and Allie*—that was partially the reason why Alice and Lenny's friendship started, as they both were obsessed it. Their friendship consisted primarily of talking about the comic strip and acting out various scenes. In fact, Lenny found out he could relate heavily to the characters in this.

The first thing Lenny did was put on black pants and a white shirt, which was his Timothy costume. Then he got out the book that they reenacted their scenes from, *Chloe and Allie's Blue Monday Book*. In one story, Chloe and Allie go out into the forest to talk about philosophy; in another story, Chloe's family takes her on an annual hunting trip that Chloe cannot stand.

Ten o'clock came, and Alice knocked on the door. She was dressed in a long pink sweater and black pants, what she always seemed to wear no matter what the weather was, even in the hot days of summer.

"Hello, Mrs. Meacham. How are you?" Lenny politely asked Alice's mother as he was instructed to do by his own mother. Lenny made sure to say hello this time—he had previously been lectured by his mother when he did not say hello to Alice's mother on their last playdate. Saying hello was hard for Lenny and he didn't seem to understand why his mother considered it a big deal when he didn't do it—or when he did.

"I am fine. Thank you, Lenny," said Alice's mother.

"You were very polite. Do you want something to drink, Sarah?" asked Lenny's mother.

"Thanks, Christina."

Alice's mother and Lenny's mother went to the kitchen to talk, and Alice and Lenny went to his room to act out scenes. *Hopefully,* Lenny thought, *my hello was enough for my mother to feel satisfied.*

"So what do you want to do first?" asked Alice.

"Let's start where we left off on page 121. But first, I want to tell you how I was picked on again."

"Did those three jerks made fun of you again?"

"Yes. I was in the bathroom, and they came in and Hector told me that if I didn't admit I was hiding from him, he would kill me."

"That's terrible. What happened after that?"

"Well, for some reason, my mother was in the hallway, and I walked out and saw her, and the three bullies told her how nice they supposedly were to me. You know how bullies are. They can fool adults and make them believe every word they say. And my mother actually believed them."

"You need to tell someone. It's not right for them to do that."

"But who can I tell? No teachers believe me. And the social worker spends her time telling me that it's wrong for me to hang out with you because you're a girl. She's even as bad as the bullies sometimes."

"Well, I actually got into some trouble, too, yesterday."

"How?"

"From the usual, teachers getting upset at me because I'm always in long sleeves and long pants."

Lenny nodded sympathetically.

"I don't like wearing T-shirts and shorts. I feel more comfortable covered up. I don't like being exposed, and people think it's weird. I don't understand why the other girls like to wear shorts even when it's cold outside."

"I don't have a problem wearing long sleeves, but I never wear shorts," Lenny said.

"Kids laugh at the way I dress, and the way I love *Chloe and Allie.*"

"Me, too." Lenny found it easy to talk to Alice because she understood him.

"That's why we're friends. It's strange, because even Claire and Tammy don't really get why I like pretending to be Allie so much, and I have to hide it from them. All they want to talk about is Justin Bieber and other stupid stuff."

"Justin Bieber is stupid." Lenny didn't really have an opinion about this, but with Alice, he found that he could keep up his end of a conversation because he didn't feel afraid of making a mistake and being teased.

"I also got into some big trouble, too. I don't know if you heard, but someone's been peeling paint in the girls' bathroom. And those three jerks that made fun of you—they set me up too."

"What?" asked Lenny.

"Yep. The principal told me that the three hall monitors—those three that make fun of you—told her that the peeling paint was found after I defended you. I did go to the bathroom and see the peeled paint, but didn't do it."

"Peeling paint? I used to do that in my room." Then he added quickly, "But I've never done it in school."

"Well, the principal decided to blame me for doing it. She told me that some girl told her that I was the one who asked these girls to peel the paint, and that unless I can find some girl to deny it, she's going to make me stay in for recess for a week."

"It's terrible," Lenny said in commiseration.

"Yep. It's really sad. I didn't peel any paint, and I don't know who did. I don't care if I do miss recess, but I don't like being blamed for something I didn't do. And she also punished two other girls."

"Do you know them too?" asked Lenny.

"I don't. Maybe they're being set up too," said Alice.

Since Alice played with Claire and Tammy during recess, Lenny typically sat quietly during recess on the playground bench and watched all of the other kids play happily with each other. It didn't bother him, though—he preferred sitting alone by himself than getting made fun of when he did attempt to play.

"I don't like it either," said Lenny. "I get blamed for everything in my house."

"Terrible," Alice echoed sympathetically.

"My mother's always upset at me. I feel like you're one of my only friends," said Lenny.

"Well then, Lenny. Do you want to play now?"

"Okay."

"Let's do Chloe and her family on the hunting trip. You still want to play the dad?"

"Sure," said Lenny.

Alice and Lenny stood up and started pretending to be the characters in the strip. In this scene, Chloe was arguing with her dad, and she didn't want to go hunting.

"I don't want to hunt, Dad! I love deer!" she shouted.

"You must, Chloe. Your family hunts every year," Lenny intoned using a fake deep voice.

"Why do I have to hunt?"

"Hunting builds discipline."

"I can't stand those guns, Dad. Don't make me hunt."

"Okay, now her mom comes," said Lenny. "You be the mom."

"Mom, I don't want to hunt!" she shouted, pretending to be Chloe.

"You need to be a true independent woman, Chloe," Alice replied, pretending to be the mom.

"What does 'independent' mean?"

"It means you need to be a free-thinking woman, and do what macho men do," said Alice as Chloe's mom.

"The deer are out, so let's just hunt!" exclaimed Lenny as Chloe's dad.

"I hope your parents give me some offerings from their trip," said Alice as Allie.

"Don't you start!" said Alice as Chloe.

"Chloe, men have hunted for years to show they are better than women," said Alice as the mom. "Shouldn't you show that you can do what men can do?"

"I don't want to hunt cute little deer," said Chloe.

"Oh, dear, oh, dear . . ." said Lenny as Chloe's dad.

"Please stop!" said Chloe.

"Dear deer, please be there for me to shoot you," said Chloe's dad.

"Dad, do you really believe that?"

"My dad told me to pray before you hunt," said Chloe's dad.

"I still don't want to hunt deer!" said Chloe.

"Your great-grandparents did not fight for their rights for you to feel scared at the hands of men with guns," said Chloe's mom.

"Well, that's the end," said Alice as herself. "You want to do another one?"

"Sure, but I need to rest."

"Okay. I love this story. The author is so cool, too," said Alice. "He was . . ."

And Lenny once again listened to her talk about the life of the comic strip's author, Mark Middleton. Lenny knew every detail, since Alice had told Lenny all about the author many times before, but Lenny always loved to hear her tell the story again, and she always seemed to want to keep telling it. She would also tell Lenny how her mother complained that she was "talking too much" about *Chloe and Allie,* but Lenny didn't think so.

"Mark Middleton was an author who believed that there were too many comic strips out there about boys, and felt that there should be a comic strip with a girl as a main character.

Inspired by the anime director Hayao Miyazaki and how his stories were mostly about girls, Mark Middleton decided to change history with *Chloe and Allie*, a story about a girl, Chloe, her best friend, Timothy, and an anthropomorphized stuffed alligator, Allie. This, he felt, was a comic strip that could help teach children to think for themselves . . ."

*If only the teachers at my school were willing to accept my friendship with Alice and leave us alone,* thought Lenny. *If only they would read this comic strip, and let us think for ourselves.*

Lenny and Alice resumed reenacting their favorite comic strip for the rest of the morning, enjoying their friendship and time together. Lenny forgot all about telling Alice that he had been diagnosed with autism, deciding just to have fun. He could tell her later.

# Chapter 8

*March 23, 2010—3:15 p.m.*
*Buffett Elementary School, Main Entrance*

On the following Tuesday afternoon, Patricia Nottingham pulled up in front of Buffett Elementary School and saw a boy sitting behind a tree. His legs were crossed tightly, his head was jammed into his lap, and he was absolutely still, like a statue of a giant pretzel. That had to be Lenny Fahrer.

"Excuse me," Patricia said to a group of three sinister-looking boys who were milling around the tree.

"You mean the Nazi?" Othello asked.

Patricia looked at him sternly and realized that the experiment could begin at that very moment.

"He is not a Nazi, just because his name sounds like a German word. How stupid can you be to make that association?"

Othello looked at her uncertainly. He was not used to adults figuring him out so soon.

"The Nazi—" Hector began, but Patricia cut him off.

"Say that again, and I'll report you to the principal. Now for the last time, where is he? And you are to refer to him by his name, not some derogatory epithet."

In her experience, she'd learned that big words were the fastest way to shut a bully up.

The statue behind the tree moved an inch, as if suddenly interested in what was going on.

Patricia walked behind the tree and asked softly, "Are you Lenny Fahrer?"

Meanwhile, Alice was walking by. She had just said good-bye to her friends and was walking home when she overheard Patricia. "Yes, that's Lenny. Those jerks are picking on him again."

Then she shouted to Hector, "He's not a Nazi, so leave him alone!"

Lenny did not say anything. He was defending himself against the bullies by cocooning. Secretly, he thanked Alice again, but he didn't want to say anything at the moment. He did not know who this woman was nor did he want to know. He was waiting for his mother to pick him up so he could escape school for the rest of the day.

"Are you Lenny Fahrer?" Patricia repeated.

Lenny still did not answer. "Is Lenny like this a lot?" Patricia asked Alice.

"Yeah, he is. He's scared of bullies. Who are you anyway?" said Alice.

"I'm Ms. Nottingham. His parents had to go out of town, so I'm picking him up," Patricia lied. "Who are you?"

"I'm Alice, Lenny's best friend. Probably his only friend," said Alice.

"So how should I get him to speak?"

"Just wait until he calms down."

Patricia used her kindest and most patient voice to say, "Lenny, I'd like you to put your head up."

Lenny did not do so. He knew better than to obey a stranger, even if Alice was obeying her. His parents had warned him about this, and his mother was supposed to pick him up at any moment.

"Lenny," Patricia repeated. She was getting impatient, but she thought about all that money and it gave her enough incentive to remain nice.

"You're not my mother! Go away!" Lenny cried, though it came out muffled because his face was still hidden in his lap.

"You're right, Lenny. I'm not your mother. My name is Patricia Nottingham, and I'm here to pick you up. Your mother and father had to go out of town suddenly, and you'll be staying with me for two months."

"Well, my mom's here. Bye, Lenny. See you later," said Alice as she ran off to meet her mother.

"Wait, Alice, if you're Lenny's friend, I need to come talk to your mom for a bit, if that's okay," said Patricia.

Alice wondered why, but didn't question Patricia, and they walked to Alice's mother's car.

"Hi, there," said Patricia. "Are you Alice's mother?"

"Yes, who are you?"

"I'm Patricia Nottingham, a friend of Lenny's parents. Lenny's going to be staying with me for the next two months because his parents decided they want to take him out of school, and they asked me to homeschool him."

"You mean he's not coming back to school?" asked Alice.

"Not for the next two months. You probably have seen how he suffers in school, right?"

"Yeah," said Alice.

"Well, his parents want to see if staying home helps."

"He'll like that," said Alice. "You're a lot nicer than Mrs. Redbear."

"We have to get going," said Alice's mother impatiently.

"I wanted to know if Lenny could keep in touch with Alice. Here," she said, realizing that she was still a stranger to them, "here's my phone number. Anytime you want to arrange a playdate, just call me, okay?"

"Those two are friends, Patricia, so sure," said Alice's mother. "It was nice to meet you."

"Thank you," said Patricia, handing her a business card. "Bye, Alice."

Lenny buried his head deeper in his lap while he waited. This couldn't be happening. His mother always picked him up. This woman must have been a kidnapper. Finally, Patricia returned and kneeled down beside Lenny.

"Excuse me, ma'am."

Patricia looked up and saw a woman standing next to her. The bullies were nowhere to be found.

"Yes?" Patricia said.

"Where's your name tag?" the woman asked.

"My what?"

"Your name tag. Unless you are the parent or legal guardian of a child in this school, you must have a name tag to speak to one of our students."

"But I'm outdoors!"

"Nevertheless, you're on school grounds, so you must sign in at the office and get a name tag."

"Fine. I'd like to see the principal. She knows that I'm here to pick up Lenny Fahrer. I'm his . . . second cousin."

"She is *not!*" Lenny said desperately, his face still in his lap. "My mother is picking me up!"

"Loreen, don't worry. Ms. Nottingham *is* here to pick up Lenny Fahrer."

Both women looked around and saw Dr. Wikedda.

"I was just doing my job," Loreen defended herself. "I've never seen this woman before."

"I've never seen her before either!" Lenny cried from the ground.

"Lenny's mother told me that Ms. Nottingham is indeed picking him up," said Dr. Wikedda. "Now stand up, young man."

Patricia felt uneasy. This was not the way to start an experiment based on trust and unconditional respect. She wondered why the principal didn't notice the terror in Lenny's eyes.

"Dr. Wikedda," she said, "why wasn't Lenny told that his mother was going out of town? This isn't right. Is it possible for him to talk to his mother on the phone?"

"I think that can be arranged, if he stands up and comes with me to the office."

"No," Lenny said. "My mother always picks me up here, and I'm not going anywhere."

"Okay, Lenny," Patricia said, "we'll wait here together."

Lenny thought about this for a moment. He realized that he was only going to be here until his mother came. It seemed strange, since no one had ever waited with him before, but finally, he said, "All right."

Lenny sat down with Patricia on a nearby bench, but not too close, since he was in the company of a stranger, who could hurt him. Soon he burst into tears.

"My mother!" he raged through his tears. "Where is she? I have to find her!"

Lenny ran back to the tree and hid behind it. Patricia remained on the bench.

Lenny cried and cried and cried. What was going on? Why didn't his parents tell him they were going away? Why wasn't this the normal end of a normally horrific school day?

He peeked out from behind the tree and saw car after car arrive, picking up kid after kid. Every time someone drove away, he felt sadder. His parents must not love him anymore because he was autistic. Why did God have to make him an autistic person?

Finally, every child had been picked up except Lenny. No cars were coming up the drive, and no one was there except Lenny and Patricia.

It was true, then. His parents had left him.

Slowly Lenny got to his feet and walked over to Patricia, his eyes staring into the air, noticing nothing, as if he were a zombie. His head tilted to the right because his body was disoriented and he had trouble balancing. The only things indicating that he was still a human being were the tears pouring from his eyes and on to the ground.

"My mother has to come!" he sobbed. "She always comes."

Patricia looked at him kindly and said, "Your mother isn't coming today, Lenny. But you will see her in two months. Until then you're going to stay with me, and we'll have fun. You'll see."

*This woman is crazy*, Lenny thought. How could she tell him that he couldn't see his parents? Even though they were mean and he hated what they did to him, they were still his parents, the only parents he had ever known. Living with someone else was a change to him, and he *hated* changes. Why didn't anyone understand that?

"Take me home!" Lenny demanded.

"Okay, Lenny," she said. "I'll take you home, but your parents aren't there. You can't stay there by yourself." Patricia called Dr. Wikedda on her cell phone, informing the principal that she was taking Lenny to his home. This alerted Dr. Wikedda to the situation, and she quickly called up Lenny's parents and told them to leave the house for a while.

Lenny walked like a zombie to Patricia's car, wondering why everyone was hurting him like this. As he climbed in, he noticed a horrible vinyl smell. He hated the smell of vinyl. It must have been a new car, not like the old wreck his mother drove, which smelled like old McDonald's French fries and the other aging food items that had fallen on the floor.

"This car stinks!" Lenny declared. "I'm not riding in it."

"It's the only car I have, Lenny," Patricia said patiently.

"This is not my car," he argued.

"But it's the only way you can get home," she said.

Realizing that she was right, Lenny held his breath. As they rode home, Lenny took only seven quick breaths, one every minute, until they pulled into his driveway.

Lenny burst out of the car, gulping in fresh, nonstinky air, and ran up to the front door. "Mommy, Mommy!" he cried, grabbing the doorknob and turning it.

The door was locked. He shoved his entire body weight against the door, in a futile attempt to break it down. Then he pounded hard, hoping that someone would answer.

Finally, he noticed a piece of paper that had fallen off the nail on the door. It said:

> *Dear Lenny,*
> *We are flying to Bolinas. Please go with*
> *Patricia. She will take care of you for the next two*
> *months, and we will see you at the end of May.*
> *Love,*
> *Mom and Dad*

Why would his parents leave him? And where was Bolinas?

"Why would my parents leave me?" Lenny asked Patricia, who had walked up to him and put her hand on his shoulder. He was so numb, he didn't notice the unfamiliar touch.

"Your parents had to go. It was an emergency. Come with me, and I'll take care of you."

Lenny walked back to the car, crying again until he had no more tears. When he realized he would have to go back and sit on the stinky vinyl, he made his body go limp, and he lay down on the back seat, playing frozen and trying to hold his breath until he fainted. At least, he had stopped crying, because one cannot cry and be frozen at the same time.

He did not know why his parents would leave him with Patricia. But he also did not know that Patricia was not like his parents.

When they arrived at her six-story apartment building in Lake Bluff, he got out of the car and followed her to the front door. He liked the fact that she was quiet, and for a moment, no one was torturing him with unwanted noise.

She opened the outside door with a key, then went to a door on the first floor and knocked. The door was opened by a huge muscular black man, someone you would not want to mess with.

"Hey, Patricia," the man said. "What's happening?"

"Here's April's rent," she said, handing him a check.

Now Lenny was terrified. This seemed to be a payoff of some kind, like he'd seen on TV. Maybe this man would hurt them if they didn't give him money.

"Thank you, darlin'," the man said with a twinkle in his eye. This confused Lenny, because the man looked like a professional wrestler but also seemed very kind.

"Wh-who are you?" Lenny whispered.

The black man chuckled, leaned over, then asked softly, "Who are *you?*"

"He's, uh, my cousin, Lenny Fahrer. He'll be staying with me for a while."

Suddenly Lenny understood. That check was indeed a payoff, to buy the man's silence about Lenny illegally living in the building. Then Patricia said, "Lenny, this is my landlord, Mr. Barry."

Lenny looked at his feet. Given all the changes that he had to process, he simply could not remember to say hello.

Mr. Barry said, "Nice to know you, young man," and he did not seem to care that Lenny did not respond.

They walked to the elevator and waited. Normally Lenny liked riding in elevators, but today his body had shut down totally, and couldn't enjoy anything. As they waited, a man entered the lobby, pounded on the landlord's door, and when the door opened, the man started screaming.

"I couldn't find work again today!" the man yelled. "And you wanna know why? It's because of people like you!"

"Hey, don't blame me for your problems! I did not leave the South Side for this!" Mr. Barry retorted, suddenly becoming stern. "But if you can't pay your rent, I'll have to evict you."

"You see?" the man said, addressing Patricia. Instinctively she put her arm around Lenny, to protect him. "People like him are taking jobs from people like me, and then throwing me on the street!"

"No, I don't see," she said, lifting her chin. "If you can't get a job, that's your own fault."

"It's *his* fault," the man insisted.

Lenny thought about this, and suddenly an important insight came to him. The landlord was being treated like an autistic person! He was being blamed for something he did not do, because of something he could not help, namely, that he was black. Lenny could not bear to see this innocent black man being bullied. It was just like being teased by Hector and his bully friends. Lenny was bullied because he was different, and so was this black man, who was getting falsely accused of something he had no power over.

"You apologize, you . . . you . . ." Lenny blurted out.

"Shh, Lenny," Patricia whispered as the elevator doors opened. "This is none of your business."

"I won't be quiet!" he insisted. "You're a bully, and it's your fault if you can't find a job!"

Lenny took a deep breath, utterly exhausted. He returned to shut-down mode.

"Thank you, son," Mr. Barry called out gratefully from his door. "I can see that young man has been brought up right."

Lenny felt as if cold water had been splashed on him. He was shocked. Someone was praising him for doing something right?

They got into the elevator and went to Patricia's apartment, No. 306. Still fearing that he might get hurt in this new environment, he ran over to the couch, threw himself down on his stomach, and started running his fingers along the design in the carpet.

Patricia saw this and decided that she would not try to get him up. When he was ready, she would tell him everything that was going to happen in the next two months.

In about an hour, Lenny had to go to the bathroom. He automatically held it in, not wanting to get up. Finally, when he could hold it no longer, he asked quietly, "Can I go to the bathroom?"

"Of course, Lenny," Patricia said. "You'll have your own bathroom. It's right this way."

His own bathroom?

Lenny followed Patricia down a hallway to a blue bathroom with a bright blue shower curtain and matching blue towels.

"This is your bathroom, Lenny. No one will use it without your permission."

Again, Lenny went into shock. He'd never heard of a child having his own bathroom.

When he was done, he went back into the living room and sat down on the sofa.

"Well, that's better," Patricia said. "Now, if you're ready, I need to tell you some things, and they may sound scary. I'm really, really sorry that you had this change shoved in your face without warning. But from now on, I promise you, I won't make any drastic changes in your life. We'll establish a routine, and stick to it, okay?"

Lenny wasn't ready to answer yet.

"Okay, you don't have to answer me if you don't want to. But I need to tell you a few things.

"One: Your parents will be out of town for two months, as you already know. I don't have the phone number of the place where they'll be staying, but you can call them on their cell phone. I'm sure you know the number. While they are away, you'll be living with me.

"Two: When you stay with me, you can eat whatever you want whenever you want. You are going to have your own room and your own bathroom."

The part about the food got his attention. He couldn't remember the last time he got to choose his own meals. Still he didn't say anything. He didn't yet trust this stranger, who might be setting up a trap.

Patricia went on.

"Three: You will not go to school for the next two months."

Lenny's eyes grew wide, and he almost made eye contact with her.

"I'm sure you will like that aspect of living here. Instead of going to school, I'll be homeschooling you, and you can learn anything you like in any way you like. You won't have to sit in a chair, and you're free to roam around, rock, twirl, or do whatever you need to do to understand me. I will speak slowly, and repeat everything as many times as you need in order to comprehend it. What do you think of that, Lenny?"

He instinctively kept his head down, but he couldn't help giving her a thin sliver of a smile.

"Four: Even though it is only four o'clock, your work day is done. In two hours, we will eat dinner, and you can do whatever you like tonight. There is no homework, and you will never have homework as long as you live with me. Now: What would like for dinner?"

Lenny looked up, then said hesitantly, "I'd like two hamburgers and, and spaghetti, please, but with no chunks of tomatoes in the sauce." Those were his favorite foods unless there were chunks.

Since most autistic children liked these foods, Patricia already had them in her refrigerator.

"Are you . . . are you going to punish me?" Lenny asked.

"Punish you?" Patricia exclaimed. "Why would I do that?"

"For what I did."

"What did you do?" she asked.

Lenny thought of several possibilities, regretting that he had brought the subject up, since sometimes just mentioning the word "punishment" got it inflicted on him.

"Well, I . . ." He decided not to go on.

"Do you mean when you stood up for the landlord?"

"Mm-hm."

"I thought you were very brave to stand up for him. It reminded me of when your friend stood up for you."

She smiled at Lenny, hoping that someday he would feel comfortable smiling back.

"Well, now, I have to go get dinner ready. Would you like to read?"

Lenny shook his head no. He had been forced to read all his life, and he hated it.

"Okay, feel free to do whatever you like. The TV is there"—she pointed—"and the computer is over there."

For the next two hours, Lenny lay on his stomach on the couch, trying to tune everything out. He wished he could tune out the fact that his parents had played a dirty trick on him by leaving him behind. What were they thinking? Although he was not under as much stress as he was at home, and he would escape the horrors of school for the next two months, he was still terrified of many things, including the fact that he would be sleeping in a strange bed.

As an autistic person, Lenny had trouble falling asleep, and he'd cried himself to sleep for as long as he could remember. He always feared the end of the day, for he knew that soon he would have to lie in bed, afraid and unable to sleep. However, he felt comfortable on this couch. Maybe Patricia would let him sleep there for the first few nights.

Lenny felt so comfortable that he actually did fall asleep. He didn't wake up until Patricia gently tapped him on the shoulder and told him that his two hamburgers and spaghetti, with no chunks, were ready.

As Lenny walked to the table, his dread increased. What if he was actually going to have to eat white vomit? However, when he got to his place, he found a plate with two hamburgers in normal-looking buns and a bowl of spaghetti with a smooth tomato sauce on it.

No chunks.

Carefully, Lenny sat down, still waiting for the trap. Perhaps the hamburger was poisoned. He took one small bite. It tasted good! He took another bite. It was great. He looked up at Patricia, waiting for her to start yelling about some rule of manners that he'd broken.

"Do you like it?" Patricia said. "It's made from grass-fed beef."

Immediately Lenny put the hamburger down. He was eating grass?

"Oh, I'm sorry, Lenny. I know you didn't understand. The cows ate the grass, and they lived long and happy lives before they became hamburger. But I shouldn't have brought it up. I'm sorry. That was a mistake."

A grown-up admitted she had made a mistake? A grown-up just apologized to him? Never could he remember a grown-up admitting that they were wrong, even though they frequently were, in fact, wrong.

This had to be the trap. Lenny tensed his body, expecting some kind of attack. To him, everyone was a dragon, and he was the knight who at any moment had to be prepared to fight that dragon.

Lenny are both hamburgers and the bowl of pasta. Patricia made no comments about his manners or how fast he ate or whether he chewed his food. When he was done, he got up to go back to the couch.

Patricia said, "I thought that since you took that long nap before dinner, maybe we could do something together now."

Immediately Lenny's heart rate doubled in fear. This was it; she was now going to punish him or force him to do something that hurt. It was as if, instead of saying, "Maybe we could do something together," she had just announced, "I am sentencing you to death in the electric chair."

Lenny hated doing things with other people, especially people he didn't know. He hated doing things that were "social," and 99 percent of the time, when someone asked him to do something, it involved something social. After all, who wouldn't be afraid to do something that usually ended up harming, terrifying, or embarrassing him? Who wouldn't be afraid of things that hurt? Fear was often regarded as a weakness to conquer, but to an autistic person, fear was a way of avoiding the things he was afraid of. Fear protected you against dangerous things. However, the word "danger" did not mean the same thing to a normal person that it did to an autistic person.

"It's up to you," Patricia said. "Since you have no homework, we could play a game. Or take a walk around the neighborhood, which is ethnically diverse and very interesting. Or we could watch TV together."

Ah, there was the trap. None of the choices involved going back to the couch and lying down . . . alone. He was free only to choose his own poison.

"Let's take a walk," Lenny said, thinking that walking was less social than playing a game.

He and Patricia took a walk along Scranton Avenue, the road she lived on. Patricia was right when she said the neighborhood was diverse. Lenny tried to minimize talking, so he would not have to worry about breaking some rule of conversation when he opened his mouth. For the first fifteen minutes or so, no one said anything. However, Lenny knew that would change—normal people always spoiled the silence by doing something called "breaking the ice."

Patricia, in fact, did break the ice.

"Although this is a safe neighborhood, Lenny," she began, "I want you to promise that you'll look both ways before you cross a street. I don't want anything to happen to you when you're staying with me."

Lenny tried to stop any conversation by not replying.

"You seem really quiet. Are you still scared?"

Lenny ignored her. He knew she was trying to get him to speak, but that would expose him to the horrors of committing a conversational faux pas.

"Why won't you talk to me?" Patricia persisted.

Lenny remained silent. He did not want to give in, and risk getting yelled at.

"I don't have anything to say," he replied finally.

"I understand," Patricia said.

They walked in silence for the next thirty minutes. Patricia decided to let Lenny do whatever he wanted to feel comfortable.

However, it just occurred to her that maybe asking Lenny to take a walk had been a mistake. Autistic people hated exercise. Realizing this, she asked Lenny if he would like to go home.

He was actually exhausted and gasping for breath, so he nodded yes.

When they got back to the apartment, Patricia wondered if she should set some ground rules for bedtime. Then she decided that she would give Lenny the right to set his own bedtime. After all, he was not going to school the next day, and could sleep as late as he chose.

"You will not have a strict bedtime," Patricia announced. "You can stay up as late as you want. Would you like to see your bedroom?"

Lenny felt a burst of renewed terror. He remembered that he would have to sleep here for the next sixty days. A new bed, a new room, new sheets and blankets, a new hallway, and a new bathroom to get used to. Could he deal with all those new things?

Silently he followed Patricia down the hall, realizing that the fear he was feeling was not unlike the fear he always felt when bedtime approached. Even in his own bed, he had a terrible time falling asleep. But at least that was a familiar sensation—being terrified in his own bed. Now he would be terrified in a bed he had never seen before.

His room was actually the guest room, the first room on the right, with a bed, a closet, a desk, a dresser, and a lamp. It was not very big, but then Lenny had never liked big spaces.

"Here's your room, Lenny. It's not Buckingham Palace, but it's good enough, I think," Patricia said. "Do you want to get settled in?"

Lenny checked the clock on the wall. It was only five minutes after eight, but if he didn't go to bed now, he might be forced to do other scary or unpleasant things. He realized that going to bed might be a way to get out of any additional torture . . . if he was able to get to sleep.

"I would like to go to sleep now," he said, even though he had no idea what to do next. He didn't have his pajamas, which he hated anyway, or his toothbrush or toothpaste.

Patricia smiled and said, "I bet you're wondering about what you're going to sleep in. Your mother gave me your pajamas, although she said you disliked them. If you want, you can sleep in your clothes."

Lenny wondered if this was the trap. Even though he loved sleeping in his clothes—since he hated changing his clothes as much as he hated any other change—he was sure that he'd be punished for doing so.

"I really mean it, Lenny. You can sleep in your clothes if you choose. You can decide for yourself. I'll close the door, and you can sleep any way you want. Now, I'll show you where your toothbrush and toothpaste are."

Together they walked a short way down the hall to the blue bathroom. Lenny's favorite toothbrush and a tube of his favorite toothpaste were waiting for him in the medicine cabinet. "Would you like to brush your teeth now?"

"My mother always yells at me about how I brush my teeth. She says I don't do it right."

"Do you want to practice?"

"I do practice, but she says I still do it wrong, even though I'm old enough to know better."

"I don't care how you brush your teeth," Patricia said. "I would like to check them when you're done, though."

Lenny brushed vigorously for the next five minutes. When Patricia checked his teeth, they were spotless.

"Now you can go to sleep if you want. Good night, Lenny."

Lenny didn't reply. As you already know, autistic people have a hard time with greeting words and phrases such as "Hello," "Good-bye," and "Good night." These words lack any meaning for them.

Lenny turned and walked slowly to his room, feeling like a child in a horror movie who is about to discover a demon hiding behind the door.

For the next hour, Lenny tried to get to sleep, but as he had feared the entire evening, he remained awake. He tossed and turned, trying to find a spot on the bed that was comfortable and the right temperature against his ear. Everything seemed so scary to him. He kept wondering if this was all a big joke, and at any minute he parents would burst in and say, "April Fool!" After all, April first was only a few days away. However, as the minutes ticked away and his parents did not appear, Lenny gave up all hope.

While he suffered through the night, terrified of telling Patricia how lonely and scared he was—for fear of getting yelled at—someone in nearby Lake Forest went to bed quickly and easily, unaware that when he awoke the next morning, his life was about to change as drastically as Lenny Fahrer's had.

# Chapter 9

*March 24, 2010—8 a.m.*
*The Fairfield Residence*

As Lenny Fahrer tossed in terror on Scranton Avenue in Lake Bluff, Illinois, Hector Fairfield was sleeping peacefully in his bed at his house on Deerpath Avenue in Lake Forest. Little did he know that he was about to get punished for even the smallest fraction—or no infraction at all—of rules he did not know existed, and no matter what he did at school, he would be punished for it.

Hector's alarm clock normally woke him up at 7:30. Hector's parents, however, were already up. It was time to start their part of the experiment. They were going to do what they had done in elementary school when they were bullies themselves.

They were going to set Hector up.

You see, the only way Hector got up on time was by the sound of his alarm clock. When his parents got up at 7:20 this morning, his father tiptoed into Hector's room and turned off the alarm. At 7:30, Hector's older brother, Dietrich, got up, threw on some clothes, ate breakfast, and left for school at 7:50.

At 8:00, Hector's mother walked quietly into his room and watched her son sleep. *Should I really do this?* she asked herself. Her maternal instincts were making her feel protective of her child. But then her bully side replied, *Of course. It's going to be fun. You've been angry at Hector since the day he was born because he wasn't a girl.*

She also reminded herself that being a parent involved wanting to hug and strangle your child all day, every day, as Calvin's dad pointed out in the comic strip *Calvin and Hobbes. I've hugged him a million times already, so now it's time to get my anger out.*

Yes, this was going to be fun.

Mrs. Lydia Fairfield kneeled down beside her sleeping son, brushed his soft hair away from his face, put her mouth next to his ear, and screamed at the top of her lungs, "WAKE UP, YOU LAZY BUM!"

Hector bolted upright, his heart pounding.

His mother jumped to her feet and glared at him.

"Mom?" he said, confused.

"WAKE UP! IT'S EIGHT O'CLOCK, AND YOU'RE GOING TO BE LATE FOR SCHOOL! YOUR BROTHER GOT UP JUST FINE! WHY DID YOU TURN OFF YOUR ALARM?"

"My alarm? I didn't touch it. It—it must be broken."

"THERE'S NOTHING WRONG WITH THE ALARM. SEE?"

Quickly Lydia reset the alarm time for 8:00, pressed the button, then shoved the clock into Hector's ear, just as it went off.

"Stop it!" Hector cried, covering his ears. "What are you doing?"

Chad Fairfield, Hector's father, stormed into the room with a raging look on his face. "HECTOR, IT'S EIGHT O'CLOCK! WHY DO YOU ALWAYS HAVE TO SLEEP IN?'"

"Do what?" Hector asked, beginning to tremble.

"WHY DO YOU ALWAYS TURN OFF YOUR ALARM? DON'T YOU CARE ABOUT GOING TO SCHOOL? YOU GOOD-FOR-NOTHING—"

"Hey, wait a minute," Hector interrupted, feeling his bully side finally waking up. "You're full of it, I didn't—"

"HOW DARE YOUR TALK TO YOUR FATHER THAT WAY!" his mother screamed.

*"What?"* Hector cried. "You can't—"

Chad grabbed his son by the pajamas and hauled him up out of bed. His bullying impulses were coming back to him, too, and he was feeling that old power surge into his muscles.

"What can't I do, huh?" He glared into his son's eyes, using the same intimidation tactics he'd used on little kids during recess.

Hector was so surprised by his father's behavior that he couldn't reply. His parents normally placed no restrictions on him, and they never disciplined or yelled at him.

"That's better," Chad sneered. "You will be confined to your room for the next fifteen minutes."

"But then I'll be late!" Hector protested.

"That's not my problem," Chad retorted. "You should have thought of that when you turned off your alarm."

"But I didn't—"

"SILENCE!" Chad roared.

"You can leave for school in fifteen minutes."

"But what about breakfast?"

"It'll be ready in fifteen minutes."

Confused and angry, Hector threw on his clothes, then pounded on the door to his room until his father announced, "Time's up," and let Hector out.

As Hector stomped down the stairs, his father called out, "Hit that door again, and I'll make you clean the toilets—with your head."

Wow, he hadn't used that line in years, but like magic, it just came back to him.

Starving, Hector burst into the kitchen, looking ravenously at the food on the table. His mother was eating a tall stack of pancakes, slurping the syrup as she chewed. He slid into his place at the table as his mother said, "Here's your breakfast."

Hector stared in horror at four soft-boiled eggs, the raw yokes oozing all over the plate.

"Gross!" he screamed. "I can't eat this crap!"

"Have your forgotten your manners? It's impolite to say food is bad and not to show gratitude," said Mrs. Fairfield, who stuffed a large bite of her pancakes in her mouth. "Eat your eggs or else you'll be late for school."

"I can't eat raw eggs. I want cooked eggs," he complained.

"Either you eat these eggs or you starve," Mr. Fairfield warned as he walked into the room. "I ate raw eggs as a child and survived."

"I don't care. I'm not eating that crap."

"Then run along now and get ready. You'll be late for school," Mrs. Fairfield said, then took another huge forkful of her pancakes.

"Why can't I have some of that?" he demanded, pointing to her food.

His father replied, "There aren't any left." He picked up a plate of pancakes and sat down at the table. "I got the last ones. Sorry."

Hector watched longingly as his father smothered the pancakes in syrup.

"I'm not eating raw eggs," Hector declared.

"Oh, yes you are. You're gonna eat raw eggs, or you won't eat for the rest of the day," said Mrs. Fairfield. She then put two more yolks onto his plate. "Now eat up, 'cause it's all you're gonna get."

"I won't eat it. I'll starve."

"Fine. Starve. Just get ready, and I'll take you to school."

Hector shook his head a few times, then said, "I'm not sure what's going on, but I'm getting out of here."

Hector got ready for school, but because he was late, his mother drove him to the front entrance of the building.

"Have a nice day, dear," Mrs. Fairfield called and burst out laughing as her son walked away.

Hector mumbled, "Bye," wondering why his parents had suddenly gone off the deep end.

When Hector got to his classroom, his teacher, Mrs. Appell, made him go to the office to get a tardy slip. As the secretary was writing out the slip, Dr. Wikedda walked out of her office and said, "Hector, because of your chronic tardiness, you can no longer be a hall monitor. I'm relieving you of your duties."

"What?" Hector cried. "Because I was a few minutes late?"

"You have been late repeatedly all year."

Now he really did think he was in the middle of a nightmare. This was the first time he'd been late in his entire life.

"No, I haven't! I'm always on time! I was late today because my parents didn't wake me—"

"Don't lie to me, boy. Your parents just called and said you stormed out of the house without breakfast."

"That's because—"

"I don't care about excuses, young man!" Dr. Wikedda declared. "From this moment forward, you will no longer be entitled to roam the halls without a pass. And if a hall monitor catches you, you'll be given detention."

"What?"

"No arguments. Now get to class."

When Hector arrived back at class, Mrs. Appell scowled at him and said, "What's your excuse this time?"

This was getting spooky. "What do you mean? This was the first time—"

"NO EXCUSES, HECTOR!" Mrs. Appell screamed, frightening the entire class. "Get into your seat. And because you are late, the entire class won't receive their reward for good behavior this week."

"What?" the kids cried, almost in unison.

A cacophony of protests erupted in the class.

"That's right," Mrs. Appell told the class with some malice in her voice. "You can thank Hector for that."

Over a dozen faces turned his way, with expressions ranging from anger to sorrow to menace.

"Just wait until recess," someone murmured.

"All right, settle down," Mrs. Appell told the class. "Before we were rudely interrupted, we were about to read the story called 'Martin and the Elephant.' Hector, you will read first."

She handed him a bad xerox copy of the story. The type was way too small, and there were black smudges and faint places that hadn't copied well.

"Why don't you come up in front of the class and read to us," Mrs. Appell told him.

"How can I read this? It's too small," Hector protested.

"Give it a try," she encouraged him. "It's probably your laziness, not the packet's fault."

"Can I have a new packet?" asked Hector.

"Nope, that's your packet, and you're not getting anyone else's."

Hector walked up to the front of the class with a sinking feeling. He put the first page up close to his nose, but he could hardly make out the words.

"'A long . . . time . . . ago, an elephant named . . .'"

Hector stared at the long foreign name, part of which had been blocked out by a black smudge.

"Go on, Hector, we're waiting," Mrs. Appell said impatiently.

"I'm trying."

"Try harder."

" . . . named . . . Ro . . . si . . . ."

"You're just not trying hard enough, Hector. Go sit down," she said in disgust. "Maddie, you continue, since Hector obviously didn't bring his brain to class this morning."

The class burst out laughing.

Maddie, the smug, self-assured genius of the class, and the girl who worked with Hector to make fun of him in the bathroom, had been in her seat sounding out the difficult word, so she walked briskly up to the front of the class and read without a pause. She also was a bully and sometimes would make fun of Lenny as well. 'A long time ago, an elephant named Rosie lived happily in the jungles of India.'"

She looked up, gave Hector a haughty sneer, then smiled sweetly at Mrs. Appell.

"Go on, Maddie," the teacher said.

"Wait," Hector said, glancing at Maddie's paper, "her copy is readable. How come mine is all smudged up?"

"What Maddie has is not your business. That's your copy, and you're not getting another one. You keep quiet, or you're off to the principal's office."

"This sucks," Hector grumbled to himself.

Mrs. Appell stared at him in exaggerated horror, as if she had never heard such a foul word. "Go to the principal's office, Hector. *Now*."

"What did I do?" he protested.

"That doesn't matter. You need to be taught a lesson." Turning to Maddie, she smiled and said, "Now, my dear, if you would please continue?"

When Hector returned from the principal's office, with a warning that next time he'd be given a detention, he found himself the subject of ridicule in gym class, and again in music. Nothing he did was right, and soon the other kids in his classes were laughing at his every move. No one was quite sure why the teachers had started a campaign against Hector, but the kids readily fell into the swing of things. It became apparent just how disliked the former hall monitor really was.

During homeroom class, Mrs. Appell rejected every idea Hector had for his student report. He came back to her desk over and over with new ideas, which she automatically shot down for a variety of reasons, including, "This doesn't follow the state rubric."

Hector had never even heard of the state rubric.

It was now lunchtime, and Hector was furious. On his way in the cafeteria, he ran into Othello and Macbeth, his old friends.

"Hey, what's happening?" Macbeth called. "We heard you got laid off."

"Yeah, too bad, so sad," Othello said jokingly, as boys do with each other.

"I don't know what's going on," Hector complained. "Everything's mixed up. Someone's out to get me."

"Yeah, sure," Othello replied.

"What did you do to piss off the principal?" Mac asked.

"Nothing," Hector protested, then to his own horror, he started to cry.

"Whoa, whoa, what's this? A crybaby?" Mac said, immediately trying to distance himself from his onetime friend.

"I—I am not a crybaby."

"Sure looks like you're a crybaby," Othello taunted him, somewhat in earnest now. "Okay, we're here to collect the lunch money. Hand it over."

"What?" Hector said, confused again. This was a trick they pulled on the younger kids, never on each other. "I'm not giving you my lunch money."

"Oh, yeah, you are," said Othello.

"Why are you doing this to me? I'm not a first-grader."

"You're a crybaby, aren't you? We'll keep it safe for you," Othello said.

"Give it to us," Macbeth warned, "or we'll report you to the principal."

Hector thought about the warning he'd just gotten—how the next time, he'd get a detention. He also knew from firsthand experience that, in this school, bullies were always right.

Reluctantly he handed over his lunch money.

As he waited in the cafeteria line, he looked longingly at all the scrumptious-looking choices. He hadn't had anything for breakfast, and he was starving. After loading his tray up with food, he went directly into the cafeteria to find a seat.

"Excuse me," said Mrs. Palmer curtly. "But you have to pay for that."

Hector turned and felt his tears welling up again.

"I gave my lunch money to the hall monitors."

"You what? Who did you give your money to?"

"Othello and Macbeth."

"The bullies? How could you be so stupid?"

"But they said they'd report me if I didn't give them my money. Then I'd get a detention."

"Hector, are you feeling all right? You know better than to give your lunch money to a student."

"But . . . but . . ."

"I'm sorry, but you'll have to pay me directly."

"But . . . I don't have any money."

"Then I'm afraid you can't have any lunch." She plucked the tray from his startled hands.

Despondent, Hector sat down by himself and starved until lunch period was over.

Then during recess, he sat down on a swing and starved some more. Since he was a bully, and the other kids didn't know what was going on, no one wanted to play with him.

When he returned to his homeroom, he sank into his chair, hoping nothing else would happen.

But it did.

"Today, class," Mrs. Appell began, "we will continue our history lesson about slavery. When the Americans first established the thirteen colonies, they separated them into three regions: New England, or the Northern Colonies; the

Middle Colonies; and the Southern Colonies. Every colony grew crops according to its own climate. The Southern colonies had the right climate for growing cotton, rye, tobacco, and indigo. These crops required the work of many men to grow and maintain, and they were grown on large farms called plantations.

"Plantation owners had to find ways to get enough people to work in their fields. White Europeans were not suited to toiling away in the hot sun, and they tried to enslave Native Americans, but the natives were steadily dying of the diseases the Europeans brought with them. These diseases, such as measles and mumps, had been unknown to the Native Americans, and they had no immunity to them. So the plantation owners started looking around for workers who could survive the white man's diseases and were used to working in the hot sun. Africans could do both.

"However, slavery was unfair and immoral," Mrs. Appell continued. "To get a feeling for what it must have been like, we're going to act out a play. Here, Steven, pass out these scripts." She handed a pile of booklets to one of her favorite students.

"Patrick, you will play the part of the plantation owner. Maddie, you'll be his wife. Steven, please pass out the scripts. You'll be the overseer. He was the one who punished the slaves and kept them from rebelling . . ."

One by one, Mrs. Appell assigned the parts. Finally, she gave the last part to Hector—he was to play Jack, the rebellious slave who is caught and punished. As Steven handed a script to Hector, he whispered, "You better watch out, loser, I'm gonna beat you up." Then he turned to Mrs. Appell and, with a bright smile, announced, "All finished."

Everyone enjoyed acting out their roles; everyone, that is, except Hector.

The kids really got into taunting and humiliating Hector, the ex-bully. They were showing the age-old human phenomenon of turning on someone when a leader—or the group—deemed it socially acceptable to do so. Hector could hardly say his lines, he was so upset. For a moment, he wondered whether he had gone back in time and really had become a Southern slave.

When school was over, he went to the curb to wait for his mother. When she didn't show up, he walked slowly home, wondering what in the world had happened to his life.

# Chapter 10

*March 24, 2010—10 a.m.*
*Buffett Elementary School, Mrs. Redbear's Classroom*

Back in her classroom that morning, Alice wondered how Lenny was doing as she listened to Mrs. Redbear give a boring lesson about the desert ecosystem and the Hopi Indians. She wished she could be homeschooled, like her friend.

Alice herself had difficulties during the school day. One of those struggles involved taking notes in class. Other students seemed to copy things down from the whiteboard just fine, but she couldn't.

Because of these difficulties, Alice learned how to compensate with her listening skills. She had a good memory, and although she could not take notes based on what the teacher said, she could still listen to the teacher and remember, sometimes word for word, what the teacher said. She tried to use these memory skills to help Lenny, who had an even harder time in school—he couldn't seem to take notes or memorize anything. She felt sorry for him, and as she was his friend, she'd tried at first to whisper information in his ear.

Until Mrs. Redbear caught her and accused them both of cheating.

"Now, class, although the desert receives almost no rain, many plants and animals still live there. The cactus, for example, has adapted to the desert ecosystem by holding in as much water as possible through its thorns and thistles. Sometimes rain can come for a brief time. When this happens, because of the sandy environment, rain can flash down an area, which causes what people call a flash flood. Who here has a parent that owns a cactus in their house?"

One student raised his hand.

"Yes, Charlie?" asked Mrs. Redbear.

"My mother owns a cactus. She says that whenever she gets angry, she imagines she's a cactus that's about to prickle anyone who gets in her way."

The entire class, including Alice, laughed. Alice also wondered why Charlie didn't get reprimanded for saying something irrelevant. If Lenny had said that, he would have gotten in worse trouble.

"Settle down. Now, Charlie, we don't need to know about when your mom gets angry. But how often does your mother water the cactus?"

"She only waters it twice a year and it still grows," said Charlie.

"That's correct. The cactus is adapted to not having much water, and if you watered it regularly like another plant, you'd overpower it with water. Now, before we settled America, one Native American tribe that lived in the desert was the Hopi Indians—"

Alice struggled to listen and keep up. She was shocked at what Charlie said but then noticed when Dr. Wikedda entered the room.

"Yes?" asked Mrs. Redbear, seeing Dr. Wikedda enter the room.

"I need to talk to the class for a bit. I've stopped in every classroom to talk about an issue in our school."

"Okay," said Mrs. Redbear.

"Class, two days ago the custodian made a shocking discovery in one of the girls' bathrooms. Does any girl know what I am talking about?"

The kids looked away or down at their desks, most of them trying not to giggle or laugh. No student raised their hand except for Dan.

"Dan, don't make a joke out of this," Mrs. Redbear warned.

"Do any of the *girls* know what I'm talking about?" Dr. Wikedda continued.

No girl raised her hand. Alice knew what Dr. Wikedda was talking about but felt scared to say anything.

Finally a girl named Edith raised her hand.

"The peeling paint," said Edith.

"Yes. Some girls here have decided to act disrespectfully and peel the paint in the girls' bathroom. Now I've been told by one of our students as to which girls have been peeling the paint, and I punished them by making them stay in for recess, which they have been doing all week. But I will be carefully monitoring the situation. If any of you know anyone else who has peeled the paint, please let me know. And if you are caught peeling paint, you will be forced to stay in for recess as well. Do you understand?"

"Yes," said the class in the unison.

"Thank you."

Dr. Wikedda left and the class returned to their lesson about desert ecosystems.

Later that day, at lunch, Alice poured out her troubles to her friends at lunch that day. Although this was her fourth and next-to-last day of staying in for recess, she still felt upset. Although she didn't always agree with everything that her friends said and did, she still stuck with them because they at least listened to her when she felt upset.

"It's just unfair that I have to stay in for recess. I didn't peel any paint, and I got in trouble," she said.

"I would hate missing recess," said Claire.

"So what do you do in detention?" asked Tammy.

"Nothing. Just sit quietly and think. Or do homework. But I don't do homework because I don't feel like doing it."

"I would hate it," said Tammy.

"I just want to find out who really did it. I wouldn't peel that yucky stuff. It'd get under my fingernails," said Alice, shuddering at the thought.

"I hope they find someone," said Claire. "You know, maybe it's not a girl, but some boy sneaking in the bathroom."

"Who would do that?"

"Maybe that gross boy Todd," Tammy remarked.

"It could be. Some boy could do that to be mean," said Claire.

"Well, I don't care what the principal thinks. I didn't peel any paint," said Alice.

"Maybe you did. How do we know?" Tammy countered.

"You're my friends, and I'm telling you the truth," said Alice.

"Anyway, okay, whatever. So when are you, like, getting out of detention?"

"I told you—the end of the week," said Alice.

"That's good. We miss you," said Tammy, but then she glanced briefly at Claire and giggled for an instant.

Even though Alice didn't always pick up on nonverbal messages, she noticed that one.

"I miss you, too," she said sincerely, hoping her friends were telling her the truth.

At that moment the lunch supervisor announced that lunch was over, and it was time to clean up. Afterwards, Alice walked to the principal's office while the rest of her grade went to recess.

"Good afternoon, Alice," said Dr. Wikedda. "How are you today?"

"Fine."

As Alice stood there awkwardly, the principal asked, "Have you seen Lenny Fahrer lately?"

"No. I haven't seen him since he left school," said Alice.

"He's being homeschooled for two months for . . . personal reasons. When you see him, would you let me know how he's doing? In fact, I'd like you to report to me on his progress. You can still play with him while he's gone. And please do this because . . . well, because I care about him," she said, putting on her friendliest motherly expression.

"Okay," said Alice, not understanding what was going on.

"I hope you can remain friends with Lenny while he's gone."

"Lenny and I will always be friends, Dr. Wikedda!" Alice exclaimed.

"Good. Now you may sit down," said Dr. Wikedda.

Alice went to a nearby chair and sat down, thinking about her situation. Right after she sat down, Lori and Mary arrived. They all sat quietly as they served their time.

She spent a lot of time thinking, wondering why she had to go to school, but wondering if her home life was any better. Although she had disagreements with her sister Colleen, there was one thing she heard from her that she did agree with, a line from a poem that Colleen had found on Facebook: "When a girl is quiet . . . millions of things are running through her mind." Millions of things often ran through Alice's mind as well.

*Why did she have to be here?* she asked herself. She truly had not peeled any paint in the bathroom, but wondered who had, and who'd blamed her for it.

Finally, after what seemed like an eternity, Alice was told by the principal she could go back to class.

After school, Alice had additional struggles to face back at home.

Her own mother, after being informed by Dr. Wikedda about the paint peeling incident, felt shocked about the whole matter.

"Alice, you're an honest person. How could you end up doing this?"

"I didn't peel any paint!" Alice cried. "I don't know who did. Someone has set me up."

"Well, I hope that's true, Alice. I love you, you know," said her mother. "I won't punish you for it because I think the school's already punished you sufficiently."

This meant a lot to Alice. She often found herself unable to get along with her mother and her sister Colleen. Alice got along much better with her father, with whom she had a special relationship, one in which she felt understood and respected. Perhaps this was because he shared several unusual traits with his younger daughter.

"Oh, and one more thing," continued Alice's mother. A woman named Patricia came to see me a few days ago and told me that Lenny's now living with her while his parents are on vacation. She gave me this number that you can use to call him if you want, okay?"

"Okay," said Alice. Her mom gave her a note card with the new number.

Alice fought with her mother over a lot of things. Her mother disapproved of how she dressed, and how she spent all her free time watching the same movies or reading the same comic books. Eventually, Alice and her mother compromised that if Alice got all of her homework done, she would be allowed to read or watch what she enjoyed.

Alice's sister came home late as she did every Thursday night after cheerleading practice. Luckily, as Alice did not have any homework that night, she got to read her *Chloe and Allie* books, and watch a new movie that she liked, *Cloudy with a Chance of Meatballs*.

"Aren't you cold wearing those short shorts?" asked Alice's mother.

Colleen rolled her eyes. "You ask me that every day, and every day I say no. Do you want me to look like some dork from Alaska?" She stared pointedly at her younger sister, with whom she still had to share a bedroom.

"In my day, we never looked like that!"

"Well, Mom, your day is not my day. Every one of my friends wears short shorts, and I'm wearing them, too."

"Don't you have any respect for your body or yourself? Boys get messages when you wear those things! They'll look at you like you're a . . . a . . ."

"Why should I change the way I dress because of how some boys look at me? I wear what I want to wear."

Alice just sat there, laughing internally at the fight. She'd listened to them argue this over and over again, and wondered if it would ever end.

"Well, isn't Alice *hot* wearing those long, ridiculous clothes?" asked Colleen mockingly. "And I wasn't referring to how boys look at her."

The argument ground to a halt at that moment, when Alice's dad came home from work.

"Hey, everyone," he said. Alice's dad worked as a trader, specializing in orange juice futures. He commuted down to the Chicago Board of Trade every day on the METRA train.

"Hi, Daddy," said Alice.

"Hi," he said, although he didn't hug her because, like Alice, he didn't like being touched. "How was school?"

"Well . . ."

"I heard about the paint. I know you didn't do it, and I'm surprised your principal would take the word of another student."

"How did you know?"

"Your mother called me. I can't change the decision of the principal, but at least you don't have to convince me that you're innocent. I already know you are."

Alice went to back to watching *Cloudy with a Chance of Meatballs*. She liked this movie because she enjoyed the story and felt like she could relate to the characters. She also liked one girl in the story, Sam, who reveals that she was made fun of in school halfway throughout the film. She was just getting sleepy when the phone rang, and she heard her mother answer it.

After her mother was off the phone, she decided, since she did not see Lenny in school today, to call him. Maybe he could get her mind off her terrible day.

# Chapter 11

*March 24, 2010—10 a.m.*
*Patricia's Apartment*

While Hector was being teased by the kids in his classroom, school was already over for Lenny. He was surprised at first, but homeschooling was a lot different from regular school. He was allowed to wiggle around when Patricia taught him, even rock and twirl. For math, they worked on graphs, which Lenny loved. Even though they were graphing his own personal exercise times—Lenny hated any exercises that involved supporting his body weight—he was motivated to complete the workout that Patricia had assigned him so he could record his times on a colored bar graph. She even allowed him to graph his heart rate and pulse, explaining that he could record them every day as a measure of his physical progress.

Patricia allowed him to read aloud and even point to the words with his fingers when it was story time, to help him comprehend the story. She did not scold him for not understanding her, and would patiently repeat over and over what she'd said until he comprehended it, often writing something down so he could read as well as hear it. For science, she let him watch a nature show on television, which she recorded so he could watch it over and over in case he missed a part. Lenny still feared that this was an elaborate April Fool's joke, and that at any moment, the punishments would come crashing down on his head.

Patricia then went to the computer and printed out a poem to share with Lenny. "I want to share this with you, Lenny. I wrote this in high school for my school magazine." She gave him the sheet of paper with the poem. Lenny read it. It was titled "One-Way Street," and it went like this:

*I walk across these hallowed halls*
*Go past the classrooms and bare walls*
*I see my friends on each school day*
*But the street, the street, is still one way.*

*I talk to them, they talk to me*
*I like them but I still can't see*
*I sometimes speak but cannot say*
*As the street, the street, is still one way.*

*What I cannot say I can still write*
*At the end of the sentence is where I fight*
*My writing is where my emotions stay*
*While the street, the street, is still one way.*

*Sometimes I lose, sometimes I win*
*With the lumps and scrapes I take to fit in*
*Yes that's sometimes the price I pay*
*As I walk the street that goes one way.*

*But I don't really care about the street's path*
*It's still worth the joy and the aftermath*
*For my friends still keep my confusion at bay*
*Let the street, that street, remain one way.*

Lenny didn't totally understand what the poem meant, but he still related to the part about not always fitting in and not being understood. He still wondered how that related to one-way streets, though.

"I'm done," said Lenny.

"Did you like it?"

"I did, but didn't understand all of it," said Lenny.

"I figured you wouldn't. I wrote it for kids older than you," said Patricia. "It's noon now, so school is over for the day. You worked hard, Lenny, and now you are free to do whatever you want."

Lenny remained silent. This could be the moment, he thought, when the punishments began.

"You're free to read, but you do not have to do so. You can play computer games, or hey, I just bought a stack of puzzle magazines from a garage sale. They look brand new. Would you like to try one? I also want to show you a movie that I got from Netflix. I have a friend whose son has autism, and she says he really likes it."

Lenny took a deep breath, afraid to answer. Offering a puzzle or the computer, or some movie that autistic people liked, might be the trick he'd been dreading, since these were the things his mother and the social worker tried to limit in his life. He looked at Patricia out of the corner of his eye. She did not seem to be trying to trick him.

"If I work on a puzzle, promise you won't tease me?"

"Tease you? Why would I do that?"

"Well, liking puzzles and computer games, says Mrs. Ting-Pot, means you're not normal. You're supposed to like people and extend the hand of friendship to them."

"Well, it's important to like people, but first you have to learn how to trust them. It doesn't sound like you've had a lot of people you can trust in your life. Perhaps that's why you like puzzles—there's always a way to figure them out. And in my home, you can work on as many puzzles as you want."

This was unbelievable. No adult had ever said that to him. He tried another tack.

"I think I get it," he said. "If I complete a puzzle in an hour, I get a check, and if I get five checks, I get a star on my chart?"

Expecting praise for good behavior, Lenny was confused when Patricia got a horrified look on her face. "Wait a minute!" she cried. "You don't have to do a puzzle if you don't want to! It's not supposed to be work. I'm not going to force you to do *anything* when you live in this house, except for a certain amount of schoolwork, but I'm going to try and make it interesting for you, and you'll be allowed to give me your opinion of how you like what you're learning."

This was so confusing to Lenny that he started to get overloaded, as if he needed to cocoon or even shut down. He put his head down in his lap.

Patricia wanted to cry. Lenny behaved like a child who had suffered from intense abuse.

"Or you can just do nothing," she said softly.

From his lap, he said, "I think I'll just do nothing." That way she couldn't punish him for making a mistake.

As she started to walk away, Patricia said, "When you're ready to do something, you can watch some TV. I have cable. What's your favorite program?"

He wasn't sure. His mother had imposed strict rules on TV watching, and he didn't understand much of what was going on anyway. He had to watch a video at least a dozen times before he could fully comprehend it. Keeping his head in his lap was a nonverbal way of saying, *I don't have one.*

Patricia nodded in silent understanding and then went to the kitchen. About an hour later, when Lenny still had his head in his lap, she came out and said, "I'm not going to force you to do anything after school, but I think you should *try* to do something."

Fearing she was about to blow up at him, Lenny said, "I—I will do a puzzle."

"Good," she replied brightly. "Here are the magazines I bought." She walked over to a shelf and pulled off a small stack.

Lenny grabbed the first magazine from the stack. He turned to Puzzle 1, which was on page 5. He wondered why Puzzle 1 would be on page 5, not page 1, but the world was often weird and made no sense.

Puzzle 1 was a maze called "Chicago," in which a person had to get from one side to another. Lenny knew that he lived in the Chicago area, but he did not like the city. It was crowded, dirty, noisy, and shocking because of the sudden car horns and sirens. He also could not stand the stench of cigarette smoke and diesel fumes.

After he had completed several puzzles, Lenny was suddenly distracted by the phone ringing. The phone was not loud, but it still got his attention. He listened to Patricia answer it.

"Just a minute, please," she said, then called out, "Lenny, it's for you."

*For me?* he thought as he walked over to the phone. Maybe it was his mother.

"Hello, who is this?" Lenny asked.

"Hi, Lenny."

"Hi, Alice," he said, surprised.

"How have you been, Lenny? I miss you."

"I'm being homeschooled today. At least, that's what my new teacher said."

"Mrs. Redbear said you wouldn't be coming to school for two months. You must really like that, Lenny. I would."

"It's fun. But I'm still scared. I don't know if my new teacher is going to stay nice to me."

"Who's your new teacher, Lenny?"

"Her name is Ms. Nottingham. And I'm living in her apartment. She seems nice. She's not forcing me to do anything after being homeschooled."

"Where are your parents?"

"They went to a place called Bolinas."

"Don't know where Bolinas is."

"I don't know either."

"So what's homeschooling like?"

"It's actually easier than school. Ms. Nottingham gives me assignments and teaches me a lesson, and we were done a lot earlier than in school. I was done at noon."

"Noon? Wow. I know this is hard to believe, but Hector was actually upset today."

"What?"

"I was walking down the hallway and saw Othello and Macbeth actually make fun of him. He apparently was fired from being a hall monitor."

"He deserved to be fired."

"It was strange though. But if bullies can bully us, they can bully themselves too."

"Hector deserved what he got," said Lenny.

"Of course he did. They all deserve getting thrown in detention. And I have to stay in for recess for a week. The principal thinks I was in charge of the paint peeling because someone told her that I was."

"What?"

"Yep. According to her, some girl told her that I ordered them to peel the paint. Someone set me up. You should understand, because people set you up all the time."

"Like those hall monitors. They're always getting me into trouble."

"Me, too. But this is the first time I've been set up in front of the principal."

"Something happened to me the week before I started homeschooling."

"What, Lenny?"

"I went to this doctor, and he said I had autism."

Alice was silent for a moment.

Lenny continued, "He said it's the reason why I'm different. It's why kids bully me."

"And why you don't understand what people say?"

"Yes. That's what he said. But how did you know?"

"Because I have trouble, too," Alice admitted.

"You do? How?"

"I have a lot of trouble understanding the teachers."

"I didn't know that," said Lenny. "You don't seem to show it."

"I don't, Lenny, you're right. But I also hear the wrong words all the time. And sometimes—please, keep this is a secret, but you know what?"

"What?"

"It's hard for me to understand other people at times."

"Really?" asked Lenny. "Do you understand me?"

"Yes. You're my friend. And I also have trouble relating to my friends. I like Claire and Tammy, but they don't like what I like and they like things I don't like, such as silly bands. But do you understand me?"

Lenny thought for a moment. "Yes. I understand you. Because you're my friend, and I'm not afraid to listen."

"Lenny, do you think that you're being homeschooled because of your autism?"

"I don't know," said Lenny. "But I still like it."

"Any kid would like it," said Alice. "Meanwhile, I've also been watching this new movie titled *Cloudy with a Chance of Meatballs.*"

"Do you like it?" asked Lenny.

"Yes. It's about this scientist who makes a machine that enables food to come from the sky. He's misunderstood just like us. And then the machines goes out of control and he has to save the day," said Alice.

"Wow, that's an interesting movie," said Lenny.

"Yeah, it's great," said Alice. "Maybe I can show it to you the next time you come over. I can show you something I like for a change."

"That might be nice," said Lenny.

He then overheard a voice screaming, "ALICE! TIME TO GO!"

"I have to go to my sister's dance recital," Alice explained. "But the principal said I could come over and play with you while you're not at school."

*The principal?* Lenny thought. *What does she have to do with this? Has she kidnapped my parents?*

"What did the principal—"

"ALICE!" the voice screamed again in the background.

"Bye, Lenny," Alice said quickly, and hung up the phone without waiting for him to say good-bye.

Lenny hung up the phone and then went back to his puzzle book. After completing Puzzle 5 on page 9, in a half-hour, Lenny turned the page. Before he started Puzzle 6, on page 10, he tiptoed toward the kitchen until he could see what Patricia was doing. She looked like any ordinary person, taking things out of cupboards and stirring a pot on the stove.

Seeing that Patricia was not plotting anything against him, Lenny went on to the 7th puzzle, a simple crossword, which he finished quickly because he was good with words in isolation. He wasn't always so good with putting them together or understanding what they meant.

Lenny finished the 7th puzzle and went on to the 8th. He decided to stop asking questions about punishment, because maybe in this house, punishment was meted out if you asked too many questions or if he did not do enough puzzles by dinnertime. He did not get bored solving puzzles, since they were, in a sense, his native language. His entire life was a puzzle, a mystery that had to be first understood and then solved over time and with great effort.

"Lenny!"

Patricia was calling him. Instinctively he clutched with fear, because he didn't know the reason she was calling him.

"Lenny, please come here," Patricia said.

Terrified, he walked slowly across the room through the door into the kitchen.

"Lenny," Patricia began as she sliced raw potatoes. "I know you hate changes and surprises, so I'm going to let you know about everything that's going to happen before it happens. And if there has to be a change, I'll let you know as soon as I find out. Dinner will be at six-thirty tonight, and we will have chicken and mashed potatoes. If you don't like those foods, we can have something else. But I have to know now so I can give you time to get used to the change."

*What did she say?* Lenny had never heard anything like this. No one ever asked him what he wanted to eat, and usually they forced him to consume things he did *not* want to eat. But still fearing a trap, Lenny just nodded and said nothing.

Patricia, therefore, continued talking to fill in the silence.

"I'd also like to ask you a question. You don't have to answer it, at least not right away. I understand that the change from your parents' house to my apartment was abrupt. It was for me, too. I did not know until a few days ago that I was going to take care of you. I want us to get to know each other since we'll be together a lot for the next two months while I homeschool you. I was thinking that we could do something together before dinner. You know, walk in the Cuneo Gardens, or along the North Shore Bike Path. Or we do not have to go anywhere. I know you are in the habit of forcing yourself to do things either to please other people or because you are afraid of them. But I want you always to tell me what's in your heart. Will you do that?"

Lenny weighed the pros and cons of saying "yes" or "no." Patricia was expecting "yes," so it was probably the safer answer. However, if he were to give the real answer in his heart, it would be "no." Deep inside he did not want to do anything with her, but he had a lesser risk of punishment if he said "yes."

So finally, after a minute, he said, "Yes, I want to walk in the Cuneo Gardens with you before dinner."

"I hope you mean that in your heart, Lenny, and if you do, I know we will have a good time tonight. But if you change your mind before four o'clock, don't be scared to tell me. I am your friend, and I'm not going to hurt you. Until then, please continue working on your puzzle book," said Patricia. "I need to get some work done. I edit books to make money."

"What does that mean?" asked Lenny.

"Publishers give me books that authors have written, and I get paid to make sure they are grammatically correct. So continue working on your puzzle book, and then we can do something in a half-hour, okay?"

"All right," said Lenny. He continued working on his puzzle book, relieved that he was successfully able to dodge a fight.

# Chapter 12

*March 24, 2010—3 p.m.*
*The Fairfield Residence*

Hector felt sudden and intense relief when the clock struck 3:00 p.m. and school ended. It was the same way Lenny had felt each day before Patricia rescued him.

Hector had been misunderstood and bullied by everyone he'd come in contact with. During the science lesson, he was partnered with a boy who kept bugging him about how he had curly hair, but when Hector complained to Mrs. Appell, she told him to "deal with it." By the end of science, she demanded, "When are you going to stop complaining?"

After a long and terrible day, he was able to go home, where he could relax and not fear being harassed or bullied. Or so he thought.

Little did he know that more was on its way.

When he first got home, though, he was overjoyed. Throwing down his backpack and coat on the floor, he raced into the kitchen and said, "Hi, Mom!"

Instead of greeting her son, Lydia Fairfield said sternly, "Hector, don't throw your things on the floor. Hang up your coat, and put your backpack in your room."

"In my room?" he said, "But I never put my—"

"Don't argue with me, young man," she said menacingly. "And go change your clothes. Your grandparents are coming over."

"Why do I have to change my clothes?"

"That's one, Hector."

Hector looked at his mother, the increasingly familiar confusion evident on his face.

"One what?"

"That's one strike, Hector. It's a new discipline technique for disobedient children, called 'Three strikes, you're out.' Each time you argue or disobey me, I'll give you a strike. After three strikes, you get a time-out or a privilege taken away."

"WHAT IS GOING ON HERE?" Hector screamed to the walls.

"That's two," his mother replied.

At that moment, Hector's older brother, Dietrich, walked into the kitchen, dressed in clean clothes, having changed from the weird T-shirt and ripped jeans he normally wore to school. Hector smiled, because his brother was a safe person.

"Hey, Dee," Hector whispered. "What's eating Mom? She's been treating me weird all day. I just walked in, and she yelled at me for nothing."

"She yelled at you?" Dietrich asked in disbelief. Hector was the baby of the family, who got away with everything.

"Yeah. It's the weirdest thing. Everybody's been yelling at me today, the teachers, the kids in my class, even my best friends were teasing me."

"Weird is right." Dietrich went to the fridge to get some juice. He poured himself a glass, then offered the carton to his brother.

"Thanks," Hector said, taking it then reaching up into the cabinet to get a glass.

DING-DONG!

The doorbell rang.

Mrs. Fairfield said, "Dee, will you go answer the door?"

"Sure, Mom," he said, chugging the glass of juice and setting it on the counter.

To Hector, she said, "Now you know you're not supposed to have anything before dinner. It will spoil your appetite." She snatched the juice carton from his hands.

"But I'm thirsty!" he protested.

"Hector . . ." she warned.

"Why did Dee get to drink something, but I didn't?"

"That's three. You struck out. Go to your room."

"WHAT? But Gramps and Grandma—"

"That's one."

"WHAT IS GOING ON?"

"That's two. Yelling is not permitted in this household!"

"But you've been yelling at me!"

"That's my privilege. Because I'm in charge. If I get to three, you will spend the rest of the day and night in your room, and miss dinner."

Hector was so hungry that he would do anything his mother said in order to get dinner.

"Okay, Mom," Hector said, starting to feel real fear.

"So go out and say hi to Grandma and Gramps."

Mr. and Mrs. Arkham were hobbling into the house, both using canes. They were the same age—eighty-eight—and had been married for sixty years. It was an embarrassing sight, but they never acted as if they were embarrassed. Mrs. Arkham had had bladder trouble for the past four years, and leaked continuously. No one ever brought up this problem except that after they left, Hector's mother had to clean the sofa with PetPro urine-removing detergent then mask the smell with Odor Eaters. If Grandma leaked on her way to the sofa, Hector's mother had to scrub away the smelly trail.

Mr. Arkham had a big scar on his cheek from falling off his bicycle the year before at the Senior Olympics. He still won the race because he was the only entrant. It didn't seem to bother him. In fact, the Arkhams seemed very happy, and despite Grandma's little problem, they were both healthy and active.

"Hector, dear," his grandma said. "Would you go to my car and get my bag?"

If this had been yesterday, he might have told her he was busy. But today, that would probably have gotten him a "strike," and one step closer to starvation.

"Yes, Grandma," Hector said apprehensively, watching his mother for a possible reprimand.

"Hector is such a nice child," Grandma cooed. "I'm so happy he's my grandson."

Lydia shook her head. "You would not have been happy to see him this morning. He overslept, would not eat his breakfast, and has been arguing with me all day."

"He wouldn't eat?" Grandpa chimed in. "But that's impossible. That boy usually eats like a moose."

"What'd you feed him?" Grandma asked.

"Soft-boiled eggs."

"Sounds healthy to me. I used to give you soft-boiled eggs every morning."

"Sounds disgusting," said Dietrich, who, like Hector, was trying to figure out what was going on. "What about Fruit Loops and Frosted Flakes?"

"Dietrich, dear, we're improving Hector's diet so he won't have so many behavior problems."

"This is getting weird, Mom," Dietrich replied.

"Now, don't you concern yourself. You're my good child." To her parents, she said, "He's never given me a day of trouble."

Hector staggered back to the front porch, carrying a large, heavy bag full of Depends, pins, Kleenexes, and baby wipes. From the smell of the bag, which in his weakened state was making him gag, Hector suspected that one of those Depends might have already been used.

"Could somebody help me?" he called out.

"As I was saying," his mother continued, ignoring him altogether, "Hector will have to learn to eat what is placed in front of him. If I give him uncooked eggs, that's all he's going to get. I'm not running a restaurant."

Hector's muscles were tiring. He tightened his grip but still felt the bag slipping out of his arms. He really needed help.

"I'll go help him," Dietrich offered.

"No," his mother replied. "He's eleven years old. He should be able to carry the bag of his grandmother. After all, he's a boy! He'll eventually grow into a man, and he'll have to be carrying all kinds of things for other people. Besides he's young. Young people don't get hurt when they work hard."

Dietrich replied, "But he's still only a kid! Why isn't anyone helping him?"

"Now, son," said Grandpa, "how's he going to get independent if someone's always helping him? Let him use a little elbow grease for once."

Dietrich looked at the adults in the room as if they had become strangers.

"Well, I'm going out to help him," he said defiantly. "I don't care what you say." This was an unusual move for Dietrich, who was usually the obedient son in the family.

"Dietrich," Grandma said sternly, "what your brother does is none of your concern. You are not your brother's keeper."

This suddenly produced ambivalence in Lydia Fairfield. She did not want Hector to get any help, but her mother's heartlessness irritated her. Lydia had never resolved her own rebellion against her parents, but had become a bully instead during high school, taking her anger out on younger children. That's why she was enjoying her role in the experiment—making Hector suffer—but she still didn't like her own mother taking control of the situation. It wasn't any of her mother's business how she was treating her own son.

"Well, I don't care," Dietrich announced. "I'm going out there."

"Do you let your son speak to you that way?" Gramps demanded of his daughter, and immediately she was transported back in time to when she was a little girl, terrified of her father as he reprimanded her for everything. She had never been good enough for him.

"No, I don't," Lydia said, even though Dietrich had never really talked to her that way before. To Dietrich, she said, "Stay where you are. I am your mother, and I forbid you to walk out of here."

"Help!" Hector called out again. "Will someone help me?"

"What's in your bag that's so heavy?" Lydia asked her mother.

"Well, I have my supplies and my pills and, let's see, my phone book—"

"Phone book?" Lydia asked.

"In case I have to call someone in the car," her mother explained.

"And my Bible—you know, the large-print edition weighs more."

"Well, no wonder it's so heavy," Dietrich commented.

"And my portable toilet seat . . ."

"Is there anything breakable?" Lydia asked.

Her mother thought for a moment, then answered, "Why, yes, my iron tonic and my cod liver oil . . . they're in glass bottles. And my instant Sanka, that's in a glass bottle, too, because you drink that newfangled flavored stuff . . ."

"And you expected Hector, who is eleven years old, to carry all that? What if he drops it?"

"Be careful, Hector!" Grandma called out. "Don't drop the bag!"

"I can't carry it anymore," he called back. "I'm putting it down on the porch." There was a knock on the door. "Could somebody let me in? I'm locked out."

None of the adults moved.

Dietrich looked around. "Well, can I go let him in?" he asked.

"Not yet," Lydia replied. "I'm teaching Hector a lesson."

"What lesson?" he asked, totally bewildered.

"I'm teaching him that when something is difficult, he has to try harder."

Fifteen minutes passed, and Hector cried out at least ten more times. It was cold outside, and he hadn't thought to put on a coat for his short errand. Lydia and her parents kept arguing about her son. As the older folks rattled on and on about discipline and tough love, Lydia felt herself get angry at them. They'd tried that stuff on her. No wonder it was so easy for her to slip into the role of bully with her own son.

"It's called survival of the fittest," Mr. Arkham told his grandson. "My father asked my puny brother to carry a twenty-pound bag of groceries into the house, knowing he wasn't strong enough. The bag broke, a jar of jelly fell on his leg and shattered. He almost bled to death and walked with a slight limp from then on, but my parents were teaching him a lesson in survival."

Lydia wanted to scream at him, "I've had enough of your theories! I'm going to go help my son." But she bit her tongue and didn't say a thing.

Finally, Dietrich jumped to his feet and said, "I can't take this anymore. Hector, I'm coming!" And he raced to the front door and threw it open.

Hector was sitting on the porch, crying. His brother had never seen him like this.

"Dee," he said weakly. "I locked myself out. It's—it's cold out here."

"I know, bro. Everyone's gone nuts in the house. Even Mom. Something's happened to her."

"This is totally screwy, I know. Here, let me carry that thing." Dietrich, who was strong and on the wrestling team, still had a little trouble hoisting the bag into his arms. "What does she have in this thing?"

Hector stopped crying and said, "Smell, and you'll know."

Dietrich put his nose close to the top of the bag, then scrunched up his face. "Ew-w-w! It smells like Grandma!"

The two boys burst out laughing, and it was a moment of relief and connection that Hector had been needing the entire day.

Holding the bag as far away from his nose as he could, Dietrich pushed open the door with his foot then moved aside so Hector could enter first. Together they walked back into the living room, where the smell of their grandmother, which had been filling the room, hit both of them, and together they burst out laughing again.

Grandpa Arkham was very displeased to see Dietrich carrying what was supposed to be Hector's burden.

"Dietrich," Grandpa said sternly. "Your grandmother asked Hector to get her bag, not you."

"But it was too heavy for him."

"Too heavy? Is my second grandson a wimp?"

Hector got angry. "I'm not a wimp. It's just that—that—" He inhaled the aroma of the bag and started laughing uncontrollably again.

Now his mother got into the argument. "Hector, how dare you laugh at your grandfather! He's trying to have a serious discussion, and you're laughing at him? That's—"

Neither she nor Hector remembered what strike he was on, but that sobered him up fast.

"I'm not laughing at him," he said in all seriousness. Then Hector glanced at his brother, then they both burst into a new round of giggles.

His face red and swollen with anger, Grandpa looked as if his cheeks would burst open at any minute.

"This is outrageous, Lydia," he declared. "That boy needs to be punished."

For a brief moment, Lydia felt herself filling with the same rage against him that she had felt as a teenager. The man had no compassion at all, no sense of fun. She thought about defending her son, who had done nothing wrong. He'd been trying to help. She looked around the room. Everyone seemed to be looking at her expectantly, waiting for her to say something.

"Hector," she said finally, "if you don't apologize to your grandmother and grandfather this instant, you will get no dinner. It's your choice."

Everyone's head swiveled to Hector, who found himself looking down suddenly, as if he wanted to escape the room. His mother had actually given him no choice at all—he would do anything, say anything, to get dinner.

"I'm sorry, Grandma. I'm sorry, Grandpa," Hector said dutifully, without meaning it.

Dietrich shook his head, put the bag into his grandmother's lap, then announced, "I'm outta here."

No one protested as he walked away.

"Well, now," Grandma said, as if nothing unpleasant had just happened. "I was cleaning out the attic the other day, and I came upon some things I wanted to show you, Hector dear. They're from your grandfather's days as a country doctor."

"I used to make house calls," Grandpa said proudly. "No HMOs in my day. I charged five dollars a visit, more if I was taking out tonsils. I'd line the kids up on the kitchen table and cut them all out at once."

Grandma reached into her smelly bag and pulled out what looked like a spiked claw.

Hector stifled a look of horror. "Was . . . was that used to deliver babies?" he asked.

"No, no, not at all." Grandpa glared at him, as if that were the stupidest question in the world. Hector decided it was safer not to say anything for the rest of the visit.

"It was actually my own invention," he said proudly, then checked to make sure that Hector was paying attention. Immediately Hector straightened up and tried to look interested, even though fear was making it increasingly difficult to look into his grandfather's face.

"What did it do, Dad?" Lydia asked politely, even though she had heard the story a thousand times.

"When I took a person's blood pressure, I used the traditional squeeze ball and cuff. But often the cuff was too big for the thin arms that I was measuring. That was before all the junk food you youngsters have these days—some people just didn't have enough to eat. Without a tight enough cuff, I couldn't get an accurate reading. So I used this device to clamp the cuff tightly enough on a thin arm. If I'd patented it, I could have made millions."

If you're thinking right now that Mr. Arkham was sometimes very strange, you'd be right. Often he thought up some odd solutions to common problems. They worked, but they also made people nervous. After getting kicked out of several medical practices, he started working on his own as a country doctor. His patients put up with his weird ways because there was no other doctor around, and he never actually hurt anybody.

Grandma Arkham pulled out more medical devices to show her grandson. Grandpa beamed with pride. All Hector could think about was food, but he nodded politely, staring at her ear to make it look like he was paying attention.

# Chapter 13

*March 24, 2010—3:45 p.m.*
*Patricia's Apartment*

While the Fairfields and the Arkhams were discussing Grandpa's odd assortment of medical gadgets, Lenny Fahrer was making a momentous decision. Although he had agreed to do something with Patricia at 4 p.m., as the time approached, he admitted to himself that he really didn't want to go.

Could he defy her, after years of being trained to obey without thinking?

She'd said that he could do what was in his heart. He decided to risk punishment to see what would happen if he followed her advice.

Slowly he walked into her office, where Patricia was working on her latest assignment as a free-lance copyeditor. He stood at her desk, trying to move the words in his mind closer to his mouth.

"Lenny, are you okay?" she asked, looking up.

"Uh, I, uh, I . . ."

"Go on. Take your time."

"You know how I said I wanted to go with you to the Cuneo Gardens?"

"Yes, Lenny?"

"I, uh, I changed my mind. I don't want to go anywhere."
There, he'd said it. Now he waited.

Patricia felt a flash of annoyance. She had already made a reservation for dinner after their walk in the Cuneo Gardens. In fact, she even considered going without him, since she was confident he wouldn't burn the house down or rob her. However, he was to be treated with unconditional respect, and that included giving him the right to change his mind.

"That's perfectly fine, Lenny. All along, I didn't think you ever wanted to go in your heart. I will go alone, if that's okay. Have you ever been alone before?"

Lenny thought about it. He couldn't remember a time when someone wasn't staring at him, at home or in school, waiting for him to make a mistake so they could yell at him.

And now she was leaving him alone? All by *himself?* It was going to be heaven.

But wait a minute. Wasn't this a trick? He recalled many other times when people had warned him, "I'm leaving now," while he sat in the corner refusing to move. Instead of doing what they had promised, they would usually stomp back to his corner, rip him off the floor, and whisk him away while he either screamed or went limp.

However, it was no trick. At 4:00 p.m., Patricia left the apartment. "I will be back in two hours," she said as she grabbed her keys. "I want you to stay inside for your own safety. But you can use the phone, watch TV, take a nap, or do what you want. I also have something that I bought for you—it's a Japanese manga book that you might like. It's called *Momo's Veggie Container Delivery School Debut.* I've heard that kids like you love this stuff."

She was a little apprehensive about leaving Lenny alone in a strange environment, but she had studied autism and knew that autistic people hated change and new things. He really had no reason or inclination to explore new things, either at a museum or in her apartment. He needed a small, dependable world with no surprises. For this reason, she knew that Lenny would not go rummaging through her drawers hoping to discover something exciting.

Lenny wasn't interested in manga, but he was too polite to tell her so. He was scared to look in drawers or to go out and explore because there was too much information for him to take in. In fact, that was why he hated modern culture. Everything was just too crowded, too noisy, too smelly—in other words, too big. And sadly, things often started out nice and small, but became big as a sign of progress, like the friendly local grocery store that moved across the street and became a giant warehouse megamarket complete with exposed pipes on the high ceilings.

All he wanted to see was the stuff he had to see in order to navigate his way through the apartment. He looked at all the doors, to the bedrooms, the bathroom, the kitchen, and the living room. Gathering his courage, he opened the front door and peeked out. Down at the end of the hall was a fire exit. Immediately he got nervous, since there was a warning about opening the door and setting off the alarm. He was afraid that his legs might walk over on their own and his hand might reach out and open the door without his being able to stop it.

Slamming Patricia's front door shut, he breathed deeply for a minute or so, trying to calm himself down. After all, he was alone. Alone! He'd always dreamed about being alone, but no one ever let him. They were always after him to do this or do that. He hated the world. To many people, the world was a nice place filled with nice people, but not to someone who had experienced the world's hostile side. To Lenny, life consisted of hoping that a single day would pass by without being reprimanded or yelled at for a mistake committed unknowingly.

So now that he was alone, what was he going to do by himself? He did not really know. After Lenny had seen all of the apartment that he cared to see, he sat down on the couch and started to think. The clock was ticking. He had seventy-five more minutes until Patricia came home. He was going to have to make the most of this time.

There was actually a lot of stuff for him to do. Walking into the office, he saw chairs and a desk with a computer against the left wall. To his right, he saw shelves of books. He decided to boot up the computer to see what games and software Patricia had. Knowing she might get angry, he kept a close watch on the computer's clock so he could turn it off before the two hours were up. And at this moment, the clock read 4:05. (The time was actually 4:20. The clock was fifteen minutes slow, but Lenny didn't know that.)

The computer booted up to Windows XP. Lenny wondered why Patricia had such an obsolete operating system, but didn't question it. After the computer booted up to the main display, he waited until the hard drive stopped humming so he could run a program. A sign popped up shortly on the desktop that said: *ZoneAlarm has loaded and your computer has been firewalled.*

Lenny didn't know what ZoneAlarm was, but when the computer finished starting up, he took a look to see what was on it. There were eight programs on the desktop—Word, Excel, Internet Explorer, Paint, Desktop, Image Expert, Windows Explorer, and Windows Media Player. He didn't find any program that he liked. It was obvious, for Patricia was unmarried and didn't have children, so she probably wouldn't have any software for kids.

He wondered what use the computer had for him. There weren't any games to play, but the computer did have access to the Internet. The Internet had a lot of interesting things to see.

He logged on to Google and then thought about what he would be interested in reading about. Quickly he typed in "Alphabet."

Instantly, 50,200,000 results popped up. Now Lenny knew that most of these results would have nothing to do with what he was interested it, but he clicked on "The History of the Alphabet."

A red screen popped up with the twenty-six letters printed along the top. As he began reading, he grew increasingly worried that Patricia would return and catch him at the computer. Every ten minutes, he would check the time, but somehow it just flew by, and suddenly the clock said 5:40. This shocked him. The passing of time without his realizing it shocked him, and made him feel as if his life was flying by out of his control. The happiness of being alone was shattered as he realized a horrible truth about his life: When he enjoyed something, time flew by like a bird, but when he hated something, time inched along like a snail. It seemed as if he had one minute of happiness for every twenty-four hours of misery.

Looking at the bottom of the webpage, Lenny saw some links that led to individual histories of different alphabets. The links were:

## HISTORIES of INDIVIDUAL ALPHABETS

**Hebrew Alphabet**
**Cherokee Alphabet**
**Arabic Alphabet**
**Armenian Alphabet**
**Mangyan Alphabet**

Not knowing what to choose from, Lenny clicked on the "Cherokee Alphabet." He then read an essay about Sequoyah, and how he decided to create an alphabet for the Cherokee language after being exposed to the English alphabet, hoping that making his tribe literate would help them defeat the white man. He read that although this was the conventional story of the alphabet's history, an alternative theory existed that Sequoyah did not invent the Cherokee alphabet. Instead, the alphabet had existed among the Cherokee for generations and was created by the tribe's Scribe clan that Sequoyah was descended from.

Well, at least Lenny had twenty more minutes to read about the alphabet—or so he thought. It was actually 5:55, and Patricia was already on the third floor walking toward her apartment.

So while Lenny was still reading, Patricia walked in and called out, "Lenny, I'm home!"

Lenny immediately tried to log off the computer. However, when he put his hand on the mouse, six ads popped up. He tried frantically to close them, but he'd only gotten rid of three when five more popped up.

"Lenny, I'm back!" Patricia called out, sounding nearer. "Where are you?"

He kept frantically trying to close all the ads as they kept reappearing like the heads of the Hydra.

"Lenny!" she repeated as she walked into the room.

He just had time to turn off the machine when she came over to him.

"Were you reading my e-mail?" Patricia asked, since he seemed inordinately flustered.

"No . . . I was reading about . . ." Lenny was terrified now. When he was little and obsessed with the alphabet, his speech therapist told his mother to discourage his interest in letters, even though they were the tools of communication that he understood the best. Adults were so weird and mean, taking away the things a child valued the most.

"Why are you home early?" Lenny asked. You were supposed to be back at six, and it's only five-forty."

"I'm not home early. I'm actually late." Then she explained, "The computer clock is fifteen minutes slow for some reason."

Lenny closed his eyes, feeling himself begin to melt down. The predictability of time was one of the few safe and comprehensible things in his life. No matter how confused a day became, there would always be a one o'clock, one-thirty, two, and on and on. Clocks were Lenny's safety nets. When the world was shattering around him, he looked at a clock to reassure himself that *something* made sense.

But here was a clock that was wrong, that lied. Lenny put his head on the desk and shut down for a time.

"If you're tired," Patricia said gently, "you can go to sleep."

In a trance, Lenny shuffled into his room, lay on his bed, and drew alphabet letters in the air with his right index finger.

When the world was falling apart and nothing made any sense, if he wrote letters in the air, he would feel safe and protected again. He did that for the rest of the evening, until he fell asleep in his clothes.

# Chapter 14

*March 24, 2010—6:05 p.m.*
*The Fairfield Residence*

The Fairfields and the Arkhams welcomed home Hector's father, Chad, from his hard day at work. Mrs. Fairfield told him that dinner was almost ready, and she ordered Hector to set the table, something he had never been expected to do before.

Fearing the descent of his mother's wrath if he protested, Hector dutifully took down six plates from the cabinet and arranged them around the table. Then he got knives, forks, and spoons from the drawer and put them at each place. Finally he got out glasses and napkins, which he awkwardly folded and set next to the plates.

Famished, he sat down at his place to wait for his food.

Mrs. Fairfield walked into the dining area, and Hector smiled briefly, expecting to receive at least a few words of praise for a job well done.

"HECTOR!" she screamed. "WHAT DO YOU THINK YOU'RE DOING?"

Confused and afraid, he hunched his shoulders as he looked up, wondering what he had done this time.

"YOUR GRANDPARENTS ARE HERE! WE DON'T SERVE THEM ON EVERYDAY PLATES! GO GET THE GOOD CHINA AND THE SILVER!"

"The . . . the what?" Hector asked, not sure what she was referring to, since he was a son, not a daughter, and had never noticed those things.

"NO BACK TALK!" she warned. "You have only one strike left. If you don't have those plates on the table in two minutes, you're not getting dinner."

Instantly Hector was on his feet, running into the kitchen, looking for the china. He opened all the cabinets. What was the "china"? It seemed like a silly name for fancy plates. What were the ordinary plates called—America?

"Mom . . ." he said tentatively, then closed his mouth.

"You have one minute left, Hector," his mother warned.

His eyes darting around, Hector felt a wave of panic rising into his throat. Suddenly he got an idea, and he ran from the room.

"Dee!" he called frantically. "Dee! Help!"

He raced up the stairs and pounded on his brother's room.

"Hey, bro, what is it?" Dee asked as he opened door.

"Where's . . . where's the china?"

"The what?"

"The china! You know, that fancy stuff that we eat off on Thanksgiving."

"How would I know? Ask Mom."

Hector felt tears welling up in his eyes. Horrified that he might cry again in front of his brother, he mumbled, "Oh, never mind," and raced down the stairs.

As he was rushing back to the kitchen, he bumped into the glass cabinet in the dining room. The contents rattled ominously. Hector stopped and looked through the class. There they were—those plates they used on Thanksgiving.

Ripping open the door, he reached in to grab the entire stack of plates. Then suddenly he stopped. What if they were too heavy, and they fell? His mother would punish him for the rest of his life. But he couldn't get them all out and set on the table in less than a minute. What if he wasn't finished when time was up, and he starved?

He stood there, unable to decide what to do, panicking because his indecision was wasting time. Finally, he picked up the stack of plates, took a deep breath, and began walking slowly to the table. It was only a few steps, but gee, were they heavy. He took a step, focusing only on the plates. Then he looked up to make sure he wasn't about to hit anything. The table was only a few feet away.

He took another step.

"Hector!" his mother called, and he lurched, sending one of the plates flying off the stack.

Hector was so terrified that time stood still. In slow motion, he watched the plate drift through the air on its way to the floor. In horror, he watched it hit with a—

Soft thud. Thank God his father hadn't pulled up the carpet last year, as he'd threatened to after the hundredth spill under the table.

The plate didn't break, but it lay there accusingly.

"Hector, what was that noise?" his mother called from the kitchen. "Did you drop a plate?"

Hector couldn't move. He couldn't speak.

His mother walked quickly into the room, saw the plate on the floor, looked at Hector holding the stack of plates, and screamed, "FREEZE!"

She sounded like a cop with a gun, and if he hadn't been frozen already, Hector would have laughed at her.

"Don't move!" she cried, then rushed to his side, carefully taking the stack of plates out of his arms and setting them on the table.

Hector crumbled to the floor and put his arms around his knees.

"What were you doing, carrying all those plates? You could have broken them all!"

"I was trying to get the table set on time," he replied in a whisper.

"That's no excuse for carelessness! Those plates belonged to your great-grandparents. They're irreplaceable. How could you be so stupid? You're eleven years old, and you should know better than to carry so many at once. Now get up."

Hector tried to get up, but his legs refused to move. He felt his energy draining out of his hands and feet and seeping into the floor.

"Get up this instant," Mrs. Fairfield warned.

Again, he tried, and managed to stand up on shaky feet when suddenly—

"BEEEEEEEEEEEEEEEEEEEEEEEEEEEEEEEEEEPP!!"

The loudest noise in the world blasted through the house. Hector fell to his knees again, holding his ears.

"BEEEEEEEEEEEEEEEEEEEEEEEEEEEEEEEEEEPP!!"

It went off again. Was it the smoke detector? Was there a fire?

No, it was the timer.

"BEEEEEEEEEEEEEEEEEEEEEEEEEEEEEEEEEEPP!!"

Tears of pain started pouring out of Hector's eyes. The noise was unbearable. He hunched his shoulders, expecting another noise like the blast of a gun. When it didn't come, Hector timidly looked around, expecting to see everyone on the floor holding their ears. Instead he saw a sea of frowning faces staring right at him.

Why wasn't anyone else reacting to the noise? Hector wondered. To him, it had been like a cherry bomb exploding down his ear canal.

Finally Hector's father asked, "Will someone explain to me what's going on?"

*Me too,* Hector thought.

"Your son was carrying a stack of our best china to the table, and in his carelessness, one fell down and could have broken. They're your grandmother's, and they're irreplaceable."

Mr. Fairfield stared at her in disbelief. "You asked *Hector* to set the table?"

At that moment, Dietrich strolled into the room. "Yeah, you should be grateful he was willing to help you. What's wrong with you guys?"

"You stay out of this," his mother warned him. "This doesn't concern you."

"What doesn't concern me?" he asked, blinking.

Mr. Fairfield gave a sidelong glance at his wife, then asked softly, "Is this part of it?"

Mrs. Fairfield shook her head slightly and whispered, "Later."

Hector didn't notice this interchange, but Dee did. Something odd was going on, and his parents knew about it. In fact, they were in on it. He decided he'd have to watch them closely from now on.

"Well, I don't know about you, but I'm hungry," Grandpa announced.

Hector thought about saying, "Me, too," but was afraid to make a sound.

"I have to decide what to do about Hector," Mrs. Fairfield explained. "I asked him to set the table by a certain time, and he should have known to use the good china, since we're having guests. Then when he got the plates, he was careless and he dropped one."

"He was so nervous, he couldn't be careful," Dee argued.

"Yeah," Hector managed to say, grateful that at least one person was on his side.

"I do not believe this!" Mrs. Fairfield cried. "Now both my children are defying me? Dietrich, see what a bad influence you are on your brother?"

"I don't see anything," Dietrich retorted, "except for some reason you're dumping on Hector."

"That's quite enough," Mr. Fairfield chimed in. "If either of you says another word, you're both going upstairs with no dinner."

"Hector," Mrs. Fairfield reminded him, "there are six hungry people in this room, and you haven't finished setting the table."

Hector looked over and saw the table completely set, just not the way she wanted it. Slowly he walked over and gathered the regular dishes and stacked them in a pile. Then carefully he picked up one of the special plates, telling himself, *Do not drop it. Do not drop it.* However, his mind was so preoccupied with that verbal warning that it forgot to tell his fingers what to do. They gradually loosened up and the plate fell on its side and rolled to the floor, this time breaking into a thousand pieces.

Everyone was so shocked that not a word was spoken. Grandma, however, started leaking on the carpet, and the steady dripping could be heard in the otherwise silent room.

"I . . . have . . . had . . . ENOUGH!" roared Mrs. Fairfield. "That's THREE!! Hector, go to your room."

Hector burst into tears again. "Oh, Mommy," he wailed, calling her by a term he hadn't used since he was five, "please don't make me go upstairs. I'll pay you back! I'll set the table for a month! I'll—I'll—"

Even in her bullying mode, Mrs. Fairfield felt a deep compassion for this pathetic child.

"Okay, okay. Go to your room now, but I'll bring your food up to you after we've eaten."

Hector's tears of terror turned into tears of joy. His mother wouldn't let him starve after all.

"But you're grounded for the next three days," Mr. Fairfield added.

Abruptly Hector's tears of joy turned to tears of frustration. He was invited to go to Othello's house after school the next day. And Macbeth was having a bunch of guys over the day after that. Hector was looking forward to that stuff in the worst way.

However, he did not say a word. He didn't understand any of what was going on.

"Well, now that we've settled that," Mr. Fairfield said, "let's eat."

But just then, from the kitchen came a loud:

"BEEEEEEEEEEEEEEEEEEEEEEEEEEEEEEEEEEEEEEPP!!"

Again, Hector fell to the floor, covering his ears.

"Now what?" Mr. Fairfield groaned, and turned toward the kitchen, just in time to see black smoke billowing out of the oven.

This time it *was* the smoke detector

The family's dinner had gone up in smoke.

"Oh, Hector," Mrs. Fairfield sighed. "Look what you've done."

"What are we going to do about you?" her husband asked, shaking his head. "You've ruined our dinner."

Again, Hector looked at the table, which was nicely set and ready to go with ordinary dishes.

"We'll have to go out," Grandma said, looking around for her bag. By now, her smell had been overpowered by the odor of the burning roast. That was the only good thing to come out of the situation.

"Such a waste," Grandpa said sadly, and even Hector silently agreed, but for a different reason.

"Let's go," Lydia Fairfield said, and silently the six hungry members of the Fairfield and the Arkham family got into the Fairfield family van and rode to a local Greek-owned restaurant. On the way, Hector wondered why his mother had made such a big deal out of a set of dishes and why everything had been his fault, and not hers for being so crazy about nothing.

# Chapter 15

*March 24, 2010—10 p.m.*
*Patricia's Apartment*

That night, both boys were feeling the effects of the "switch."

You've probably noticed that a lot of things happened on that first day. The truth is, a lot more things happened than I've actually written about.

For an autistic person, every aspect of a new thing, down to the smallest detail, is scary and has to be gotten used to. As you have probably figured out, someone like Lenny has a good reason for fearing new things. New things can hurt you. And even Hector, who until today was just an average normal bully, was now starting to fear new things. After only one day of living an autistic life, Hector was starting feel autistic himself.

However, it is not my job, as the writer, to ramble on, presenting theories and beliefs about first things. It is my job to entertain you with a story, which is the reason you bought this book or I gave it to you if you are an autistic person and too poor to buy it. Therefore, our story continues on the second day of the experiment, which for Lenny, began at midnight.

Even though Lenny fell asleep early, by midnight he was wide awake, tossing and turning and unable to get comfortable.

He stared at the new ceiling until the newness of all the cracks and brush strokes in the paint overwhelmed him and he had to put his face into the pillow. Finally he stared out the window, watching the sky turn from dark to smoky to pale to rosy. He knew Patricia would be waking up soon, even though he was finally getting really tired. This was not an uncommon situation for Lenny. In fact, this was how it usually was—he was unable to sleep until the rosy fingers of dawn appeared in the sky.

Patricia woke at 7 a.m. on the dot, thanks to her alarm clock. She got dressed, then walked softly over to Lenny's room. Peeking in, she saw Lenny fast asleep in what looked like an uncomfortable position. His arms and legs were bent at funny angles, and his head was inclined backward. She decided it was important not to wake him up, for she had heard him tossing and turning during the night and knew he must really feel exhausted and need that sleep. Besides, she saw no reason to get him up at a particular time, and getting enough sleep would be an aspect of the experiment.

Patricia made herself a cup of coffee, then sat down and planned her lessons for the day. She would begin by reviewing what they had covered the day before, so Lenny wouldn't be confronted by something new right off the bat. Together they would check over his work, although she would not give him grades, since that was a worthless system of evaluation. It didn't matter whether Lenny got the problems right, only that he learned what the problems were supposed to teach. Thinking over Lenny's reactions the day before, she realized that she should also keep track of his behavior and how it changed.

The major problem she had was that she didn't really know what she was doing for Lenny except treating him with kindness and respect, something every child deserved. In her brief reading, she'd learned sadly that the current treatments for autism, by definition, were not based on kindness and respect, but rather fear and force. In her training to be a teacher, with the goal of starting a charter school someday, she learned that child abuse gets started when a parent or caregiver tries to change a child, according to the parent's mental image, in ways that are impossible for the child to achieve. If the child resists, the parent gets increasingly insistent and abusive, as if yelling and punishment would somehow change a child's essential nature.

All therapies that attempt to change a child's basic nature, therefore, are a form of abuse.

And most methods of educating children are based on forcing them to sit in uncomfortable chairs among individuals they have not chosen to associate with, learning things they are not interested in. It sounded like a form of abuse to Patricia. Her school would be based on what children really need—lots of room to run around and explore, guided by an adult who encouraged rather than controlled them.

Lenny presented a special opportunity for her, because if she could get through to him, she could easily succeed with normal children. And the four thousand dollars would give her some start-up capital for her school.

## 10 p.m.
## The Fairfield Residence

Meanwhile, Hector was sent back to his room after his family returned from the Greek restaurant. He had been screamed at by his parents for placing his elbows on the table, something he had always done before without giving it even a second thought but had not been reprimanded by his parents for doing so. He wondered what could have happened. Hector's brother, Dietrich, sat silently in shock, wondering why his parents and grandparents were acting so strangely.

"For your elbows on the table, go to your room. We'll tell you when it's time to go to bed," said Hector's mother.

When he got to his room, he lay on his bed and began to cry. What had he done to deserve this? He didn't know when he could come out of his room, but he didn't even want to come out.

The door opened. Hector's heart began to pound as he feared his mother or father might scream at him again. However, it was not them—it was just the cat Pointy. The Fairfields had owned Pointy for three years after adopting her from the Heartland Animal Shelter. Pointy was the tabby cat that Hector had selected three years ago because it looked like a tiger, and Hector admired tigers because of their fierceness.

Hector liked the cat. Pointy was a strong cat who often chased and killed mice throughout the house. Hector loved watching her chase her victims through the house's many rooms, and he imagined what it would be like to be a cat, chasing a mouse, and enjoying the fear that he engendered in a weaker animal.

But now he wasn't interested in seeing Pointy chase a mouse. He hoped Pointy would notice his sobbing and his crying, and that he felt upset. He wondered how Pointy would react seeing him this way. The cat had never actually seen him sad before.

Pointy walked around the room, and eventually climbed on to Hector's bed. "Hello, Pointy," Hector said, continuing to sob while he lay down on the bed. "I'm really sad now."

The cat meowed at Hector and moved toward him, lying right next to him.

"At least you won't scream at me," said Hector. "Everyone else seems to be pissed off at me."

The cat just meowed, like Gary the snail from the show *Sponge Bob Square Pants*. The cat seemed to Hector now as the only living being that would not yell or scream at him. The cat just lay there, looking at Hector and meowing. Hector looked at the cat, too, wondering what the cat was thinking. He couldn't know what the cat was thinking entirely, but at least it was not thinking about another way to entrap and yell at him again.

"I don't know what's going on," Hector said to the cat. "I know you might not be able to understand me, but at least you can listen."

The cat meowed again. And then, magically, the cat moved closer to Hector. He lifted his arm and put it around the cat. Hector didn't know if this would upset the cat, but it didn't. The cat just stayed there. Hector started petting the cat. The cat didn't object. It just sat there and rested by Hector while he kept petting its back.

"All day, everyone has been acting really strangely. My parents yelled at me, and my friends acted mean to me. I feel like there are no more people that I can talk to anywhere. But at least you don't . . ."

The cat began to purr as Hector talked to it.

"At least I can talk to you without getting screamed at. And you don't have to worry about everyone the way I do. You can just roam around the house and have fun chasing mice. You don't have to go to school tomorrow and worry about whether the people that used to be nice to you will act mean to you the next day. Maybe everyone will go back to normal tomorrow, and I can feel better."

The cat climbed on to Hector's chest.

"And my teachers acted mean, and my mother and grandfather screamed at me, and I'm even too scared to go to sleep tonight because I might sleep in again. I don't know what to do, Pointy."

Pointy fell asleep on Hector's chest. Hector was shocked that the cat was so comfortable there. But then, Hector had never cried in front of Pointy before. He was glad that the cat was there and not leaving him.

Pointy was soon snoring the way she did when she went into a deep sleep. Hector now realized that he could go to sleep, too. He gradually drifted off as he felt the weight of the cat on his chest, slowly breathing on him.

Hector's mother finally opened the door one hour later. She saw him fast asleep with the cat on his chest, on top of his black comforter on his bed. She wondered whether she should scream at him and make him put on his pajamas and brush his teeth, torturing him some more. But she chose not to. Even she had her limits, although she'd enjoyed the experiment so far and what she was doing to her son. She still had to admit that she loved him. She remembered a comment that she had read from an old *Calvin and Hobbes* cartoon: *Being a parent is wanting to hug and strangle your child at the same time.*

"I hope you learn your lesson. I hope you become a better person after all this is done," she whispered, then quietly walked out of the room.

# Chapter 16

*March 25, 2010—9:42 a.m.*
*Patricia's Apartment*

The next day, Lenny woke up, tired but not exhausted, and walked to the kitchen. His body told him that he needed to use the bathroom, but his mind couldn't concentrate on waking up, walking, and listening to inner signals at the same time.

Patricia was at the kitchen table, looking over his work from the previous day.

"Good morning, Lenny," she said.

Lenny remained silent.

"What would you like for breakfast?" she continued.

Lenny continued to remain silent. He had a bad dream and had woken up afraid. It took him a moment to realize that he was in Patricia's apartment, having slept in a strange bed, and he had no idea what was going to happen to him. As he stood there in the kitchen, his tears welled up, and he realized that he wanted to go home. He was pretty sure that Patricia would understand, but he knew that she would never let him stay there alone.

The tears started falling down his cheeks.

"What's wrong?" Patricia asked, even though she already knew.

"I want to go home," cried Lenny. "Take me home. I don't care if my parents aren't there. I just want to be in my own room."

Patricia was starting to feel really terrible about the entire arrangement, but she could not take him home. At this point, she didn't care about ruining the experiment—she was more concerned about Lenny's feelings—but if she took him home and he learned that the entire story about his parents going out of town was a hoax, he might have even less trust in adults than he had now.

"Lenny, you know I can't take you home. Your parents aren't there."

"I WANT TO GO HOME!" Lenny screamed.

Patricia thought this would be the normal reaction of any ten-year-old in Lenny's situation, but he was actually suffering from a surge of anxiety called a panic attack, something normal kids usually did not go through. Overcome by the fight-or-flight response to extreme stress, the urge to get away was pumping chemicals into Lenny's bloodstream that made him feel as if he was about to explode. When he was with his parents, they called it "reaching his limit," which meant that no matter where they were, they had to drop everything and take Lenny home.

"I WANT TO GO HOME! I HAVE TO GO HOME!" he screamed.

Patricia tried to remain calm, even though anger and frustration were welling up in her, so that she felt the growing impulse to scream right back. However, that wouldn't help either of them. And besides, if she ruined the experiment after only one day, she'd undoubtedly have to give the money back.

"All right, Lenny," she said finally, unable to choose money over the suffering of a child. "I can understand how scary all this must be. I'll call your parents and see if I can take you home."

"Th-Thank you," Lenny choked out, then got on the floor, put his head in his lap, and cocooned.

Patricia walked into the next room, picked up the phone, and called Lenny's house.

"Hello?" his mother said after two rings.

"Hi, my name is Patricia Nottingham, the person who's taking care of Lenny for the next two months."

"Oh, hello. How's everything going?"

"Well, to be honest, it isn't working. Lenny's been crying and insisting that he wants to go home."

"Oh, yeah," Mrs. Fahrer said, with more irritation than sympathy. "He's reaching his limit, right?"

"Hmm, that's an interesting way of putting it. He's very upset about being away from home. I'm going to talk to the principal and call this whole thing off."

Mrs. Fahrer was struck by instant dread. "You can't do that! I've had only one day . . . I mean, well, don't you think you should just stick it out? It's supposed to help Lenny in the long run."

Patricia sighed. "How can this help him? He's so terrified, he's sitting on the floor rocking back and forth and humming the same thing over and over."

"Yeah, I know. He does it all the time. You don't know a lot about autism, do you?"

"Well, I thought I did. That's all the more reason to call this whole thing off. I'm bringing him home."

*"No!"* Lenny's mother protested.

This was very confusing to Patricia. That woman didn't *want* her son to come home.

"Mrs. Fahrer, we are being cruel to Lenny. Think of your son's feelings."

"My son doesn't have feelings the way you and I do."

"Oh, my God, is that what you think?"

"Mrs.—what's your name again?"

"Patricia."

"Okay, Patricia. It's clear you don't know a lot about autism. I don't either, but I've raised Lenny for the last ten years, and you don't understand him. If you took every one of his outbursts seriously, you'd never get anything done."

Now Patricia was really mad, and she was beginning to understand why Lenny was such a mess and why it was necessary for her to continue the experiment.

"Mrs. Fahrer," Patricia said firmly. "I am bringing Lenny home right now. If you want to continue the experiment, and you want it to be a success, we are all going to have to take his feelings seriously. I'm going to drive him to your house, and my suggestion is that you not be there. You and your husband are supposed to be in Bolinas, remember?"

"Oh, right. Okay, I'll leave now."

"If Lenny decides that he doesn't want to live with me anymore, I'm calling the experiment off, and I'm going to explain everything to Lenny and hope he can forgive all of us."

"Oh, please don't. He'd never understand what's—say, I have an idea."

"What is it?"

"What if you continued the experiment here, at our house? My husband and I will live in a hotel for the next two months. I'm sure he won't mind. He's enjoying—I mean, he's just as committed to the experiment as I am."

Patricia thought for a moment. She would need time to pack, but if Lenny felt more comfortable in his own bed . . .

"I'll consider it. We're going to do what's best for Lenny. I'm bringing him home now. So if you don't want to see him, please go out for a few hours. When we're there, I'll ask him if he wants to stay, then I'll let you know what he says. Could you leave a key for me somewhere?"

"There's one in the garage. Lenny knows where it is."

"Good. We'll stay for only a few hours, until, say, noon at the latest."

"All right, I'm leaving. Good-bye," Mrs. Fahrer said, then hung up.

When Patricia returned to the kitchen, Lenny was still cocooning. Respecting his need for privacy, Patricia got Lenny's backpack and filled it with his books and school supplies.

Finally, she said softly, "Lenny, it's time to go home. I called your mother, and she said you know where the key is."

At this, Lenny perked up and lifted his head. "It's on the left wall in the garage, the third shelf."

"Let's go then," Patricia said.

Lenny got to his feet, but did not look at her as they walked to the car. He'd stopped crying, but he was silent, obeying Patricia mechanically, not expecting her to take him home. However, when she went south on Green Bay, then turned left on to Westleigh Road—the correct route to his house—he straightened up and looked out the window, watching the familiar landmarks roll by.

In a few minutes, Patricia was parking the car in the Fahrers' driveway. Lenny burst out of the car, ran up the drive, banged the garage code into the lock box impatiently, ducked under the garage door as it was rising up, grabbed the key, and then ducked under the door again, since it had still not risen to the top.

Feeling like Allan Parrish returning home in *Jumanji,* Lenny turned the key in the front lock then pushed open the door.

"I'M HOME, MOM!" he screamed, mimicking Robin Williams.

Like Robin Williams, Lenny was greeted by the silence of an empty house.

"Hey, wait for me!" Patricia called out, racing up the front stairs.

Lenny was so happy to be home that he ignored her. Looking around, he noticed that all the furniture was the same. The messes and piles that were usually on the floor were gone, but the aroma of the house, a combination of soaps and cleaners, had not changed.

"I'm home," he said more quietly. "I want to stay here. I don't want to go back to your place."

"Lenny," she said gently. "You can't stay here. Your parents are in Bolinas."

"You can stay with me," he suggested.

"I can't do that. Your parents wouldn't allow it."

"Ask them."

Patricia couldn't explain to him why his parents wouldn't let them stay there—namely that they weren't really out of town—but then she recalled Christine's idea of his parents staying in a hotel. Sure, why not? If the purpose of the experiment was to see how Lenny would react to an environment of respect and trust, then it certainly was a mistake to make him feel as if he'd been banished from everything that was familiar to him.

"You're right," Patricia said resolutely. "I'll ask your parents if we can stay here. But you still won't be able to see them."

Lenny thought about this for a moment. The fact that he wouldn't see his parents for two months didn't bother him a bit. He didn't miss them, only his home, his room, and his things.

"I don't care," Lenny said, rushing up the stairs to see his room again.

"Don't stay up there too long," Patricia called after him. "You have to begin your lessons."

"Okay," he shouted down the stairs.

Patricia rummaged through her purse until she found Christine Fahrer's cell phone number. She dialed the number, and Christine answered on the second ring.

"Hello, is this Patricia?" Christine asked, obviously having looked at the caller ID.

"Yes, it is, and I'm at your house. Lenny is overjoyed at being in his own home again, and frankly, I don't have the heart to make him go back to my place. I felt like I was kidnapping him."

"Nonsense," Christine retorted. "Lenny doesn't have the ability to feel anything deeply."

"That's where you're wrong. He's—" Patricia began.

"You're another one of those know-it-alls who's had exactly one day interacting with an autistic person. Try every day for a decade, and then come and tell me if you have any heart left."

"Mrs. Fahrer, I agree, yesterday was, um, quite a challenge. I don't know how you've managed to deal with such a sensitive child."

"Sensitive? I'd call my son many things, but 'sensitive' is not one of them."

"You know what I mean. It seems as if every little thing bothers him, and half the time, I'm not sure if he's listening to me."

"All you have to do is blow up a paper lunch bag and pop it right next to his ear. He'll listen to you real fast, and if he doesn't, just threaten to pop another one."

"What?" Patricia asked in disbelief.

"Temple Grandin's nanny used that technique. And look how successful she became."

No wonder Lenny had developed the ability to tune everyone out, Patricia thought. "Okay, let me put it to you this way: The purpose of this experiment is to treat Lenny with kindness and respect, not turn him into a kidnap victim. If you want me to keep doing this, Lenny is going to have be able to live at home. You're free to stay here, I can just be the live-in tutor or something. How about that?"

That choice filled Christine's shrunken heart to the narrowed brim with terror. She'd had only one day away from Lenny, and she'd been promised two whole months!

Patricia continued, "Do you want to talk it over with your husband?"

"No, no," Christine said hurriedly, "he, uh, he wants the experiment to continue as planned. Are you in a room where Lenny cannot hear?"

"Yes, I am. He's in his room."

"So, you've been with him one day, and already you're letting him hole up in his room."

"Well, that's not exactly—"

"Oh, yes, it's exactly what I've been telling everyone. That boy is impossible."

"Look, Mrs. Fahrer, I'm sorry I ever agreed to this experiment in its original fashion, but—"

"You can't back out now. I—"

"Back out? I have no intention of backing out. I've already seen some changes in Lenny, and I'm not going to abandon him when we've just gotten started."

"Fine. I'm not coming back home because *I* need a break."

Patricia realized that the discussion was going in the wrong direction. Even though she was still in this for the money, she didn't want to hurt Lenny anymore.

"You'll get your break, but there is no way I can treat him with kindness and respect unless we stay here. He thinks that you and your husband are in Bolinas for two months and that the house is empty. I do not blame you or Dr. Wikedda for concocting this story, but now your lie is causing you trouble. There really isn't any reason I can give him for why he can't stay in his own home. So I'll kindly ask you and your husband to go to a hotel for two months, as you suggested."

Christine sighed. "Oh, very well. Although it really isn't fair to ask us to leave our own home."

"It's what you were asking Lenny to do."

"That's different. He's a child."

"And that makes it even more unfair—to him. So take it or leave it. Either you let us stay here for two months, or I'm going to explain the whole situation to Lenny, and the experiment will be over by the end of the day."

"All right, all right," Mrs. Fahrer conceded. "You've got me in a trap. At least I need some time to pack my things."

Patricia decided that she didn't like this woman at all. No wonder Lenny had problems.

"Come and get your things when Lenny's asleep."

At this, Christine Fahrer laughed. "And after one day, you've figured out how to get Lenny to sleep?"

"Well, uh, not really. He didn't sleep well last night."

"He doesn't sleep well any night. It's part of his condition."

"But when he finally did settle down, he slept in and got up late. That's one of the benefits of homeschooling."

That statement made Christine pause for a moment. If the experiment could help Lenny stay asleep longer, then that would make it worth the trouble of staying in a hotel for two months. She realized that after ten years of listening to Lenny toss and turn in his bed, she herself was exhausted.

"Okay, we'll come at five p.m. He's usually tired then, and he'd sleep if I let him. Let him take a nap."

"I know of a sleeping medication that is safe for children. I'll give it to Lenny this once."

Christine snorted. "Good luck getting it down him! We'll be there at five." Then she hung up.

Shaking her head, Patricia walked into the hallway and called up the stairs, "Lenny, are you ready for your lessons?"

He didn't answer in words, but dutifully walked down the stairs.

"Are you ready for your lessons?" Patricia repeated.

"What did my mother say?" Lenny asked.

Patricia felt a flush of embarrassment. "Did you hear what I said?"

"Yes," he replied. "But I didn't understand it. Will she let us stay?"

Patricia smiled, for once happy about his language comprehension issues. "Yes, we can stay."

Lenny didn't answer, but there was a shadow of a smile on his face.

"Right now?" he asked.

"We have to go back to my apartment just one time so I can get my things, and you can pick up the things that belong to you. But yes, you'll be sleeping tonight in your own bed."

Lenny looked at her for a long time, not knowing what to say. Finally, he said, "Thank you."

"Now," she said brightly, "what subject do you want to study first?"

He thought for a moment, then said, "I want to start with science."

"Fine. Here's your book. Start with the second lesson."

Lenny threw himself down on the floor—his own floor—and got in the twisted position that helped his eyes work the best.

**1.2** *The Digestive System*

*Humans, like all other living creatures in the world, need to take in nourishment in order to survive. Food is fuel to us the way cars burn gasoline. Therefore, our body, just like other every other body in this world, has a system devoted to taking in, digesting, and processing food to create the energy we need to live and engage in the activities necessary for life.*

Lenny thought he understood what the book was trying to say, even though some of the individual words were difficult. He continued to read, but his mind wandered to a dozen other things.

*Food is obtained in different ways by different types of living things. Plants do not have a digestive system, because they can make their own food. Animals cannot make their own food but must take in raw materials, which are then digested. Some animals are meant to eat meat, and they are called* carnivores.

*Other animals eat plants, and they are called* herbivores, *or* vegetarians. Frugivores *eat only fruits, while* omnivores, *such as human beings, can eat meat, plants, and fruits.*

As Lenny was reading, his mind kept wandering to other things. Finally, Patricia said, "That's enough reading for now. I'd like to ask you some questions." She pulled out her teacher's manual.

"Okay," said Lenny.

"First question: What is the digestive system?"

Lenny could remember the first few sentences very well. "The digestive system is a system devoted to taking in, digesting, and processing food to create the energy we need to live and engage in the activities necessary for life."

Patricia thought over what he said, then asked, "Lenny, do you know what that means?"

"Yes," he said.

"Could you tell me in your own words what that means?"

Lenny wiggled his foot. Like many autistic people, he could take in visual material rapidly but processing it took more time.

When it was clear that he wasn't going to answer, Patricia said, "Let me ask you a question, then. What are the different kinds of digestive systems?"

Understanding auditory information, such as a spoken question, took even more time.

Lenny looked at her blankly. "Could you repeat the question?"

"All right. And I'll slow down. What . . . are . . . the . . . different . . . kinds . . . of digestive . . . systems?"

Now Lenny understood the question. However, when he thought over what he had read, the answer to this question was not there. He'd learned that there were different kinds of *animals*, but that was not what Patricia had asked. She wanted to know the different kinds of digestive systems.

"Uh," he said finally. "I don't know."

"Let me see your book." She began reading the second lesson. "Here," she said, "the answer is here." She pointed to the second paragraph. Lenny repeated the question in his mind, then looked at the second paragraph. He did not see how that information answered her question.

"This paragraph talks about different animals, not different digestive systems."

Patricia reread the paragraph, then looked at her teacher's manual, and realized that he was right.

"Lenny, I apologize. The question was poorly worded. It's not your fault." She closed the teacher's manual and thought for a moment. "I have a better idea. Let's not do any reading today. Let's talk about ourselves. What do *you* like to eat? Are you a carnivore, or an omnivore, or another kind of 'vore'?"

Lenny started giggling, almost uncontrollably. "I don't know what kind of vore I am. I can't eat a lot of foods. Like wheat. It gives me a headache."

"Well, that's good to know. Why don't we make a list of foods that you can eat, so that I can feed you and not give you a headache. Okay? Then we can figure out what kind of vore you are."

Lenny loved lists. He showed Patricia where the computer was, booted up Microsoft Excel, and together they made category headings and listed the items that Lenny ate in each category. His mother always complained that he was a picky eater, but after an hour, they had over fifty foods on the list, if you counted vanilla ice cream and vanilla ice cream with sprinkles as two different foods. Then Lenny selected the bar graph format, to see which category had the most foods. Carefully he chose the colors, printed the graph out, and put it up on the refrigerator with magnets.

# Chapter 17

While Lenny was listing and graphing all the foods he could eat, Hector suffered all morning in school and still could not understand way. When he protested that he had done nothing, Mrs. Appell warned him to stop lying.

Yet Hector wasn't lying.

When gym class came, Mr. O'Beas played his part in the experiment. In fact, he was actually looking forward to mistreating Hector and getting away with it.

"Now everyone pick a partner," Mr. O'Beas instructed, and the students instantly paired off. But since there was an odd number of students, someone was always left out. To his surprise, Hector was the one who was left out on this day. His friends, Othello and Macbeth, had paired off immediately, and even sneered when he walked over and tried to stand next to them. Even though they had no knowledge of the experiment, the kids had unconsciously sensed a change in Hector, an insecurity, enough so that he had become an instant outcast. Generally, the odd ball would have Mr. O'Beas as his partner, but the gym teacher decided to treat Hector the way he treated Lenny—by making him sit against the wall and watch, excluding him from the game because no one wanted to be his partner.

"Can you be my partner?" Hector asked somewhat timidly.

"Not today, Hector."

"Why not?" he persisted.

"How can you talk to me that way? One more crack like that, and you're getting a detention."

*"What?"* Hector yelled in disbelief.

"That's it," the teacher declared. "Hector, while the other kids are playing their game, you're going to do ten laps around the gym."

Hector gave him a murderous look.

"What is going on here? I can't believe this!" Hector screamed.

"GET GOING. NOW!" Mr. O'Beas roared.

Because Hector was an athletic boy, he could run ten times around the gym without too much effort. This was quite unlike Lenny, who couldn't even run one lap, because of his low muscle tone, and would run only when the teacher was watching him. As soon as Mr. O'Beas looked away, Lenny would immediately slow down to a walk, running again only when the teacher turned toward him again. This would anger the other kids, who'd push Lenny to run faster and not hold them up. Sometimes they'd push him along, while other times, they'd push him out of the way and he'd fall.

When Mr. O'Beas realized that ten times around the gym was not a particularly bad punishment for Hector, he came up with something that was: jumping rope. Hector was a muscular boy, which made him a powerful runner but a lousy jumper—too much bulk banging on the soles of his feet. After a hundred jumps, he was exhausted and sat down heavily on the floor.

Mr. O'Beas turned his head and said angrily, "Hector, get on your feet. No sitting during gym class."

However, when the class started, the teacher had specifically asked Hector to sit against the wall because he didn't have a partner. Hector started to point this out, when suddenly his mouth froze in fear. Whatever he said these days was somehow used against him.

Hector staggered to his feet, swaying a little before he got his balance. Someone noticed and snickered.

Fortunately the bell rang for gym, which ended at 11:30. The class did not return to their classroom but instead went directly to music. Music class also lasted a half hour, ending at noon, and was taught by Mr. Birdson. Today he was going to introduce the class to the percussion family of instruments.

"Today we're going to talk about percussion instruments," Mr. Birdson began, "something that former Beatle Ringo Starr knew about very well. Can anyone give me an example of a percussion instrument?"

A dozen hands shot into the air.

"Yes, Justin?"

"Drums," he said.

"Very good, Justin. And what does the drum normally do in a song?"

Only a half-dozen hands shot up this time.

"Yes, Mary?"

"Uh, it gives you the beat."

"Right. It determines the beat, or the tempo, which means how fast or slow the song is. Sometimes it also indicates the style of the music, since drumming is different in jazz than, say, classical music."

He walked to the corner, where he'd assembled a number of percussion instruments.

"Drums aren't the only percussion instruments. There are also cymbals, xylophones, various types of bells, the tambourine, the triangle, and perhaps the most dramatic instrument of them all—the gong."

Mr. Birdson looked around. "Who wants to hit the gong?"

The same dozen hands shot up in the air. As the teacher looked around, he noticed that Hector did not have his hand up. In fact, he seemed a bit nervous.

"Hector," the teacher called out, "because you're sitting there so quietly, we'll let you hit the gong."

Hector didn't want to hit the gong. In fact, he was feeling a strange fear about the noise it would produce. However, he couldn't look like a chicken in front of his classmates, so he went up and took the mallet from Mr. Birdson.

"I want you to hit it as hard as you can," he told Hector. "Everyone else, cover your ears if you want to."

A few people did while the class tittered with excitement. Now Hector was really afraid. He didn't want to seem like a wimp in front of all those kids. So he swung the mallet back, and with all his might, he crashed it into the gong with a loud

BBBBBBBBBOOOOOONNNNNNNNNGGGGGGGG!!!

Hector felt as if a bomb had gone off next to his ear. Dropping the mallet, he walked slowly back to his place, hunching his shoulders in an instinctive attempt to block out the sound.

"Whoa, cool . . ." another student said.

"Yeah, cool."

"Totally."

Someone banged Hector on the back as if to say, "Good job," and he flinched as if he'd been hit. Immediately the other kid raised his hands in mock surrender and said, "Hey, it's cool. Sorry." Then the other kid looked around the room at his friends, and rolled his eyes in Hector's direction, as if to say, *What's with that guy?*

Mr. Birdson looked at Hector sternly. "Well, that was *too* loud. Did you forget that there are other people in the room?"

Hector was about to say, "What?" After all, Mr. Birdson had told him to hit it as hard as he could. But again, detention was on the horizon, and Hector couldn't figure out what would set one of his teachers off.

"No, I . . . I didn't forget. I'm sorry. I didn't realize it would be so loud."

"Didn't I *tell* you it was going to be loud? Were you not listening?"

"No, I was—I mean, yes, I was listening. Sorry . . . sir."

"Don't do it again. In fact, the gong is off-limits to you for the rest of the week. Justin, would you like to hit the gong?"

Hector tensed. His ears were still ringing from the first blast.

"Yeah," Justin said, jumping up and rushing over to Mr. Birdson, who handed him the mallet.

Immediately Justin banged the gong as hard as he could. It made an even louder:

BBBBBBBBBOOOOOONNNNNNNNNNGGGGGGGG!!!

Now Hector was almost in pain. He held his hands over his ears while the kids laughed around him. Why were the kids laughing at him? At *him?* No one used to laugh at him.

No one used to yell at him either. Let me remind you that throughout his life, Hector had been misbehaving and treating other kids badly, but no one had reprimanded him. Now, it seemed, everything he did was wrong.

# Chapter 18

*March 25, 2010—12:30 p.m.*
*Buffett Elementary School, Front Hallway*

Today was Alice's fourth day of staying in for recess, along with Lori and Mary, the two other girls who were accused of peeling the paint. No one had confessed in this short amount of time, but it didn't really matter since her punishment would end on Friday. Still she hoped that someone would come forward.

Alice also couldn't understand why every day Dr. Wikedda would ask her if Lenny had changed. Alice refused to answer, and told Dr. Wikedda that she was following the federal privacy laws. Dr. Wikedda told her she shouldn't talk back to the principal, but admitted she couldn't force Alice to speak.

Alice now walked from lunch to the principal's office for the last time. On her way, however, she stopped when she noticed something peculiar. She saw Hector, Othello, and Macbeth arguing with one another. This seemed strange—were they not the best of friends? She decided to stop and watch.

"Hey, Hector, I got a deal for you," said Macbeth.

Hector felt scared now. He had just been set up by his friends, and wondered if he could trust them anymore. But

Hector decided he would listen to his friends, as they had been there for him before.

"Well, we just heard today in class that there were a bunch of girls peeling paint in the girls' bathroom. So we'd like to make a deal with you. You sneak into the girls' bathroom right now, peel some paint, and show it to us, and we'll be your friends again. We won't yell at you for being uncool, and we'll still hang out with you," said Macbeth.

"How come?"

"Just to test how much you're willing to be friends with us. Consider it a dare," said Othello. "Do you accept?"

Hector thought about it for a while and then agreed. "I do," said Hector.

Alice decided not to just watch but to get involved. She felt that the dare was wrong, especially since she might get blamed again if more paint was peeled off. She ran to the bathroom door and blocked Hector from entering.

"Get out of my way, Alice," Hector warned.

"Don't you get it?" she retorted. "If they don't want to stay friends with you, they won't, no matter what you do to prove it. Besides, what's going on with you anyway?"

Hector shook his head, forgetting his tough guy stance for a moment. "I don't know," he said honestly. "My friends say that they hate me, and my parents are acting strange, too."

"Well, no matter what's going on, you shouldn't go into the girls' bathroom."

"Get out of my way, or I'm going to push you aside," Hector said, reverting to his menacing tone once more. Alice, fearing the physical contact of being pushed, stepped aside. Hector opened the door, but Alice entered behind him. When they got into the bathroom, both were shocked by what they saw.

A girl was already in there, peeling paint off the walls. She was pulling it off rapidly, using her long nails like scraping tools.

But what shocked Alice was that she knew the girl.

And it was not just any girl.

It was *Tammy.*

"You!" Alice screamed.

"Alice!" Tammy gasped, turning around.

"What are you doing?" asked Alice.

"What are you doing, Hector?" asked Tammy.

"So . . . are you the one who's been peeling the paint?" asked Alice.

"I . . ." Tammy stopped and stuttered. "I . . ."

"I don't believe it! Why? Why are you doing this?"

"Okay, Alice," Tammy said, straightening up defiantly. "This day had to come, and I'm just going to tell you the truth."

"What truth?" asked Alice.

"About the paint peeling."

"Okay, tell me," said Alice. "Are you the one's been peeling all the paint?"

"Yes. I have the whole time."

"Why?"

"Because of my friends. My other friends, Lisa and Wendy—not you and Claire. Friends I enjoy being with."

"What do you mean?"

"Alice, you are one of the craziest people I've ever met. I have no idea why Claire actually likes you because I don't."

"Tammy, you're one of my friends! What are you talking about?"

"You are not my friend, Alice. You've never been my friend."

"What do you mean?"

"You've always been weird. You've bored me with your comments about that crazy comic book and your friend Lenny. I don't know what you see in him. He's such a dork."

"He is not!" shouted Alice.

"He's weird and crazy, and he's a boy," said Tammy.

"So what? I enjoy playing with him," said Alice.

"The truth is, I've only put up with you because Claire told me that she was your friend, and that she wouldn't let me make fun of you. And Claire's my friend. But I've also wanted other friends. I wanted to be popular. So I finally got to be friends with the two popular girls—Lisa and Wendy."

"Them?" asked Alice. "They're so stuck up and mean and they make fun of me! Why would you want to be friends with them?"

"Why wouldn't I?" said Tammy. "They're some of the nicest girls I've ever met. I love it. I get to be popular. Everyone knows them. And together we came up with this—it's a joke."

"So they put you up to this?" asked Alice.

"Yeah," said Tammy. "They did. But we've been doing it all together."

"And what about Lori and Mary, the two girls that also got in trouble? Did they do anything?"

"No, of course not," said Tammy. "But I didn't set them up. Lisa and Wendy went to the principal themselves and framed them."

"So you just went along with what they said? Even if it got other people in trouble?"

"It was fun. I didn't care if you got in trouble, as long as they liked me. After we became friends, we started hanging out together. Not during lunch and recess, but sometimes over the weekends. And I call them up all the time."

"So that's why you couldn't hang out with me after school two days ago? You weren't really forced to go to your grandma's house?"

"Nope," said Tammy. "Grandma had nothing to do with it. I was actually hanging out with Lisa and Wendy."

"Well it doesn't matter now. But was your friend Liz involved with this?"

"Nope, she wasn't. This was just between me, Lisa, and Wendy."

"So how did the peeling of the paint begin?" asked Alice.

"When we started becoming friends, they asked me if I could do something to prove myself to be loyal to them," said Tammy. "They told me they wanted to pull a joke on the school, and asked if I could help them. So they asked me if I could peel the paint in the bathroom as a joke. And I did, and they've been my friends ever since."

"They're not really your friends," said Alice. "They just did that because they want to set you up. They're popular girls. They don't actually really care about you."

"How do you know how my friendships work? You aren't really my friend," said Tammy. "You're a weirdo. They are not. And Claire, she's also my friend. But not you."

Alice was in shock. She just could not believe that Tammy . . . a girl she had thought was nice . . . would do this to her.

"I did this for my friends, and in return, they have listened to me, hung out with me, and become friends far more loyal than you'll ever be. But at the same time, we also knew that the principal would find out and have to blame someone, so I told the principal that I saw you peel the paint and told the other two girls to do it, too. We needed to blame someone. I set you up, Lisa set up Lori, and Wendy set up Mary."

"So you're the reason I stayed in for recess!" said Alice. "And got into a fight with my mother and everything!"

"Yeah. It was worth it—to me."

"All right, you guys. What's going on?"

Claire had entered the bathroom.

"I just caught our 'friend' peeling paint," Alice said.

"What?" Claire asked, amazed. "Tammy?"

"Oh yeah, it's me. Now that the truth's out, we can both ditch Alice and stay friends. This is your chance to be popular, Claire. Lisa and Wendy want you to join our group. Just ditch Alice and you're in."

"Tammy, no!"

"I thought that's what you wanted, right?"

"No, you wanted that. You thought Alice was weird, I didn't," said Claire.

Claire could not believe this was going on either. She was friends with Tammy, but she also liked Alice. Why would Tammy do this?

"I'm sure Lisa and Wendy are secretly laughing at you behind your back," said Alice. "They'll ditch you the moment this is done."

"Shut up, Alice," said Tammy. "No, they won't. We'll be friends forever."

"Well, you should have just told Alice you didn't want to be her friend, rather than setting her up," said Claire. "You know what, Tammy? I do consider Alice my friend, no matter what you think. And you know what? I actually like Lenny, even if he is a boy. I only rejected him when he came up to play with us out of respect for *you*. I'd actually like to be his friend."

"What?" asked Alice. "Really?"

"Yes, really. I like Lenny just like you do, Alice," said Claire.

"Well, then you're not my friend either!"

"Fine," said Claire. "I don't want to be friends with you anymore!"

"Fine," said Tammy. "I've got Lisa and Wendy now."

"Good riddance," Claire said, then she turned to Alice. "What are we going to do about this?"

"You won't tell," Tammy said. "And even if you did, no one would believe you."

"Are you all crazy?" asked Hector, who had been too shocked to leave.

"Hector? Why are you still in here?" asked Alice.

"Get out of here, Hector," Claire said. "Right now. This is a girls' bathroom."

"What's going on here?" an adult voice called out.

Dr. Wikedda entered the room. Her presence shocked everyone.

"Hector, I don't know what you're doing in here, but as punishment for being in a girls' bathroom, you will have a detention after school today."

"I caught this girl peeling paint, Dr. Wikedda," he replied, pointing at Tammy, who was standing next to the vandalized wall.

"You're no longer a hall monitor," the principal retorted, "so you have no authority. Now get out."

Hector immediately rushed out of the bathroom. Othello and Macbeth still stood there, having waited for him outside.

"So, did you bring us some paint?" asked Othello.

"Naw. I just overheard a stupid girl fight," said Hector. "And now I've gotten detention."

"Well, we're sorry, but we can't be your friend anymore," said Othello.

He and Macbeth left.

"So what's the problem with you girls? Alice, why didn't you come to the principal's office? I came in here to look for you when I heard your voice from the hallway."

"We caught Tammy. She peeled the paint, Dr. Wikedda. She led the paint peelers. And she just peeled some more paint right now. I'm innocent, Dr. Wikedda."

"Is this true, Tammy?" asked Dr. Wikedda.

"Look at her. She just peeled that wall," Claire said.

Tammy stood there, her hands behind her back. She couldn't show them because there was paint under her fingernails.

"Tammy, show me your hands," the principal ordered.

"No."

"Show them to me. If you didn't peel anything, you have nothing to worry about."

"Okay, Dr. Wikedda." She showed her hands as they were—full of paint, peeled from the walls.

"Why would you do this, Tammy? So has everything Alice said been true?"

"Yes," said Tammy, now trying to pretend as if she was innocent and had actually been exploited by Lisa and Wendy.

"It started out as a joke, but now my friends keep bugging me. I just wanted to please them. And Lori and Mary are innocent too—they didn't do anything either. You have to understand, Dr. Wikedda."

Alice hoped that Dr. Wikedda would finally punish the real culprit and not find a roundabout way to blame her again.

"Tammy, I don't know why you did this, but you're going to serve a week in detention, starting next week. Alice, I won't punish you anymore since it seems you were innocent all along, but you will still stay after school, since you missed your last detention in my office today. After that, however, your punishment is done—you will not have to come Friday. As for you, Tammy, you will come with me my office. I'll be sending for Lisa and Wendy to join us. I'll decide their punishment after talking to them."

Claire showed Dr. Wikedda her two clean hands. "Dr. Wikedda, I didn't peel anything. My hands are clean, see?"

"No, she didn't," said Tammy. "Alice and Claire both are innocent."

"Well, that's good. Tammy, you're still coming with me to my office. Recess is almost over, so you both should go back to class, Claire. And Alice, I apologize for falsely accusing you."

"Thanks," said Alice.

Claire and Alice went back to class, both feeling glad they had not gotten into any more trouble. Tammy went to the principal's office, now that her scheme had been revealed, not knowing what would happen to her in the office.

Meanwhile, Hector spent the rest of recess by himself, sitting alone on the playground. It was a place he used to enjoy with his friends, but now he was considered an outcast, and nobody would go near him.

# Chapter 19

*March 25, 2010—11:30 a.m.*
*The Fahrer Residence*

On that same day, Lenny had completed two subjects and it was time for lunch. Patricia was thinking how best to give him his sleeping pill. She pulled out her bottle of sleeping pills, which the doctor had said were safe for children, and read:

INSTRUCTIONS: Take with food 30 minutes prior to desired sleeping time. Promotes restful sleep for up to eight hours. Safe for children over the age of six.

WARNING: Keep out of reach of young children.

Patricia foresaw a problem. She wanted Lenny to take the pill with a meal, but four thirty was not dinnertime. The only solution was to give him the pill with his lunch and ask his mother to come earlier.

When she called up Lenny's mother, Christine said, "Now what?" She sounded annoyed.

"I'm wondering if you could come at around one o'clock. I want to give Lenny the sleeping pill with his lunch, around noon."

"I don't care what time I come. Just figure out some way to keep him sleeping so he doesn't see me."

"I promise," Patricia said, then hung up, glad she wouldn't have to see that grumpy woman for the next two months.

After the phone call, she walked into the living room and told Lenny it was time to make a graph of his physical exercise.

"I'm going to take your pulse now. Then I want you to run around the room as fast as you can for one minute, and I'll measure your pulse again. Every day we'll do this, and let's see if your overall pulse rate goes down, which means you're training your heart muscle."

"We did that in school once. After twenty seconds, my legs gave out," Lenny told her.

"Well, do the best you can. We'll graph the results on the computer every day."

Although Lenny would always hate running, he liked graphing numbers, so he got up.

"All right. When I say 'go,' run as fast as you can around the living room. Ready, set, go!"

Lenny ran as fast as he could around the living room, taking big breaths. In ten seconds, however, his legs started getting tired, and he huffed and gasped. Then he ran slower and slower until he fell to the floor. He had been running a total of twenty seconds.

Patricia obviously saw how weak Lenny truly was, but it wasn't his fault. And it wasn't her job to make him stronger. It was her responsibility to make sure he was happy and to be his teacher.

"Let me take your pulse again," she said gently, and she did. It was 145.

"Now, let's put both numbers on a graph."

"We can make it on my computer," he said proudly.

Lenny sat down at the computer and booted up to Microsoft Excel again. He entered in the days of the week and chose the bar graph. Finally, he saved the file as "Lenny's Pulse."

"Good work. Now it's time for lunch. You can be at the computer while I get it ready."

Patricia decided to open up the sleeping capsule and put the powder in Lenny's food. She found spaghetti and instant mashed potatoes in a kitchen cabinet, so that's what she prepared for lunch. She loaded the potatoes with butter and milk and emptied the capsule into Lenny's serving.

By 12:10, lunch was ready. "Lenny," she called out, "it's time to eat."

Lenny looked at the clock, and he became angry. Yesterday he'd eaten at noon. Now his lunch was ten minutes late.

He stormed into the kitchen and demanded, "Why are we eating late?"

"Lenny, we're not following a strict schedule. That's one of the advantages of homeschooling."

"But yesterday I ate at noon! I'm supposed to eat at noon!" He started to cry.

"You are?"

"Yes. That's my lunchtime at school."

"I never set a strict schedule. I'm sorry if you thought that."

"Yesterday my lunch was ready at noon. Today you broke the rule."

Patricia felt herself getting annoyed again, but she suppressed her anger. Without realizing it, she was now in a situation that autistic people experienced all day long—breaking a rule she didn't even know existed. And she was starting to feel the way an autistic person feels—irritated and on edge. This made her feel somewhat compassionate toward Lenny, at least for the moment.

However, more trouble was on its way. For when Lenny started to eat his mashed potatoes, they felt a little weird on the roof of his mouth. He detected some kind of powder in them.

"Why is there powder in my mashed potatoes?"

Now Patricia was really angry. She had been found out, and she didn't like it. "I don't know," she lied. "Just eat your lunch."

"I'm not eating mashed potatoes with powder in them."

Patricia felt cornered. She had to get Lenny to take the sleeping pill, but how?

"Well, I confess, Lenny, I put some vitamin powder in your mashed potatoes. I didn't think you'd notice. How do you usually take your vitamins?"

"In juice. My mother puts vitamin C powder in my apple juice every morning."

"I'm sorry. I didn't know. Here, let me give you your vitamin C."

She'd noticed a bottle of powdered vitamin C on the counter, so she put a little bit in a glass of apple juice, and when Lenny wasn't looking, she emptied another sleeping capsule into the juice.

Lenny, however, refused to drink it. That was because he always drank his vitamin C in a special blue glass so he couldn't see the color of the juice. Plus he didn't trust Patricia, so he needed to find some safety in his special blue glass.

"Why don't you drink it?" Patricia asked wearily.

"It isn't in my blue glass," Lenny explained. "I have to have it in my blue glass."

*What does it matter which glass it's in?* Patricia thought, but this time, she managed to suppress her anger.

"Why, Lenny? Doesn't it taste the same in another glass?"

Lenny thought for a moment, then said, "I don't know what it tastes like. But it doesn't *look* the same."

Realizing that in the scheme of things, this was a small matter, Patricia decided to let Lenny have his preference.

"All right, where is the blue glass?" she asked finally.

"On the shelf over there, by the sink."

Patricia opened the cabinet door and found the blue glass. However, she was afraid that Lenny would detect the different taste in his juice. She was not sure what to do when she remembered that she'd also brought along some liquid Benadryl, which would make Lenny drowsy and maybe keep him asleep for up to three hours. Quickly pouring more juice into the blue glass and adding a teaspoon of the liquid Benadryl, she handed it to Lenny, then she held her breath as he drank it down. She didn't have to worry because Lenny didn't really taste anything. He ate and drank according to what looked and felt right.

After he drank down his apple juice without a complaint, Patricia asked him if he would like to lie down after lunch.

This surprised Lenny, since he was always sleepy after lunch. Sometimes he felt so full that he was unable to sit up. But no one had ever allowed him to lie down after he ate.

"Can I lie down in my room?" Lenny asked.

"Of course. We'll continue homeschooling later."

Lenny went to his room to lie down. When he got into his bed, he slowly got himself comfortable. By 12:30, Lenny was asleep. Fortunately, his mother was five minutes late, because of unexpected traffic on State Road 176.

Christine walked into the house at 12:35. She didn't think to knock, since it was her own home.

"Hello," Christine said. "You must be Patricia."

"Yes, I am. Just give me a minute." She ran up the stairs to make sure that Lenny was asleep, then closed his door tightly.

By the time she ran down the stairs, Christine was fuming. This was, after all, her house, and she was feeling like a visitor.

"Lenny is asleep. I gave him some Benadryl. Please don't go into his room."

"Are you telling me what to do in my own home?"

Patricia tried to smile, but she was still feeling angry herself, and this was making it worse. "No, not exactly. But since you told Lenny you were in Bolinas, I don't think you should confuse him by being here. None of this was my idea, by the way. I was hired by Dr. Wikedda, and I'm only doing it because I'm getting paid."

"Of course. Who in their right mind would spend time with Lenny unless they were getting paid?"

Patricia looked at her sharply. Even though she agreed with Christine completely, she had to put on a false face.

"Lenny and I are learning to get along. He's adjusting to the experiment. So I would ask you not to go into his room and wake him up."

"All right, all right. I won't interrupt the experiment. Just don't tell me what to do in my own home."

Lenny's mother went right to work packing up her things. As she was filling her suitcase, Patricia asked, "So what do you want to come out of this experiment?"

"I want my son to be normal!" Lenny's mother cried. "I don't know why he isn't. I couldn't take the burden of an autistic child!"

"You seem to have done well for the last ten years," Patricia replied.

"You think I've done well? Ha! I have not. Anyway, let's not talk about it. All I want to do now is pack."

"Fine, I'll let you pack."

It took Lenny's mother the next two hours to pack up her things, but by 2:45, everything was ready to go. Lenny stayed asleep the entire time.

"Well, it was nice meeting you," Christine said finally. "I hope my son doesn't drive you crazy!"

Patricia watched Lenny's mother load up her car, then waved as she drove off.

At 2:50, Lenny woke up. He tried to open the door to his room, but it was locked.

"Patricia!" he screamed. "Let me out!"

She ran up the stairs and pushed open the door. "It wasn't locked. You could have opened it yourself."

Patricia didn't realize that Lenny didn't have the physical strength to pull open a door that was tightly closed.

"What time is it?" he asked.

"It's about two fifty."

"Two fifty!" he cried, shocked. He'd never slept that long during the day. He was also shocked that almost three hours of his life had passed and were gone forever without his having realized it. Life was going by at the speed of light, but he was traveling at the speed of sound.

One hour later, Alice called up Lenny to arrange their playdate.

"Hi, Lenny!" said Alice. "How's homeschooling?"

"Great," said Lenny.

"Would you like to come over to my house on Saturday?" asked Alice.

"I don't know. I've never been there before," said Lenny. He initially felt scared about leaving his home again so soon, but he really wanted to see Alice. "I'll ask Ms. Nottingham."

Lenny put the phone down and walked over to Patricia. "Hey, Ms. Nottingham, Alice asked me to come over to her house. Can I go there?"

"Yes, you may," said Patricia. "I know you like Alice."

Lenny went back to the phone. "Ms. Nottingham said it was okay."

"Okay," said Alice. "See you Saturday at noon. Bye. Oh, and I have a surprise for you when you get here."

# Chapter 20

Nine minutes before the final school bell rang, Hector's class had just finished their history lesson. Word had come to Mrs. Appell that Hector had misbehaved during gym and music, and she was unhappy. She had warned Hector that at the end of the school day, she would institute a behavior program for him—before he went to detention in the principal's office.

"Hector," she said loudly so everyone in the class could hear, "the gym and the music teachers both told me what a bad boy you were during their classes. I have a zero tolerance policy for misbehavior, and I'm going to make sure it never happens again."

The kids giggled and whispered among themselves.

Hector suddenly felt terrified of what she had planned for him, even though teachers had never intimidated him before. Why was everybody blaming him for things he hadn't done, and things he didn't know were wrong?

While the class watched, Mrs. Appell took a large sheet of paper, walked over to Hector's desk, and taped it on top. At the top of the sheet, she wrote in big letters: HECTOR'S BEHAVIOR CHART. Then underneath, she wrote in two columns: *Hector Behaved* and *Hector Misbehaved*. By now, everyone's eyes had turned to Hector's desk, watching Mrs. Appell embarrass Hector. On the left side of the paper, she wrote the days of the week, and under the *Misbehaved* column, in the space for Friday, she wrote three big fat black checks.

"If you get five checks in the *Misbehaved* column, you get a punishment. If you should get five checks in the *Behaved* column, then you'll get a reward."

"I didn't misbehave!" Hector cried.

"You did just now when you told that lie," said Ms. Appell, and she picked up the pen to write another check in the *Misbehaved* column.

"That's not fair!" Hector screamed.

"And talking like that to a teacher gets you another check. You just earned yourself a half-hour in detention."

"But I'm already in detention! I got set up by my friends."

"Hector . . ." his teacher warned.

Hector felt an urge to attack Mrs. Appell, to put his hands around her neck and choke her. However, his fear of worse punishment kept him in check. He was so angry now, he couldn't move or speak. No one else had ever been humiliated this way in the class.

Mrs. Appell continued, "Your ultimate goal will be to earn five checks in the *Behaved* column and none in the *Misbehaved* column. If you get five checks in one week for being good—at least one per day—then you and the entire class will be rewarded. Therefore, your fellow students will want you to behave, for their sake. If you fail, everyone will be punished. This will encourage them to help you, rather than bully you and attempt to make you misbehave. Remember, I'll be watching you, and my decision regarding the placement of a checkmark is final. Remember, too, that in one week, parent-teacher conferences will begin, and I know that you want me to give a good report to your parents."

Hector looked away. He was so embarrassed, he tried to shrink into his desk. Everyone in class was laughing at him now.

"To teach you good behavior," she went on, "I am including a new game that our class will play every day. It's called Hector's Behaving Game. In this game, your classmates will put you in specific social situations in which you are expected to behave appropriately. If you misbehave, you'll get a—"

BBBBRRRRRRRIIIIIIIIIIIIIIIIIIIIIIIIIIIIIIINNNNNNNGGGG!!!

The school bell rang, and the children leapt up to leave.

Hector was too afraid to move. "You may go to the principal's office now," said his teacher, tapping him on the shoulder.

At the end of the school day, Alice also went to the principal's office to sit quietly for her last detention. Hopefully, Dr. Wikedda wouldn't pester her again about Lenny. Alice refused to tell her anything about Lenny's new life. To her, that was none of Dr. Wikedda's business.

"Hi, Alice," said Dr. Wikedda. "Have you noticed any changes in Lenny?"

"Dr. Wikedda, please don't ask me again."

"Just go and sit down then," said Dr. Wikedda.

She went into the small detention area and sat quietly. At least this was the last time she had to sit there, and her name had been cleared. But unlike the other times, she had a lot of thinking she had to do this time.

She felt as if she had lost something that day. She had been friends with Tammy for the last two years and now . . . she was actually gone. Tammy, someone whom she had met in the second grade, and whom she had gone trick or treating with two years in a row dressed as Allie the alligator, was not there for her anymore. And not only that, but she had gotten Alice into trouble.

Was it true? Did Tammy really not see her as a friend? Did she really just think Alice was weird? Alice had no idea that Tammy had thought this of her. If Alice had known, maybe she would not have bored Tammy every once in a while with her love for her comic strips.

Alice realized that one thing her mother had told her was right. She'd said that a friendship had to work both ways. The person you were friends with had to consider you their friend as well. If one person didn't consider the friendship to be one, it was not a friendship. And if Tammy did not see Alice as a friend, then it must not have been a friendship, according to her mother.

Her thinking came to a halt when Hector entered the room. Alice wondered why he was there until she remembered—Hector had been ordered to stay after school, too. Hopefully, he wouldn't bother her.

"Uh, hello, Alice," he said, then proceeded to sit down next to her. He was secretly hoping that she, at least, would be nice to him. After all, they were fellow outcasts.

"Don't talk to me or come near me," warned Alice. "You've made fun of me enough times."

"I'm not going to make fun of you," said Hector. "People have been making fun of me."

Alice couldn't believe it. She thought Hector was making it up. "Don't lie to me," she said. "You had no reason to enter the girls' bathroom today."

"I don't want to hurt you," said Hector. "I just . . . wanted to say I was sorry."

Alice couldn't believe it. Hector . . . saying he was sorry?

"What?"

"I didn't want to hurt you," Hector repeated. "But since a few days ago everyone has been mad at me. My mother, my father, my teachers. My friends don't even want to talk to me anymore. They've rejected me."

"I don't believe you," said Alice.

"Please, please believe me. They've been making fun of me."

"I thought you were friends. You've made fun of other people together," said Alice.

"Well, now they rejected me. And I'm sorry for going into the girls' bathroom. They told me they'd be my friend again if I did."

"Don't you realize that they were just setting you up?"

"No, I thought they really were true friends."

"Lenny has been told by kids to do bad things, and he's been told that he'll be their friend. And then Lenny does them and the kids reject him," said Alice.

"That happens to Lenny?"

"Of course it does," said Alice. "And don't forget that *you* set him up many times yourself."

Hector did not even realize that he had done such a thing to Lenny. He just sat there silently.

"You once told Lenny to call a teacher by his first name. And he did because he thought you'd be his friend."

"That was a setup?" asked Hector.

"Yes, it was," said Alice. "I hope this teaches you a lesson," said Alice. "It's not right to make fun of other people. Don't bully me or Lenny again."

"Quiet in there!"

Dr. Wikedda, after talking to a teacher about a student whose parents had been late picking her up, was done and thus heard them talking. "No talking when you are staying after school!"

Alice and Hector didn't want to get into any more trouble, so they stopped talking. Twenty minutes later, they were told they could go home. Alice came outside to find her mother waiting for her beside the car. Without saying anything, Alice's mother hugged her.

"Alice . . . I'm so sorry," said Alice's mother. "You weren't lying to me about the paint peeling."

"I'm sorry, too," said Alice.

"I just got a call from Dr. Wikedda. She told me that she found out that Tammy had peeled the paint, and that you never did anything. I am so shocked. That's not like her."

"I know, Mom," said Alice, beginning to cry. "I know."

"Well, at least I know that you weren't acting up or rebelling or anything," said Alice's mother. "If I were you, I wouldn't talk to Tammy again. Good thing Claire's still your friend."

"I won't, Mom. I don't want to anyway."

Alice and her mom got into the car and they headed home.

"You know, Alice, I'm actually shocked that this would happen to you. Usually you don't get set up by your friends."

"I know, Mom. I'm shocked, too," said Alice. "And Claire told me she actually liked Lenny and pretended not to because of Tammy."

"I don't know if this is the right time to tell you, Alice, but I've actually thought that you might have autism, too. Not as bad as Lenny, but higher functioning. I've read on the Internet that girls with autism often don't get diagnosed because their issues aren't always noticed."

"What do you mean, Mom?"

"Well, Lenny's mother told me that Lenny was diagnosed with autism by a doctor named Dr. Griffiths in Lake Bluff. I've heard from other people that he's a really nice doctor. So next week I'm going to take you there to see if you have autism. I hope you n't, but I just want to make sure. Is that okay?"

"I don't mind. Maybe that could explain why I love my comic strips and why I consider Lenny to be my best friend."

"I also read that girls with autism sometimes get along better with boys than with other girls," said Alice's mother.

"Where did you read this, Mom?" asked Alice.

"There was an article on the Internet about girls with autism. And the article described a girl who seemed similar to you."

"Well, at least if I have autism, I can understand what happened to me today," said Alice.

"The article also said that autistic people like to wear long-sleeve shirts and long pants. And obviously that's how you are," said Alice's mother.

"You can say that again," said Alice.

"You know, I think I need to make it up to you after what you went through. This weekend, you have my permission to invite Lenny to come over, okay?"

"Thanks, Mom!" said Alice. This made Alice very happy. "I'll call him up when I get home."

"Okay. Tell him he can come over after eleven a.m. Saturday. And you can also invite Claire over. Maybe she wants to see Lenny too."

"She might. She did say she liked him, after all," said Alice.

When Alice got home, the first thing she did was call Lenny at his new place. When there was no answer, she tried his home number. She didn't understand why he was there, but it didn't matter—he was coming over on Saturday, and they could they could continue to act out *Chloe and Allie.*

# Chapter 21

*March 27, 2011—11 a.m.*
*The Meacham Residence*

Friday came and went. After another horrific school day on Friday and after school detention, Hector returned home. His friends had abandoned him that day, telling him he was no longer cool enough to be their friend, and that they didn't hang out with people who got in trouble with the principal. He was happy to return home yet hoped that his mother would be sympathetic.

His mother, however, was not. She immediately took him to get his haircut, where the barber seemed to be quite sadistic and pulled his hair while cutting it, making him scream and shout. And his mother told him he was being a brat the entire time.

Finally, after doing his homework, he went to sleep after bonding again with Pointy, wondering what had caused this nightmare.

Lenny, meanwhile, enjoyed another day of homeschooling with Patricia. He got more relaxed and realized that Patricia truly was a good person and not someone to be scared of.

Today Lenny happily anticipated his visit with Alice. He had never been to her house before—she had always come to his house. He wondered as he looked at the houses he passed in Patricia's car which one would be Alice's house. He saw homes of different sizes—big mansions and small ranches—and remembered his father telling his mother how the neighborhood was changing into a mix of old and new as developers tore down some of the older homes to make room for new mansions.

Lenny knew better than to ask, "Are we there yet?" He had already known from movies that to do so would result in getting screamed at. Instead, he waited patiently until finally Patricia pulled into a driveway.

"I'll pick you up in two hours," she told him.

Lenny got out of the car and looked at the house as Patricia drove off. It was an old house, not a new mansion, he immediately noticed. It also looked like a split-level house, since the windows on the left side of the house were situated differently than on the right side. But he didn't care. He went to the front door and knocked. Mrs. Meacham answered the door.

"Hello, you must be the infamous Lenny," Alice's mother greeted him as he entered the living room of the house. Lenny didn't hear what she'd said, though, as he looked around. The living room was just as big as his, with a couch centered toward a TV that was playing a song sung by some really high-pitched singer, in a music video set in a bowling alley. Colleen, Alice's older sister, was sitting on the couch watching it.

Actually, he did not recognize Alice's mother, because he had only seen her before when she'd dropped Alice off at his house or picked her up from school. He had never seen her in this unfamiliar environment, and therefore, he did not know who she was.

"Oh," he answered, because that was all he could manage to say until he had processed the fact that she was in a new context.

"You'll have to wait for one more minute. Alice is still in her room having a time-out."

That got his attention. "Why?"

"Well, Alice may be your best friend, Lenny, but sometimes she misbehaves, too. She talked back to me this morning when I told her that she had to get a little homework done before you came over. I'm sure your mom has sent you to your room."

"Yes," said Lenny, who was telling the truth.

"Still, I'm really glad that you're Alice's friend. She doesn't have a lot of kids she can actually call. Did she tell you about what happened to her this week?"

"No." Lenny was starting to loosen up since this mom required only one-word answers.

"Well, it turns out that she was telling the truth when she said she hadn't peeled the paint in the girls' bathroom. A friend of hers set her up."

"Oh," said Lenny. He had been set up many times before by Othello, Hector, and Macbeth, but Alice getting set up by one of her friends? That was a shock. "Who?"

"It was her friend Tammy."

"What?"

"Yes," said Alice's mother.

"Hey, Lenny!"

Alice came down the stairs that led to the upper split level of the house.

"Well, I'll leave you two to play," said Alice's mother cheerfully, and walked back into the kitchen.

"Hi, Alice."

"Hey, Lenny. Do you want to watch *Cloudy with a Chance of Meatballs*?"

"What's that?"

"It's a cool movie. I want to show it to you. You'll like it and probably relate to Flint the way I relate to Sam. Also, they become friends, and I think Flint and Sam's friendship is similar to ours," said Alice.

Lenny initially felt scared that he wouldn't like the movie, but realized he should be polite to Alice and let her show it to him. "Okay," said Lenny, and they walked back up the short staircase to her room.

Lenny liked Alice's room at first glance. Inside was a TV and DVD player, a dresser, a phone, a bed with a red cover over it, and a big *Chloe and Allie* poster. This picture showed them in color, with Chloe in blond hair, a white shirt, and yellow pants, and Allie the Alligator with her green body and skin.

"I'm sure you like my poster," said Alice.

"I do," said Lenny.

"I got it from a garage sale," said Alice.

As they sat down on her bed, Alice said, "Claire told me she wants to be your friend."

"What? I thought you told me not to play with Claire." Now that they were in the privacy of Alice's room, Lenny could talk just fine.

"Well, Claire's changed, and it turns out she wants to play with us. Remember the surprise that I told you was going to happen?"

"Yeah, what is it?" asked Lenny.

"Claire's also coming over today. She wants to play with us."

"Really?" Then Lenny became silent. He didn't know how to react as this would be new for him.

"I hope it doesn't upset you," said Alice. "She really wanted to come see you. She told me Tammy told her she couldn't talk to you."

"Why not?" asked Lenny.

"I don't know," said Alice. "But Claire and I aren't friends with Tammy anymore. Our friendship's over."

"Why?"

As if on cue, the doorbell rang.

"Alice, Claire's here!" said Alice's mother. "Colleen, let Alice answer the door."

"Okay, I'll get it. You can come if you want, Lenny," said Alice.

Alice and Lenny walked downstairs from her room to the door. Alice answered the door and Claire entered. She had on a pink shirt, black pants, brown glasses, and her usual straight brown hair.

"Hi, Alice," said Claire. "I'm so sorry Tammy did that to you. I told her I'm not going to be friends with her anymore after what she did. She can hang out with those other girls all she wants."

"It's not your fault," said Alice. "You didn't know."

"Is Lenny here?" asked Claire.

"Yeah, he's right here," said Alice.

"Hi, Lenny," said Claire. "What's up?"

"I've been homeschooled for a while," said Lenny.

"I'm so sorry I ever told you I couldn't play with you," said Claire. "Tammy told me that I couldn't."

"Why?" asked Lenny.

"Because she didn't like you. And I didn't want to be mean to her," said Claire. "But Tammy and I aren't friends anymore."

"And neither am I," said Alice. "And I found out who peeled the paint."

"Yeah, your mom told me it was Tammy."

"Yup, it was," said Alice. "I won't talk to her anymore."

"Tammy set Alice up for it," said Claire. "She lied to Dr. Wikedda and said that Alice peeled the paint, when Tammy was doing it with her two friends. And Dr. Wikedda believed her."

"That usually happens to me," said Lenny.

"QUIET DOWN OVER THERE!" shouted Colleen from the living room couch. "I'm trying to watch this. If you want to talk, go to Alice's room."

"Colleen, I'm ashamed of you!" said Colleen's mother. "That was rude. Say one more thing and the TV goes off."

"Fine, I'll be quiet," said Colleen.

"Let's go to my room," said Alice. "I don't want to bother my sister. We don't get along."

"Enjoy yourselves," said Alice's mother as Lenny, Claire, and Alice walked up to her room. "Oh, and remember that Lenny and Claire have to go home in two hours."

"Okay, Mom," said Alice.

They entered the room. Lenny sat on the floor, and Alice and Claire both sat on her bed.

"I like your poster," said Claire as she saw the *Chloe and Allie* poster.

"So, Lenny, I had to stay in for recess because of her," said Alice. "And then I caught Tammy peeling the paint when I went into the bathroom to stop Hector."

"Hector?" asked Lenny.

"Yeah, he was also getting set up, too. Things have been weird at school. Hector's been acting strange, and it looks like his two hall monitor friends have dumped him," said Alice.

"What?" said Lenny.

"Well, it happened. Hector was dared by them to enter the girls' bathroom when I caught Tammy. And then Dr. Wikedda found all of us in the bathroom," said Alice.

"Those boys are really mean," said Lenny. "I can't believe they're even mean to each other."

"Well, Tammy now has a detention and has lost two friends," said Claire. "And now I can be friends with you, Lenny. Hope she learns a lesson."

"If she wants to hang out with those two other girls, she can," said Alice.

"Who are they?" asked Lenny.

"She told me she peeled the paint with two other girls who were her friends. Lisa and Wendy," said Alice.

"I don't know them," said Lenny.

"You shouldn't. Lenny, do you think that's the right thing to do? I mean, we were friends for over two years, but I just don't think I can forgive her for this."

"It's up to you, Alice," said Lenny. "And Claire."

"At least Claire's still my friend. But you know what's even crazier? Dr. Wikedda has been asking me about you every day," said Alice.

"Why?"

"She wants to know if I've noticed any changes. I can't understand why," said Alice. "It's like she's up to something."

"I guess you can't understand adults," said Claire. "But then they don't seem to understand us either."

"Maybe she wants me to come back to school so the state will pay her more money," said Lenny.

"It could be. But I don't know . . ."

"What did you tell her?"

Alice replied, "I told her to follow the federal privacy laws," then she and Claire both giggled.

"That's all? Did you say anything about homeschooling?"

"No. It's none of her business. But do you like it?"

"Yeah, it's great. No bullies."

"You're lucky. I'd love to be homeschooled," sighed Alice. "Well, now that you're here, Claire, can we watch my favorite movie? It's called *Cloudy with a Chance of Meatballs*."

"I like that movie," said Claire. "I especially like the spaghetti tornado."

Alice went to the television and turned it on. The DVD was already loaded, so she turned on the DVD player, got the remote, fast forwarded the previews, and then started the movie.

Lenny, Alice, and Claire all sat down and enjoyed the movie together. Lenny enjoyed the movie as much as Alice and Claire did. He was glad Alice had shown this to him. Alice was right—he did relate to Flint, especially since Flint, like him, felt misunderstood and was different than the other people in the town of Swallow Falls. Lenny sat there, amazed at Flint's determination to invent his machine.

"He really is just like me," said Lenny. "Like an autistic person."

"Yep. And I'm just like Sam," said Alice. "You'll see her later."

However, when Flint ended up inventing the machine that enabled food to fall from the sky, Lenny started to feel sorry for the residents of Swallow Falls.

"I feel sorry for them, having to eat what the weather serves," said Lenny. "I'm a picky eater. I wouldn't always want to eat what came out of the sky."

"Good thing you don't live there," said Claire.

Sam came into town to do some reporting, and then met Flint. They entered his Jell-O castle and enjoyed themselves until finally they sat together on a bench in the castle.

"This is my favorite scene in the whole movie," said Alice. "I feel like I connect with Sam."

Sam proceeded to give her whole scientific explanation about Jell-O. This fascinated Lenny. At least now he had an explanation for why Jell-O was so gross to him. However, he did disagree with Sam about the next part—that it tasted good. To him, it was disgusting.

He watched on to hear Sam's revelation that she was a nerd back in school, that she thought the kids did stupid things while she did her nerdy stuff, and that the kids called her four eyes because of her glasses.

"That's terrible. I'm glad no one has ever called me that because of my glasses," said Claire.

"You look nice with your glasses on," said Alice.

They continued watching as Flint created a hair scrunchie for Sam out of Jell-O, which revealed part of Sam's inner beauty. Sam initially felt scared at first, but liked the way she looked after Flint's transformation. Finally, the scene ended when Sam confessed that she had a lot in common in Flint.

"I'm having a lot of fun here," said Claire. "It's great being with you and Lenny. We should be our own little club."

"Definitely," said Alice. "Tammy can be with her friends. We're just fine with each other."

"I liked that scene, too," said Lenny.

And they continued watching the movie together, happy that they were together. Lenny felt like he could connect to Flint the way Alice could connect to Sam. In addition, although he previously would have been uncomfortable playing with more than one other person, for the first time he felt comfortable interacting with more than one kid in his life. The experiment had started to work its wonders on him.

# Chapter 22

*April 1, 2010—10 a.m.*
*Elaine's Apartment*

Five miserable days had passed since that horrible afternoon when Hector endured the most painful haircut of his life. Even his mother was feeling pangs of guilt and found herself facing an intense moral dilemma. On the one hand, she really wanted to help her child, but on the other hand, even she hated what she was doing to him.

What happened during those five days was essentially what you've already been reading about, but if I told you everything, the book would go on way too long, and you'd get bored and accuse me of being repetitious. Hector's parents and teachers were doing the same horrible and unfair things to him every day, day after day, without change. It was Hector who was changing, however, ceasing to struggle and learning to submit.

Lenny was changing, too, but in the opposite direction. The block of ice he had encased himself in during years of being bullied and misunderstood in school was slowly melting. For the first time in his short life, he wondered whether he had the potential to actually be happy.

One week after the experiment began, Lenny and Patricia were going on a field trip. Lenny was going to learn about how people lived in the 1950s by visiting an elderly woman who lived on the floor below Patricia's apartment. She was hoping that the woman would entertain Lenny while she went up and packed more of her things, for she would be away from home for the next two months.

That morning, when she announced that they were going to see a very old woman, Lenny was initially terrified. Then he remembered that when he was in kindergarten, he was forced to sing to a bunch of very old people at a nursing home, and those very old people were very nice to him. So he could feel better about the change in their routine, Patricia announced that they would be leaving the house at exactly 10 a.m.

Therefore, at 10:00 sharp, Lenny got into Patricia's car, and they drove to her apartment in Lake Bluff. This time when they entered the building, the black man did not come out of his apartment to greet them. Instead they walked right up to the second floor, to Apartment 206.

After Patricia knocked, they heard someone inside calling out, "I'm coming. Don't leave. I'm an old woman and can't walk fast."

Lenny felt his anxiety level go up. Maybe this was a trick, and Patricia was going to abandon him? But no, he reminded himself of the very nice old people at the nursing home, and that calmed him down.

Slowly the door opened, but instead of an old woman, an old man answered.

"Who are you?" the old man demanded loudly without saying "hello" or even trying to be courteous. Maybe he had autism, and that calmed Lenny down even more.

"This is the son of a friend of mine," Patricia said, bending the truth a bit.

"Does he live here?" the old man shouted, as if he was hard of hearing.

"No."

"Then where does he live?"

Lenny got more comfortable by the minute. He felt at home with rude people, as long as they didn't bully him.

"In Lake Forest," Lenny supplied.

"What are you doing here?" the old man asked. "Shouldn't you be in—"

"George, don't interrogate these people," said a female voice from inside the door. "I was expecting them."

"Expecting them?" George asked suspiciously.

The door opened wider to reveal a short, misshapen, doughy woman dressed in a strange printed sack.

"Yes, honey. For a history lesson. They want to know what life was like in the 1950s. This must be Lenny," she said, smiling broadly and reaching out to touch him on the face.

Instantly Lenny became rigid. He preferred George's aloof style.

"Say hello, Lenny," Patricia instructed him.

"That boy doesn't have to say hello," George interjected, "if he doesn't want to."

Lenny really liked that.

"Father, don't badger my guests. Now step aside and let them pass."

"I was on my way to the grocer's anyway, Mother." As he passed, he whispered in Patricia's ear, "I don't really have to go to the grocer's. I just don't want to hear all those stories about her cats!"

As the man walked slowly to the elevator, Lenny entered the apartment and looked around. It was identical to Patricia's but full of the weirdest furniture he had ever seen. The old woman walked slowly back toward the sofa. She seemed really, really old. Older than Lenny's grandparents. He wondered how old she was, so he asked her.

Patricia immediately replied, "It's not polite to ask a woman her age. Apologize to Mrs. Benson."

"Now Patricia," Mrs. Benson chided her. "You're too hard on the boy. Maybe that's why he's so shy."

"Still, I don't want you to feel uncomfortable."

"That's quite all right. Obviously he doesn't know what is and isn't polite to ask. That is the innocence of childhood." Turning to Lenny, she said, "To answer your question, I am eighty-eight, and my husband is eighty-nine."

"Thank you, Elaine," Patricia said. "Now I'm just going to leave him—"

"Leave him?" Lenny echoed in horror. "Why leave him?" He had visions of being abandoned a second time.

"It looks like he doesn't want you to leave," Elaine said. "So why don't you stay and listen to the story of my two beloved cats."

"All right, I'll stay for a little while. And when I leave, I'll try to be quick about coming back. I just need to pack up a few things."

"I thought I was going to learn about the 1950s," Lenny said.

"Hmm. I don't remember you saying that," Elaine told Patricia. "I thought you wanted me to tell Lenny about my cats."

Patricia exhaled a weary sigh. "Fine," she said. "Tell Lenny about your cats."

"Yes," said Lenny, for he realized that this woman must have been hurt by the world also, because of her age and forgetfulness.

Lenny sat down in a nearby chair. A small white dog trotted into the room a few minutes later, climbed into Lenny's lap, and curled up into a ball.

"I hope that's okay. That's usually his chair, but he doesn't mind that you're there," said Elaine.

Lenny didn't mind either. He loved animals, especially dogs. At one time, he actually wanted a pet after he went to a petting zoo and discovered that the animals didn't reject him. Just as Hector had learned with his cat, animals didn't scream at him or judge him the way people usually did.

Unfortunately, Lenny had never had a pet because his parents adamantly refused to buy him one. But whenever Lenny came near a dog or a cat, he loved to pet it, and he was thrilled when the animal didn't shrink away from his touch.

Lenny stroked the dog's back. Its fur was totally white. "Hello, dog," said Lenny. "I hope you're okay with me here. I won't hurt you." To Mrs. Benson, he asked, "What type of dog is this?"

"It's a young Dalmatian. He hasn't got his spots yet," said Elaine.

"Like in the Disney movie?"

"Yes."

"I hope your dog isn't kidnapped," said Lenny.

"No, he probably won't be."

"I hope you like your spots," Lenny told the dog. "The dogs in that movie did."

"You know, Dalmatians were useful animals at one time. They say that before we had electricity and cars, Dalmatians were used to lead firefighters to fires. Dogs can smell things a lot better than we can, and can be bothered by smells that don't bother—"

"You're just like me then!" cried Lenny, still addressing the dog. "I get bothered by smells that don't bother others."

"Really?" asked Elaine. "Like what?"

Lenny looked up, so relaxed that he was able to make brief eye contact with the old woman. "I can't stand the perfume my mother's friend wears when she comes over," he said. "And I can't stand the smell of certain foods, like salmon."

"Well, this dog can't stand the smell of perfume either," said Elaine.

"We really do have a lot in common," Lenny said to the dog.

"But then, young man, as I told you I would, let me tell you about my two cats. In 1952, I lived in Batavia, Ohio, a farming town east of Cincinnati. It was where I raised by two children with my husband, George. You met him just now. Ten years ago we moved to Illinois to be near my daughter because she got a job here, and I wanted to be closer to her. As a farm girl, I always liked to go to the local store, so I was sad when they tore down all the small stores and built that great big mall. Now I can't even find a corner grocery, and I get lost in that big old Walmart. But back then, in 1952 . . ."

Patricia started to get annoyed with the rambling, but Lenny liked it because that was how his mind worked—jumping back and forth between past and present.

"As I was walking home with my shopping cart—we didn't have a car in those days—I saw two cats crossing the street. There wasn't a car in sight, but I was afraid someone would come speeding around the bend and run them over. They made it successfully, but I approached them and saw that they had no tags. They looked like strays. Realizing I wanted to help them, I put them in my shopping cart and took them home. My children instantly took to them, since they had always wanted a pet.

"We loved taking care of them. My cats had the softest fur in Batavia—in fact, my next-door neighbor said they were so soft that we should put them in a petting zoo. One of the cats was all black with green eyes, while the other was white with red eyes. Maybe they were the softest cats in Ohio, or the Midwest, or America, or the whole world!

"My mother always told me what her mother told her what her mother told her—that no two living things created on Mother Earth are exactly alike. So it was that my cats were as different as night and day . . . black and white . . . green eyes and red eyes . . ."

As Elaine rambled on and on, Lenny looked at Patricia, who seemed bored to death. But Lenny was interested because he could understand what she was saying. For one thing, she spoke slowly, so he had time to hear and process each word. For another thing, Elaine kept wandering off her topic, filling in details, which helped Lenny get a better idea of the story.

Finally, Patricia got up to leave.

"Ms. Nottingham," Lenny said politely, "where are you going?"

"To the bathroom. I won't be long."

"Okay," Lenny said, feeling pretty confident that she wasn't going to abandon him.

Elaine continued, "Although the cats tried to escape captivity at first, they soon adjusted to their new home. We called the black cat Janet, and the white cat Martin because we figured out that they were a girl and a boy. About a year later, Janet had kittens, even though we never figured out when they had spawned, and I didn't even know that Janet was going to be a mother until I came home one day and we no longer had two cats, we had seven! I loved my cats. They always could give me company when I needed it.

"I loved those cats. I played with them every day, and whenever I felt sad, they would let me cuddle them and I would feel happy again. And every morning at the stroke of seven, they would wake me up by meowing on my bed or biting my toes when they were kittens. And I would always wake up and feed them and clean the litter box.

"It was a lot harder to take care of seven cats than it was two, so we called a family meeting to decide what to do. The kids, of course, wanted to keep all the kittens, but we just couldn't manage after they started running around the house. The first thing we did was go to the vet, to fix Janet and Martin so they wouldn't have any more kittens. Then we found homes for three of the kittens, then kept the other two, so before we knew it, we had four grown cats to take care of. As the kids grew up, our cats got old, and soon Janet and Martin, almost at the same time, started acting strangely. They stopped eating, stopped doing what cats normally do, you know, purring and cleaning themselves . . ."

Elaine stopped talking. Lenny wondered what was going on, but he dared not say anything in case it was the wrong thing, and he might hurt this nice old woman.

He waited for a while, then she looked up and said, "Oh, there you are, young man. What was your name again? Benny? Is that it?"

Lenny was too afraid to correct her, in case there was some rule against it, so he said, "Yes."

"Benny, yes. What were we talking about? Oh, I was telling you about my cats . . . oh yes, I remember now, I was going to show you some pictures."

She pulled out a drawer in the end table next to the sofa, then took out two framed pictures. Or rather, they were simple children's drawings, and not very good. When the two cats died over forty years ago, the kids drew two pictures so they could remember them.

"What happened?" Lenny asked, then wondered whether it was impolite to ask this, since obviously the cats were sick and about to die in the story. Would this question hurt Elaine's feelings?

"Well, they got a disease that only cats get, and they both died around the same time in 1962. They were old for cats, and we buried them in the pet cemetery near the cemetery where my Aunt Martha is buried, in San Francisco. She loved those cats and wanted them to be near her for always. We tacked a bunch of their pictures up at the grave site. But in 1989, an earthquake struck the Bay Area, and the pet cemetery was destroyed. But at least I have these two pictures left."

Lenny resisted the impulse to tell her that they were crummy drawings, not actual pictures, It was not her fault that she was getting old and couldn't tell a picture from a drawing. And he did not understand how Patricia could be bored by such an interesting story.

He looked at the clock and realized that he had been there for forty-five minutes. Thirty-five minutes of that time period, he had been with Elaine alone. But he hadn't felt lonely or abandoned or even afraid. He did not think he could start a conversation with her, but he felt a strong rapport, an invisible bond that he had only felt with Alice, since usually people hurt him and he hated them for it. But this woman was obviously hurt herself. Lenny could tell. Someone had hurt her, but it wasn't her fault.

Then something else came into his mind, and it wiped out all feelings of rapport and sympathy. Where was Patricia? It didn't take anyone that long to use the bathroom, did it?

Lenny got up, startling the dog, who scampered out of the room.

"Where are you going?" asked Elaine.

"To the bathroom," Lenny replied then walked into the hallway.

"Hurry back. I want to tell you what happened to the kittens."

Lenny walked to the bathroom to see if Patricia was there. She wasn't. Immediately he felt as if the world were falling apart and caving in on him. He wanted to run out of the apartment and find her.

He looked toward the front door and realized that she was probably in her apartment, packing up her things. He knew that in his mind, but his nerves were pounding and throbbing in fear. If his parents could leave him without any warning, certainly a stranger could do the same.

Without saying anything to Elaine, he walked out of her apartment and took the elevator up to the next floor. Now he recognized the hallway. He walked to the right and came to Patricia's doorway.

"Miss Nottingham!" he called and banged on the door.

"Yes?" a voice responded through the door.

"Why are you up here?" he asked.

Patricia opened the door. "I was using the bathroom."

"For forty-five minutes?"

"Well, no, but I had to pack some things up, too."

Lenny didn't believe her. He decided that she was hiding something, the way he hid things all the time.

"But for that long?" he persisted.

"Well, I also ate some lunch, too. I got hungry," said Patricia.

"Oh. Okay. I'm hungry, too. Are we going back to Elaine's?" Lenny asked.

"Do you want to?"

"I want to hear what happened to the kittens."

When they walked down to Elaine's floor, the front door was ajar. They walked in, and Patricia called out, "We're back, deary."

Elaine looked up from the sofa and cried, "Benny, where have you been? You suddenly disappeared, and I didn't know what happened. Or did I just forget you were here?"

"He was perfectly safe," Patricia reassured her. "And his name is Lenny, not Benny."

"Hmm, I guess I'm just getting old. My memory isn't what it used to be."

"You didn't tell her where you were going?"

"I didn't think she'd let me go."

Patricia decided not to scold him, since it was an honest misunderstanding. In other circumstances, she would have reprimanded a careless child, but in this experiment, Lenny was to be validated and agreed with one hundred percent.

"Well, it actually is time to go. I'm glad you were able to tell Lenny the story of your cats. Thank you kindly."

"I'm glad to be of help," Elaine said proudly. "But wouldn't you like something to eat before you go?"

"No, I'll feed him," said Patricia.

As they left, he felt his tears gather in his eyes and trickle down his cheeks. He might never feel that close to another person—or dog—ever again.

# Chapter 23

After one week, Hector now failed every subject at school. Every day he was embarrassed when asked to play Hector's Behaving Game, in which he was put in situations in which he had to confess to crimes he had actually not committed, as well as be the victim in humiliating situations. Even though he tried to fight against his feelings, he lost the battle, and it seemed as if he was getting in trouble with everyone—the music teacher, the gym teacher, his homeroom teacher, the lunch aides, and now his art teacher. The day before, in art class, he needed to water down some of his watercolors, and although he was careful, some water dripped on the floor by accident. The art teacher flew into a rage, screaming at him for intentionally making a mess.

Hector could not take it anymore. Every day, even though he tried as hard as he could, the checks were piling up in the *Hector Misbehaved* column, while there weren't any checks in the *Hector Behaved* column, no matter how hard he tried to do the right thing.

It was now 1:10 p.m., and Mrs. Appell was reading to the class after lunch. At least, the attention was not focused on him, Hector thought, and for a moment, he felt some relief. Then she closed her book and announced, "Reading is over for the day. It's time to play Hector's Behaving Game. If anyone has a new scenario, please raise your hand."

Ten students raised their hand, and this alone embarrassed Hector.

Mrs. Appell scanned the room, then pointed to Tommy. "What's your idea?" she asked him.

"What if someone trips Hector by accident and then Hector has to accept his apology?" Tommy offered.

"That's a good idea. Who wants to trip Hector?"

Again, ten hands shot up in the air amid a lot of giggles.

Hector couldn't believe this was happening. Wasn't it against some rule to trip a person, even in a skit?

"Me! Me!" someone called.

"All right, Macbeth," Mrs. Appell said, pointing to him.

Although the class had been torturing him for one whole week, Hector could tell by the gleam in his former friend's eye that this would be the worst. He stood up, preparing to meet his doom.

Hector and Macbeth walked to the front of the room.

"Now, boys, pretend you're walking down the hall, and you, Macbeth, accidentally collide with Hector and trip him. You got that?"

"Yes, Mrs. Appell," Macbeth said politely, using the phony voice that Hector himself once used.

"Hector, you go to that wall, and Macbeth, you go to the opposite one." After the boys had gotten into position, Mrs. Appell called out, "Three . . . two . . . one . . . go."

Hector didn't move. He felt glued in place. Macbeth came at him menacingly.

"Hey, retard," he hissed. "Come out here. The social worker says you have to be my friend."

Hector didn't move.

Mrs. Appell cut in, "Now, Hector, you have to start walking. Otherwise, I'll start counting."

Taking baby steps, Hector inched away from the wall, watching Macbeth's feet. In his mind, he was imagining the impact, already falling to the floor. He was so preoccupied with worrying about falling that he didn't see Macbeth's foot snake out and trip him.

"Ow!" Hector cried out, keeling over. His classmates howled with laughter.

"Oh, sorry!" Macbeth said dramatically, not meaning it.

"Why'd you do that?" Hector demanded.

"I didn't mean to!"

"Of course you meant it. You're a big fat—"

"Cut!" Mrs. Appell announced.

For a few seconds the laughing ceased. Then gradually a titter here and a giggle there burst into full-blown laughter. Hector wanted to cry.

Turning to the class, she asked, "Now, what was wrong with that scene?"

A number of hands flew into the air. Mrs. Appell called on Cynthia.

"Hector didn't accept Macbeth's apology," Cynthia said smugly.

"Very good. You're right. Hector should have accepted Macbeth's apology. Anything else wrong with the scenario?"

The class remained silent.

"Macbeth," she continued. "Let's give Hector one more chance to win his good check for the day. Go ahead."

"I'm sorry I tripped you," Macbeth repeated.

Hector again felt unable to move.

"Go ahead, we're waiting," Mrs. Appell prompted.

"Would this help?" Macbeth asked, then he kicked Hector behind the knees, causing him to fall forward, hit his head on the corner of a desk, and crash to the floor.

"Ow-ow!" Hector said while the class burst out laughing.

"Hey, sorry, bro," Macbeth said, grinning and taking a bow as the audience clapped.

Hector didn't respond, and just held his head and groaned. Mrs. Appell stated, "Now remember, Hector, it is important to always accept another person's apology. Right now, you *have* to accept Macbeth's apology, or you will get another check in the *Hector Misbehaved* column. In fact, it's your turn now to apologize to Macbeth."

When he still didn't respond, she picked up the chart and put a big black X in the *Misbehaved* column. "Well, that's it. You will now stay in for recess along with your detention after school."

The kids continued to laugh and laugh, while Hector held his head, waiting for the pain to subside.

"Did you hear what I said?" Mrs. Appell demanded.

Something inside Hector snapped. He couldn't stand this anymore. He was going to ask to go to the bathroom, then run away. This seemed like the only way he could escape, since fighting didn't work.

As it turned out, he didn't even have to ask to leave the classroom. His golden opportunity presented itself. At that very moment, the loudest, most annoying noise you could imagine pierced the silence so quickly that it had the same effect as hearing a guillotine coming down to chop off your head. It was a noise right out a horror story or a nightmare.

When this horrible noise had blasted Lenny the previous month, he fell apart. His body went into such shock that he couldn't concentrate for the rest of the day. Initially he burst into tears, but no one would sympathize with him, and he felt all alone in his misery. No one knew, no one understood, and no one cared about the pain that he felt when that noise attacked his ears. And when he tried to explain how horrible the pain felt, everyone told him he was exaggerating, for what was a routine event for most children sounded like a nuclear explosion to Lenny.

*It was the monthly fire drill.*

Feeling the same inexplicable pain, Hector covered his ears and kept groaning, since now both his head and his ears hurt.

"Get up, Hector," Mrs. Appell ordered, "and everyone get in line."

Hector complied, but even though he was supposed to line up according to his last name, the kids kept accusing him of budging, and shoved him to the very back, after Tony Zweibel. As they walked through the halls, the flashing blue strobe light that accompanied the fire drill pierced Hector's eyes like daggers. Now three parts of him were in pain.

These were the same strobe lights that had always bothered Lenny. They reminded him of the lights used for disco dancing or in haunted houses, and whenever he heard a loud noise, it reminded him of the fire drill, which reminded him of the strobe lights and the pain it caused his eyes. Lenny dreaded it for weeks until it happened, and could relax only between the day of the fire drill until the end of the month. But promptly on the first of the month, the dread returned. In fact, sometimes he shivered every second of the day fearing the time when the sound would go off again. Now Hector was having the same reaction.

The reason for the pain was the element of surprise. If only Lenny's, and now Hector's, body were given advance notice, it could prepare for the attack. Even though the principal promised Lenny that she'd tell him about an upcoming fire drill, she never did. And she certainly wouldn't have told Hector, had she known it was bothering him. She would have jumped for joy that her experiment was working.

However, this particular fire drill also provided Hector with a means of escape. With everyone exiting the building, he could disappear into the neighborhood and never be seen again. While his classmates evacuated the school, he figured out how he was going to make his escape. The side exit doors were always locked during school hours so when it was time for the students to reenter the building, each class would appoint a student to run to the main entrance to be admitted, then run to the appropriate exit and open the door outward. Pretending that he wanted to perform this service for his class, Hector volunteered, but instead of running to the front door, he ran away. As he rounded the corner, on his way to what seemed like the front door, he darted into the street. His school was on Sheridan Road, so he sprinted north on Sheridan and kept on running.

He knew where he wanted to hide—the Skokie River Forest Preserve. It was quite a hike, maybe two or three miles, but it would be worth it. Maybe he could hide out for days before someone caught him. Only a week ago, he'd had absolutely no reason to run away. Well, now he had a reason. He was angry. He wanted his parents and teachers to worry about him, and maybe when they became desperate, they'd stop picking on him. Maybe he'd stay for a month, or maybe he'd head home later that night. He couldn't make plans at the moment—he only wanted to run.

The forest preserve had an entrance near Witchwood Lane in Lake Forest. It would be a perfect place to hide. No one would suspect he was there, because they'd be searching the streets of Lake Forest first.

He passed the intersection where Sheridan Road turned abruptly to the west, and he continued north on Moffett Road, still running as fast as his legs would carry him. The stress of what had been going on was building into more and more anger, which gave his muscles greater power.

Within five minutes, Hector made it to East Witchwood Lane, but he was still quite a distance from the preserve. He realized that he would have to find some food, so he kept on running. There had to be a small store somewhere.

After what seemed like an hour of running past large, affluent homes, he still hadn't found a store. He'd already left the main part of Lake Forest, however, which was crucial to his escape. Still on Witchwood Lane, he crossed the railroad tracks, hoping to find a store. Instead he found more large houses. It seemed as if everyone lived in a castle around there.

Instinctively, he followed the tracks, figuring they had to lead into a station somewhere. Soon he got to the edge of a short business district, and like an oasis in the desert, a small convenience store loomed across the street. Reaching into his pocket, he pulled out about ten dollars in bills and coins, which was the normal amount of money he carried in school just for status. His hand shook from exhaustion, and he was breathing heavily.

Around the same time, Hector's mother returned from a social event, and she was greeted by two terrifying voice mail messages. One was from Hector's principal, Dr. Wikedda, and the other was from the Lake Forest Police.

"OH MY GOD!" Mrs. Fairfield screamed, after she had listened to both messages. "MY SON! WHAT'S HAPPENED TO HIM?"

Jumping into her car again, she raced over to the school, parked in a handicapped spot because it was the closest to the school entrance, then dashed through the front doors into the office.

"I need to speak to the principal!" Mrs. Fairfield shouted, racing past the secretary's desk.

"Name tag," the secretary, Mrs. Hamm, reminded her, pointing to the sign-in book.

"What are you talking about? This is an emergency! My son's missing, and the principal told me to come here right away."

"Yes, ma'am, but you still need a name tag. Please sign in at the front door and get a name tag, then come back here."

"Wh-what?" Mrs. Fairchild asked in a daze.

Mrs. Hamm looked at her condescendingly, as if she were a special ed student. Pointing, she instructed, "Go back out the door, toward the exit, then you'll see a sign-in book and a stack of blank name tags. Please sign in, then write your name on a blank name tag."

In disbelief, Lydia Fairfield rushed out of the office and back toward the front door. Spotting the sign-in book, she scribbled her name and the date furiously, but when she looked for the stack of name tags, all she found was a small plastic cube filled with crumpled-up triangles—the peel-off backings from already used name tags.

Lydia stormed back into the office. "I *demand* to see the principal," she screamed.

Mrs. Hamm replied, "I don't see your name tag."

"There aren't any more, you—" Lydia caught herself before she called the vile woman an appropriately vile name.

"DR. WIKEDDA!" Lydia shrieked. "It's Hector's mother! I have to see you right now!"

The secretary jumped up. "Oh, I'm sorry! You're the mother of that boy? How can you stand him?" Then she pulled open one of her drawers, withdrew a name tag, and handed it to Lydia, who scrawled her last name in the middle of it and shouted, "Dr. Wikedda, I need to see you!"

"I'll take you, Mrs. Fairfield," Mrs. Hamm said. "If you could please just put that name tag on—"

"Oh, for God's sake, what's wrong with you?"

"It's not my rule, but school policy. I hope you understand."

Lydia understood nothing. "Where's the principal?" she demanded.

"Please calm down. I'll take you to her."

As Mrs. Hamm walked down the short hallway to the principal's office, Lydia had the impulse to push the irritating woman out of her way. Finally, when they reached the principal's office, Lydia did push the woman out of the way and barged through the door.

The principal was looking over some forms.

"What HAPPENED?" Lydia screamed.

"Hector ran away from school," Dr. Wikedda stated matter-of-factly.

"WHY?" she shrieked.

"Now please calm down, Mrs. Fairfield. Hector has been misbehaving in school all week, as I predicted. He's learning that he is not the crown prince, and he is reacting badly to our experimental treatment of him. It's as I predicted."

"You're crazy," Mrs. Fairfield said, shaking her head. "I never should have agreed to this ridiculous setup."

"Oh, come now," Dr. Wikedda said, looking her in the eye, "you can't tell me that you haven't felt a certain measure of satisfaction making that spoiled brat of yours squirm a bit."

What the principal said was true, but Lydia wasn't about to admit it.

"As soon as the police find him," she said, "this experiment of yours is coming to an end. Understood?"

Dr. Wikedda was about to protest, but she saw the murderous look in Lydia's eyes and murmured, "Understood."

"I'm on my way to the police station now. If anything happens to Hector, I'm holding *you* responsible."

"Wait. I'll come with you. A teacher thought she saw Hector running north on Sheridan Road during the fire drill. We were all outside, and Hector volunteered to go through the front doors then run to the fifth grade entrance to open it for the rest of his class. We always keep those side doors locked, you know. For the safety of our kids."

"You didn't keep my son very safe, did you. You're crazy," Lydia Fairfield spat.

"Please calm down, Mrs. Fairfield. We gave a full description to the police, and they are looking in the area north of here. Fortunately, it's an affluent area, and there are never any children outside playing. They're all at their scheduled activities. A boy walking alone is sure to be noticed."

When they got to the police station, they were seen by an Officer Crowe, who asked Mrs. Fairfield a series of questions. The school had already filed a report.

"Can you suggest a motive as to why your son may have done this?" the officer asked finally.

Lydia glanced at Dr. Wikedda, then thought for a moment before answering, "No. I—I can think of no motive whatsoever. Hector has always been a happy boy."

"It's such a shame," Dr. Wikedda said, wondering if she had enough data for a partial write-up of her experiment.

# Chapter 24

*April 1, 2010—4 p.m.*
**Skokie River Nature Preserve**

At the same time, Hector had reached the Skokie River Nature Preserve after an hour of running. He only made one stop—at the small convenience store to pick up some sandwiches, several cans of Sprite, and two candy bars so he would have something to eat. He would ration the food as much as possible to make it last. When he got to the preserve, he saw a sign that it was closed for the season. This was good—people would probably not suspect anyone to be inside the preserve, and not look for him there.

He would still have to be careful, however, since there were trails in the forest preserve, and someone might get suspicious if they saw a boy walking alone carrying food. The police might have even put up "Missing" posters, and he might be recognized. So he avoided the trails and went deep into the forest. Pretty soon he was lost.

But he was not scared, for the woods were peaceful and inviting. And in order to find his way out, he would simply have to walk north.

Meanwhile, Hector's mother and Officer Crowe were driving around in a squad car looking for her son. They were now driving on Woodland Road after they'd covered Spruce Avenue. The officer made sure he searched every side road and looked down every driveway. Very few kids were out except to get off buses or out of cars and disappear into their houses for the night.

When they had finished searching most of the Lake Forest streets that were east of Sheridan Road, they crossed over and went west. As they drove, Officer Crowe asked Mrs. Fairfield more questions.

"Are you sure you have no idea why Hector would do this?" he inquired.

Mrs. Fairfield pretended to think, since she was not going to tell him the truth. "No, I can't think of a single reason. He's usually a . . . very well-behaved and happy child."

"Well, this doesn't make any sense now, but there has to be some explanation. I'll keep looking on Deerpath, Western, and Green Bay. If I can't find him in Lake Forest, I'll call up the Lake County sheriff so we can ask every community in the county to start looking for him. When it gets dark, though, you should go home and rest."

Mrs. Fairfield started to protest, then changed her mind. There wasn't much she could do just sitting in a police car.

"All right," she said.

Officer Crowe got Officer Stanley on the radio. "Any sign?" Officer Crowe asked.

"Nope," came the reply. "But I'm about to go to the business district and ask in the stores if they've seen a boy fitting Hector's description. Maybe he stopped by for an ice cream sandwich or something."

"That's a great idea, George. We'll start checking out gas stations and convenience stores on our way, okay?"

"Okay."

Little did these adults know that they were far away from where Hector was hiding.

He'd been wandering for what seemed like hours, but it was only 4:39. Feeling safely hidden, he wondered what he was going to do now. Actually, there was nothing for him to do because he had run away from school before the teacher had assigned the homework for the day. So he decided to wander around a bit more and figure out where the hiking trails were then keep away from them. Since it was springtime it wouldn't get dark until 7:00, so he decided to eat at 6:00, then find a place to sleep. The next day he would return home at 4:00—after school was over—and explain to his parents why he had to run away.

And he really did have to do it. For more than a week, everyone had been out to get him, and he had been badly hurt by his parents and teachers. He wanted to let them know that they couldn't get away with what they'd done, even if they were adults.

Hector kept walking deeper into the woods. No one would find him here.

Finally, during his wanderings Hector reached the backyard of US Highway 41, the highway that bordered the forest preserve. It was now 5:10, and he'd been walking through trees for forty minutes. The forest seemed like a happy little world, his own little Garden of Eden. No one was going to hurt or humiliate him or make him do something he hated. In the forest, he didn't have to go to school. Unlike people, the animals around him went about their business of survival and didn't pay him any attention, except to keep their distance. He knew he couldn't talk to the animals in the forest, but he wondered what they would say to him if they could.

For the first time in days, Hector felt happy. He had escaped the cruel human world. It was as if civilization had ceased to exist, and everything had turned into trees. Here no one could yell at him for misbehaving or for breaking rules they had suddenly invented as a trap. Here there were no rules at all.

He decided to sit down next to a gnarly old oak tree and observe any animals or plants he could see. Although the trees were bare, he noticed that the leaves that had fallen the previous autumn were still on the ground. No lawn service here to whisk away all evidence of the changing seasons. He tried to see any squirrels moving or birds flying, and wondered . . . what were they thinking in this forest? Did they enjoy their lives, or did they feel the encroachment of human civilization all around them?

He also wondered about the plants in the forest as well. The plants could not move the way the animals did. They just had to stay put wherever they sprouted, or wherever someone planted them. If an animal tried to eat them, they could not defend themselves or escape. He wondered if they thought things and judged each other the way kids did. Did they think things, have friends, and make fun of each other, too? He couldn't know, but he wondered what it would be like if they did.

He recalled the Disney movies he had seen as a young child before he grew to hate them as sissy stuff, movies that sometimes involved talking plants and animals, and he wondered if plants and animals really could engage in conversations, but he and other human beings just couldn't hear or understand them.

He also remembered the time he bonded with his cat in the bedroom a few days ago when he was upset, and he felt that he had actually communicated with Pointy. He wondered if other people came to the forest to talk to the animals and plants that lived there. If he could talk to them, he would have voiced his anger against the people who were mistreating him.

A red bird that looked like a cardinal flew down and landed in a branch on a nearby tree. The bird looked at him cautiously, perhaps sizing him up, and then looked away as it stayed there. Hector wondered if the bird was afraid of him, then felt a sense of great relief and satisfaction when the bird started to tweet with other birds. He looked at the tree and saw that the bird was near a nest in a nearby branch, where another bird, brown with red accents, was sitting inside.

In fact, the birds now seemed to be ignoring him, tweeting away. It just seemed to live its life. Finally, the bird that landed on the branch calmly took off and flew away, and Hector waved good-bye sadly, as if he were losing a dear friend.

Hector did not realize it as he sat in the forest preserve, but he was now thinking like an autistic person. He was seeing the human world as his enemy and as something that was out to get him. Like an autistic person, he had become afraid of anything having to do with other people.

He had run and walked for a long time, and he was hungry. With nothing else to do, he decided to have dinner early, so he unwrapped one of the sandwiches and leaned back against the tree to eat it.

Hector's mother was beginning to lose hope that she would find her son by the end of the day. She and the other officers had scanned all of Lake Forest east of Highway 41. She wasn't worried about her son Dietrich returning to an empty house because, according to the Department of Child and Family Services, at thirteen, he was old enough to be home alone.

"Mrs. Fairfield," said Officer Crowe as they drove along Green Bay Road, "I understand how you feel. That boy must be your whole world. Sometimes we never find missing kids, or they turn up dead, occasionally in pieces."

"Yes, he is my whole world." She started to sob, not noticing how socially inappropriate some of the officer's comments were. Even Lenny knew not to talk about dead kids in front of parents.

"I'll take you home," he continued. "You have your other son to think about."

When they pulled up in front of the Fairfield house, Mrs. Fairfield thanked the officer, then ran inside. Dietrich was lying on the couch doing a math problem.

"Hi, dear," she said. "I take it you know what happened."

"We need to talk," Dietrich said coldly.

"I've just spent two hours searching for your brother in a squad car, and that's all you can say?" she wailed. "Why do we need to talk?"

"Because you've been acting really weird and mean toward Hector," he retorted. "What is going on? You never treated him like that until a week ago."

"It's none of your business how I treat Hector! I'm the parent, not you."

"Well, then, let me be more specific. Why have you been feeding him raw eggs for breakfast?"

"HOW DARE YOU ASK ME THAT? HE'S MY SON, AND I CAN FEED HIM ANYTHING I WANT!"

Dietrich looked at his mother as if she had gone crazy. "Why are you yelling at me? Is there something going on that I don't know about?"

Mrs. Fairfield didn't have a good answer to that question, but she realized that if she kept up with the experiment, she might lose both her sons.

"All right, I'll tell you," she began, feeling a sense of defeat and resignation, "but things are about to go back to the way they were. Eight days ago, I got a call from Hector's principal, Dr. Wikedda. She wanted to conduct a scientific experiment that would change Hector's life . . ."

# Chapter 25

*April 1, 2010—9 p.m.*
*Skokie River Nature Preserve*

Hector spent the night sleeping next to the trees in the preserve. He heard occasional animal noises—a squirrel chattering, geese flying overhead, and even an owl hooting from time to time. However, he didn't once feel afraid or threatened because he trusted the animals. They had better things to do besides watch him misbehave, and they misbehaved a lot themselves and no one was there to scold them. It was an adjustment to sleep on the hard ground rather than a warm bed, but Hector was willing to deal with it so he could get away from his parents and teachers for a while.

Even at night, the distant lights of civilization allowed him to see the silhouettes of the plants and trees around him. He wondered if they went to sleep and woke up like he did. He remembered his mother saying that outdoor trees did not like all-night Christmas lights wrapped around them, since trees needed darkness at night like people did, but he'd never really listened to her. Now, however, he wondered if what she'd said could possibly . . . maybe . . . have some truth to it. He felt bad that he'd never even considered that trees had needs and rights.

Before he fell asleep, he also looked at the different dry grasses, dead and brown now because of winter but still standing. He noticed a little section where he saw some tree stumps. He wondered who had cut down those trees, and needing to move around to warm himself up, he wandered over to them and found a plaque, which he could just make out in the dim background light coming from the outside world: *This area is being maintained by the Friends of Native Plants, who try to remove as many invasive species in the area, such as purple loosestrife and buckthorn. To volunteer, contact www. friendsofnativeplants.com.*

Hector wondered what the sign meant, not knowing what invasive species, purple loosestrife, or buckthorn were. He did, however, memorize the website address, realizing that he could have a reason to return to this home away from home. Maybe he didn't need to beg his old friends to take him back—he would find new friends who were not bullies, but people who cared about plants and animals.

He remembered the night when he had bonded with his pet cat. Perhaps he would never go back to hanging out with people again. He looked down at his feet as he returned to his tree trunk, heard them crunch the dry leaves and dead vegetation, and felt at one with his environment. It seemed like a whole new world. He remembered something his aunt had told him about the forest preserves in the Chicago area—that they seemed small from the outside, but inside they were quite large.

When it was time to sleep, he initially tossed and turned, trying to make himself as comfortable as possible on the hard ground. He knew his clothes probably had become dirty, but he didn't care. Fortunately the ground was not wet, and it was too early in the year for worms and crawling insects.

After finding a restful position, Hector finally went to sleep, lulled by the peace and friendliness all around him.

*9 p.m.*
## The Fahrer Residence

Meanwhile, Lenny Fahrer was at home reading an American Girls book before he went to sleep. Patricia wasn't shocked when he revealed his interest in the history of girls and women—like autistic people, they had suffered from centuries of oppression because of who they were born. In fact, she took him to the library to check out as many books as he wanted.

As Lenny lay on the couch, reading about the lack of child labor laws at the turn of the twentieth century, Patricia was cleaning up the kitchen, thinking of the progress he had made. For in truth, Lenny was not the same boy that he was when she'd first met him. No longer was he frozen and cut off from other people. In one week, he had thawed. Leaving school was like coming out of a freezer. Lenny was still autistic, with the quirks and anomalies that defined who he was, but the terror that had struck him repeatedly every day was nearly gone. Looking at Lenny emerging out of his ice block, Patricia was convinced that she should follow her dream to start a charter school for autistic children, in which she would *not* do what public schools and IEPs did to these kids.

When she walked into the living room, Lenny looked up from his book and actually smiled.

"What are you reading about?" Patricia asked, then sat down next to Lenny on the couch. He stayed where he was and did not immediately move over to give himself more space.

"I'm reading about how kids had to work in factories a hundred years ago, and there were no laws protecting them. They got hurt, lost fingers, and nobody cared. Sometimes they were orphans and didn't belong anywhere."

"Is this upsetting to you?" Patricia asked.

Lenny thought this question over. Generally, he understood what it meant to be hurt, but he had accepted it as a fact in the lives of all people who were different.

"Yes," he said.

"Well, why don't you close that book now, and let's talk about something fun that I have planned."

Lenny closed to book and looked toward Patricia, not afraid of seeing her anymore.

"I'd like to take you on a field trip next week. Do you remember my telling you about the toy museum in Fox Lake? Well, next Thursday we're going there by train."

Every year Lenny's school went on a special spring field trip, and this year it would be to the Parnell Toy Museum. The whole school did not go there at once—each individual grade went on designated days. Patricia knew of that trip from looking at the school schedule, and she'd decided to take Lenny there herself so he wouldn't miss the one thing he might have actually enjoyed. It was her own personal side experiment, to see whether Lenny might actually try to interact with some of his former schoolmates. She also knew that Lenny loved to read train schedules, so she'd decided to take the train.

"Okay, Lenny," she said, "we're leaving in the morning and returning in the late afternoon. I'd like you to do some research for our trip. When does the museum open, and when does it close? Figure out how many hours you want to spend there, then find the two trains that will give us that amount of time. If you want to do something extra, look up the restaurants in Fox Lake and figure out which one you want to have lunch at."

Now Lenny felt very excited. He knew about the Parnell Toy Museum at the intersection of Grand and Rollins Road. They had toys from all different eras, including the 1950s. Elaine, Patricia's downstairs neighbor, had told him about the toy museum, and was supposed to describe the toys to him, but hadn't gotten around to it. Now he would see them for himself!

And the best part was that they would be taking a train. His parents had driven him everywhere, so he had never been on a train before. *Suddenly after reading schedules for so many years, he would actually be riding on a train.* He was so excited, he could hardly stay still. He and seen—and felt—many trains pass the two stations in Lake Forest. And finally he was going to feel what it was like to ride in one of those trains. He was happier than he could ever remember being.

# Chapter 26

*April 2, 2010—10 a.m.*
*Skokie River Nature Preserve*

Hector spent the morning wandering through the forest preserve. He had eaten the rest of his food and was starting to get hungry.

He decided that he wanted to go home. He had enjoyed his visit to the forest, spending time with the nonjudgmental plants and animals, but he was now looking for the entrance gate so he could walk home and tell his parents why he had run away. He said goodbye to the birds, the owls, the squirrels, the trees, and the plants, even though he wondered why

He successfully found the gate by walking into the eastern sun. From there he would walk home.

Except that he didn't have to. When he got to the entrance, a police car was just driving in.

At first, Hector backed up and hid behind a tree. However, the officer had already spotted him because he turned on his strobe light and slowly drove toward Hector's hiding place.

"Hector Fairfield," a voice came from a portable speaker. "Don't be afraid. I've come to take you home."

Hector felt a terror unlike anything he ever remembered experiencing. He was so afraid that he couldn't move a muscle, couldn't speak, and could hardly breathe. His nerves expected that at any moment, the car window would open and a rifle would appear, aiming right at him. His hearing became hyperacute, and when he did hear the sound of the window being lowered, he fell to the ground and covered his head with his hands.

He listened to the sounds of the car being parked, a door opening and closing, and a voice saying, "I've found Hector."

Inside the car there were the muffled sounds of a dispatcher speaking. Hector strained to pick out the words being said. It took his mind off the immediate terror that he felt, the way an autistic person will focus on house numbers to appease the terror of being driven to a new place.

Hector, at this point, was becoming increasingly autistic as a means of survival.

He was so focused on listening to the dispatcher that he forgot to listen for approaching footsteps until two big black leather shoes planted themselves right next to him on the ground and a voice from above said, "Hello there, son."

Hector was too afraid to look up and see who it was—and whether he had his gun drawn.

The voice continued, "You've given your parents quite a fright. Would you like to tell me why?"

Hector replayed the voice's question in his mind, trying to determine whether it would be safe to answer. Finally he whispered, "I wanted to prove a point."

"I see . . . And what was that point?"

Scrunching his head farther down against his knees, Hector did not answer. In truth, he did not really know how to explain the point he'd been trying to make.

After about a minute, the officer said, "I'm required to take you back home, Hector, and I'll give you two choices. Either you come willingly, or I can pick you up and take you home kicking and screaming."

Hector finally took a quick peek upward and saw the stern look on the officer's face. Was he is serious trouble? He had only wanted to prove a point, but doing so did not mean he wanted to fight a cop.

"I will come willingly," Hector said softly.

"Fine. Good boy," the officer said. "Now please get up and walk with me to the car."

Hector did so, and the officer instructed him to sit in the backseat.

Grabbing his radio transmitter, the officer reported, "This is Officer Martin. I have Hector Fairfield with me. He is quiet and cooperative, and I'm taking him home."

There was a garbled question, then the officer continued, "I found him at the entrance to the Skokie River Forest Preserve. His mother was right about him crossing the city limits."

As they drove, Hector followed the street signs of the route he took from the school. Suddenly this seemingly boring activity took on a special meaning for Hector, because those signs represented an adventure in self-assertion that he would never forget. And as we have seen before, Hector was now thinking like an autistic person, and they love the order, predictability, and unchanging nature of streets and their signs.

The officer turned his head toward the backseat and announced, "The dispatcher is calling your mother now. You'll be home soon."

Hector wasn't sure what his mother's reaction would be, although he sensed that he was in deep and serious trouble. She had already been jumping on him for every little thing, and this was truly a very big thing.

They drove along Green Bay Road, then crossed the railroad tracks. Hector would be home in five minutes.

The dispatcher said something incomprehensible, then the officer picked up his mike and said, "I'm approaching the child's house now. I'll talk to you later. Over." He hung up the radio just as he pulled into Hector's driveway.

The officer parked the car, then said, "I'll accompany you to the door, Hector."

Hector mumbled, "All right," but kept his head down.

Together they got out of the police car and walked to the front door. Before they could even knock, the door flew open and Hector's mother stood there, glaring at Hector.

"Mrs. Fairfield?" the officer said.

"Yes," she replied, trying to sound civil.

Hector stood there, frozen to the spot. His legs refused to move. Even though he had wanted to prove a point, he had forgotten what that point was. In fact, he had forgotten how to speak.

"Sorry for all your trouble, Officer," Mrs. Fairfield said, reaching out to grab Hector by the shoulder. He didn't flinch or even react as she pulled him toward her.

"I'm glad we could be of assistance," he said. Then smiling a policeman's fake smile, he said, "Bye-bye now."

Hector didn't respond, but Lydia poked him in the back and ordered, "Say thank you to the officer."

He still didn't respond. He was unable to.

Lydia shook her head in disgust, then gave the officer an equally fake smile. "Bye-bye," she said, then pulled Hector through the door, slammed it shut, and flung him toward the living room.

Immediately Hector crept over to the sofa and lay down.

He did not look at his mother but felt her approach, hovering over him like a black storm cloud.

"I want to know . . . why you did this."

Hector had found his voice, remembered the point he was trying to make, so he began, "I did it . . . because—"

"I DON'T CARE WHY YOU DID IT!" roared Mrs. Fairfield. "WHY DID YOU EVEN THINK OF RUNNING AWAY?"

"I did it because—"

"DON'T GIVE ME ANY EXCUSES! HOW COULD YOU BE SO STUPID AS TO THINK YOU COULD GET AWAY WITH THIS?"

*How could you not know why I did this?* Hector thought. *How could YOU be so stupid?*

"I didn't think—"

"OF COURSE YOU DIDN'T THINK! THAT'S ALWAYS BEEN YOUR TROUBLE—YOU NEVER THINK!"

"That's not what I meant. I—"

"IT DOESN'T MATTER WHAT YOU THINK!"

"Please let me—"

"Look," Hector's mother said, a little more calmly. "It's ten twenty, and you should be in school. So I'm not going to punish you right now. In fact," she added with a wicked gleam in her eye, "the kids will probably figure out a way to punish you on their own. But when you return home, you're grounded for the next two weeks, with no TV or computer unless it's essential for schoolwork. And I get the final approval on whether it's essential or not."

Hector looked away. He didn't want to go to school. Not ever again.

"DID YOU HEAR ME?" Lydia Fairfield screamed right near his ear, causing him to jump back.

"I—I—"

"Good. Now get your backpack. It's in your room. The school gave it to me yesterday after you ran away without it."

Hector walked slowly down the hallway to his room. But when he put his hand on the doorknob to open the door, he suddenly felt sharp, searing pain on his palm.

"OW-OW-OW!" Hector screamed.

"Hurry it up," his mother called, "and quit complaining."

He tried the door again, and once more he was hit with a sharp, cutting pain. Looking down and under the knob, which was an old one and actually made of glass, Hector saw a crack, which had caused two broken, jagged pieces to separate, and form a sharp edge. When he studied his palm, he saw a trickle of blood where the sharp edge had cut him like a razor.

"My hand was cut when I touched the doorknob!" Hector cried.

"That's crazy!" Mrs. Fairfield said. "How can a doorknob hurt you? One more lie from you and there'll be no TV and computer for *three* weeks."

Hector did not reply. What was the use? No one believed him anymore. No one was nice to him anymore. Carefully he tried to the knob again, but again he cut himself.

"Ow!" he screamed.

"No more noise!" his mother warned.

"But I'm bleeding!" Hector protested, then instantly regretted telling her the truth.

"And no more lying."

"See for yourself," he said, the extended his palm out to his mother, who had come alongside him.

His mother scrutinized his hand, then shrugged. "You probably just did it to get my attention."

"I have no reason to do that," Hector argued.

"You have every reason. If you're hurt, you can get out of going to school."

"How could I do this to myself?"

"I wonder," she scoffed, then turned the doorknob herself. Magically it opened, and she showed him her hand, without a scratch.

Hector walked into his room and sat wearily on the bed. He did not understand why his mother was going crazy. Or maybe he was going crazy, for how could she have opened the door and not gotten hurt?

In the car on the way to school, Hector realized that there was no way he was going to get his old life back. There was no way he was going to win against his parents, his teachers, his so-called friends, and the rest of the world. He would just retreat from everyone, placing himself behind an iron curtain so that nothing got into his brain and nothing came out. He would ignore the rest of the world, and it seemed that he would be doing the world a favor.

When they got to school, Hector walked silently to the office with his mother, got a tardy slip, and went to his classroom.

As he walked in, all the kids turned and stared.

"Well, hello, Hector," said Mrs. Appell. "Welcome back. I hope you learned your lesson."

Hector wasn't sure which lesson she was referring to, but he nodded his head yes and walked over to his seat, tuning out the glaring looks of the other kids. Nothing mattered to him anymore.

"Now, to continue what we were learning in science," Mrs. Appell announced to the class. "Long ago, the earth did not look the way it does now. This is because the earth's surface is divided into pieces, or plates, that when formed together . . . *blah blah blah blah blah blah . . .*"

That was what Hector was hearing now. *Blah blah blah blah.* He did not care about whether he failed the lesson. If he was to live in a hostile world, then he would have to protect himself, and it seemed as if this was only way. Everything that anyone said would become *blah blah blah* to him, and he imagined himself inside a giant balloon—able to see everything without being seen.

As the teacher's words faded away, Hector felt a new contentment inside his balloon sanctuary. No one could hurt him in there.

What Hector did not know, however, was that Lenny Fahrer had placed himself inside a similar sanctuary for years. From the first traumatic day when Lenny entered school until the day he left it for good, Lenny had hidden behind self-erected barriers, protecting himself not only from his teachers but also from students such as Hector.

As Mrs. Appell droned on and on, Hector hunched into himself, trying to block out all sound. He stuck his index fingers in his ears, but that only blocked out background noise, and he could actually hear Mrs. Appell a little better. So he tried something new, in which he stuck his fingers in his ears, then pulled them out, then repeated this rapidly over and over, causing a pattern of hearing-silence-hearing-silence, which garbled the words he heard, similar to the way a strobe light's pattern of on-off-on-off confuses what you are seeing.

Unfortunately he was caught. "What are you doing, Hector?" Mrs. Appell demanded.

He thought for a moment, then realized he didn't know what he was doing. He was creating his own private world by protecting his ears.

Finally he replied, "Ear privacy."

The whole class erupted in laughter.

"What's that?" the teacher asked.

"It's what I'm doing," Hector replied, continuing to press his fingers in and pull them out of his ears.

"That's not an answer, young man," Mrs. Appell said. "If you continue to do this, I'll have to send you to Mrs. Ting-Pot, the social worker."

Hector now felt as if he had come full circle. He was once the terror of the hallways, sending scared kids running to Mrs. Ting-Pot. Now he was being sent to her himself.

He stopped plugging and unplugging his ears but stayed inside his balloon, imagining the noise to be far away instead.

When it was lunch time, no one approached Hector or said a word to him, to his relief.

No one talked to him at lunch, or during the rest of the day.

As Mrs. Appell was reviewing the homework assignments at the end of the day, she reminded the class that next week was their class's field trip to the Parnell Toy Museum in Fox Lake, and that everybody should bring a sack lunch. As much as Hector dreaded school, he was dreading the field trip even more. He knew from his own experience as a bully that bus rides and field trips provided ideal conditions for terrorizing weak kids. Now it was his turn to experience what he'd always thought of as "having a little fun." He now knew in his heart that it was not fun for the chosen victims—not fun at all.

# Chapter 27

"Does Mrs. Appell's class have my undivided attention?" asked Mrs. Carson.

At the Parnell Toy Museum, the tour guide was taking Mrs. Appell's class around the contemporary floor. The entire fifth grade had come on the field trip, as well as a half-dozen room parents and student chaperones from the middle school, including Hector's brother, Dietrich.

"If you look to your left, you will see our Crazy Bones collection," Mrs. Carson told the class. "They were very popular in the late nineteen-nineties, but they fell out of favor when the next craze, Pokémon, arrived on our shores from Japan. Take some time and look at all the shapes. Does anyone have any questions?"

One girl raised her hand.

Mrs. Carson nodded toward her. "Yes?"

Giggling a little, the girl asked, "Well, like, what do you *do* with these things?"

Several other kids nodded and had questioningly looks on their faces.

"Kids collected them," Mrs. Appell explained. "And traded them. Like Pokémon cards, some were considered more valuable than others."

The kids milled around, looking at the shapes and wondering how anyone could possibly want to collect small blobs and hunks of cheap plastic—and they felt superior to those bygone kids, because kids today collected things that were much more sophisticated and useful, like animal-shape rubber bands, which could be worn on the wrist as jewelry.

Mrs. Carson then announced, "All right, Mrs. Appell's class, I am now going to take you on a treasure hunt in our playroom. You will be divided into groups and will look for toys. If you find a toy, please show it to me. You can play with it, but you cannot keep it."

She led the class to the playroom on the second floor at the other side of the museum. The building had two floors, but all the exhibits were on the first floor. They climbed one flight of stairs then walked down a long hall to get to their destination.

"Mrs. Appell," the tour guide called out, "will you divide up the groups?"

"Certainly," she replied. "Since there are eighteen students and six buddies, we'll have six groups consisting of three students and one buddy."

Hector was assigned to Group 4, along with Carly Veerman and Robert Anderson.

The three children were assigned one corner of the playroom, where there were five stacks of boxes. In each box several toys were hidden amid a lot of shipping materials. Immediately Carly started kicking the stacks of boxes and squealing when they fell down. Finally she ripped open a box and pawed through the stuffing until she found a small wrapped box.

"What did you find?" Robert asked.

"I don't know," replied Carly.

"You sure did a good job knocking down that stack," he said.

Then Robert thrust out his foot and kicked down another stack of boxes, laughing as they flew out in all directions.

Meanwhile Hector was sitting down in the corner, ignoring everyone. He wanted to pretend he was alone. A few times he glanced quickly at Carly and Robert throwing boxes at each other, often tearing one open, finding a toy, then tossing it on the floor. Sometimes Robert would kick a box if it got in his way.

Fortunately, the buddy that was assigned to Hector's group was his own brother, Dietrich. Unfortunately, Hector by now assumed that everyone was in on the plot to destroy him, including Dietrich. When he saw his older brother walking toward him, Hector jumped to his feet and pretended to be playing and having a good time.

He ran up to one of the stacks of boxes and kicked it with all his might. The boxes flew in all directions.

"Hey, what do you think you're doing?" Carly screamed.

"Yeah, what did you just do?" Robert demanded.

Hector looked at their angry faces and felt confused. "I—I did what you were doing," he replied.

"No way. You could have hurt someone."

"But—but—"

"We don't want you in our group," Robert sneered.

Hector felt close to tears. He didn't know what he had done differently from the other two kids, who were getting along just fine.

Dietrich had witnessed the entire scene, and he knew it was time to confront his brother. However, he didn't say anything when Hector went back to the wall and slumped down on the floor. He didn't want to humiliate his brother, who had suffered enough.

"Welcome to the Parnell Toy Museum," said Mr. Garter, the man at the entrance. "The suggested donation is five dollars. Here is a map of the museum. Would you like to join a tour, or walk around by yourselves?"

Patricia turned to Lenny and asked, "Which would you prefer?"

Immediately Lenny answered, "I'd like to walk around by myself."

Patricia put a ten-dollar bill in the donation box then together she and Lenny entered the museum.

"What would you like to see first?"

"I don't know," said Lenny, becoming fascinated by the map itself. He looked at the organization of the floors and saw patterns and designs in the hallways that led from one room to another. On the second floor was a large open space called PLAYROOM. The word "play" had always inspired terror in his heart, since it generally involved other children, so he looked at the other headings. Finally he noticed the TRAIN ROOM on the first floor.

"I'd like to see the Train Room," Lenny said.

"Sure thing," Patricia said, and Lenny pointed down the hall in the direction of the Train Room.

It was fun just walking down the hall, seeing in three dimensions what he'd first encountered in two on the map. This was one of Lenny's supreme joys, seeing how something represented in two dimensions actually existed in three-dimensional reality. Perhaps this is one of the reasons that autistic people like maps so much, because they provide a certain predictability to the confusing and random world around them.

The room itself, however, was filled with noisy, overactive, unpredictable kids. Lenny took one look at the horde and said, "Let's go somewhere else."

"Why don't you be my tour guide?" Patricia suggested. "You can take me from room to room."

"Okay."

Lenny studied the map, then led Patricia from room to room, each time glancing inside and deciding that there were too many kids running around. However, it didn't matter. He was having a wonderful time pretending to be a tour guide.

When they had looked into every room on the first floor, Lenny asked Mr. Garter, "What's the Play Room? It's on the second floor."

"Oh, that's where kids can go and get rid of some of their excess energy. They're allowed to run around, make noise, and knock things over in a safe environment. They don't have to be well behaved like they do on the first floor."

Lenny thought, if the kids on the first floor were supposed be well behaved, what were the kids like on the second floor? In his mind he pictured the scene from *Pinocchio*, when all the boys were wrecking the model house on Pleasure Island, right before they turned into donkeys.

Seeing the horrified look on Lenny's face, Patricia said, "We don't have to go up there. But you might enjoy it."

Lenny decided he would climb up the stairs and peak inside the Play Room, just to confirm that the map was correct.

Slowly they walked up the staircase while Lenny stared at his map. He could hear loud noises already, shouting and the sounds of things crashing to the floor. When they got to the door, Lenny recognized fifth grade students from his school. Instinctively he turned away. Then out of the corner of his eye, he noticed someone sitting on floor playing frozen. This was intriguing to him, since he didn't know any other autistic kids in his former school. the room and went toward the boy playing frozen against the wall.

He didn't go right up to the boy, but instead stayed a few feet away since playing frozen meant you didn't want to be with anyone.

Hector noticed the shadow of someone approaching him. At first, he covered his head more tightly with his arms.

Lenny waited patiently for the boy on the floor to react. He was now using his personal knowledge of autism to feel empathy for the other boy and to predict how he was feeling.

Finally Hector looked up at Lenny, and their eyes met. Hector recognized Lenny right away.

But Lenny did not recognize Hector.

"Lenny," Hector whispered.

This terrified Lenny. Who, other than Patricia, would know his name? Quickly he turned and started walking away.

"Lenny!" Hector called out, and jumped to his feet. "Wait! Stop!"

Lenny kept walking away, looking around for Patricia, who was deep in conversation with another adult.

Hector didn't call out again. He did not want to frighten Lenny any further. Instead he walked slowly toward Lenny, while Dietrich noticed that his brother had gotten up and began walking toward the two boys.

When Hector got close enough, he said quietly, "Hi, Lenny."

Lenny turned around and asked, "Who are you? I'm not supposed to talk to strangers."

"He's not a stranger," Dietrich chimed in as he approached. "He goes to your school."

"I'm Hector Fairfield."

"Don't tease me!"

"He's not teasing you. He really is Hector. Don't you recognize him?"

Lenny glanced quickly in Hector's direction. Even though he had a hard time noticing changes in other people, even he noticed the huge difference in the bully. For one thing, he didn't look like a bully anymore. He looked . . . Lenny didn't know how to describe another person in words, but he felt that Hector somehow looked autistic now. Gone was his confidence, and he looked scared, uncertain—and defeated.

"No," Lenny said. "The real Hector is a bully."

Hector thought about this for a moment, then said, "Maybe the real Hector used to be a bully, but not anymore. The real Hector is just like you. I don't know what's been going on for the past two weeks, but everyone is out to get me. I'm sorry for all the times I went after you. I had no idea what I was doing."

"Don't lie to me!" Lenny cried. "Who'd want to hurt you?"

"Everyone. I don't know what's been happening, but since this started, my life has been hell. People have been jumping on me for every little thing, yelling at me for no reason, and the only way I can escape is to sit on the floor and roll into a ball."

Lenny knew exactly how Hector felt. Still, it didn't make any sense.

"Why would anyone try to hurt you? You're making this up."

"I'm not making it up!" Hector felt a little desperate. He wanted Lenny to believe him.

"No, he's not making it," Dietrich said quietly.

By then Patricia had walked up to the three boys. "Lenny, what's going on?" she asked.

"I'm Hector Fairfield," Hector said. "I go to Lenny's school."

"I'm Hector's brother," Dietrich said. "Who are you?"

"My name is Patricia. I'm taking care of Lenny while his parents are away."

Dietrich looked around at the three faces and figured out what was going on. He already knew part of the story, but he'd figured out the rest. Lenny was the name of some weirdo kid his brother used to tease. This must be the kid who was the other part of the experiment. He was going to get in big trouble by revealing what was going on, yet he had to tell them the truth. His brother and this boy had been involved in a giant plot involving parents, teachers, and other students. It had to stop.

"Look, Hector . . . Lenny . . ."

"Young man . . ." Patricia warned. "Be careful what you tell them."

"I have to tell them. At least as much as I know," he told her, then turned to face Lenny and Hector. "I'm not quite sure why this all started, but apparently, bro, you've been a real pain in the ass at school."

"Yeah, I know," Hector said, looking down and even smiling a tiny bit in embarrassment.

"So the principal and some shrink thought up a plan to make you less like a bully. The shrink got the idea that kids like Lenny are quiet and scared because everyone gets angry at them and yells at them and teases them. So this guy talked everyone into yelling at you and punishing you and humiliating you for no reason—to see if you'd change."

"No way," Hector said.

"Way. Sorry, but that's what happened. And then—"

"That's enough," Patricia interrupted.

"No it's not," Dietrich declared, then continued, "Lenny was the other half of the experiment." To Lenny, he said, "What's been happening in your life?"

"My life changed, too," Lenny replied. "At first, my mother didn't pick me up from school, and I was terrified. But then Patricia told me that I was coming to live with her for two months while my parents were away."

"Are they really away?" Dietrich asked, scowling at the woman he knew was also in on the scheme.

Patricia bit her lip, realizing she'd been caught. Finally she said, "No, Lenny, your parents aren't in Bolinas. They're living in a hotel nearby."

Lenny suddenly had mixed feelings about this revelation. On the one hand, he wanted to see his parents again, but on the other hand, he liked living with Patricia and didn't want to go back to his old life.

"Is he right?" Lenny asked. "Am I part of an experiment?"

"Yes, Lenny," Patricia said sadly. "Dr. Wikedda and the psychologist wanted to prove that autism, like bullying, is environmental. They felt that you behave the way you do because your environment is confusing, you don't understand how to behave, and everyone is always telling you that you're wrong or that you're breaking a rule you didn't know existed. They thought that if they changed your environment, so that it was comprehensible and predictable, you would no longer be autistic. So they asked me to homeschool you for two months to see if you'd become normal."

Lenny thought about this for a moment then said, "Well, I have been much happier than I ever was before. And I'm not afraid of everything anymore. Life is even worth living, now that I don't have to go to school and be bullied."

"That's wonderful," Patricia exclaimed, clapping her hands once.

"But I'm still autistic," Lenny said. "That's what I am, and it won't change."

"And Hector isn't," Dietrich complained. "I think this whole thing was ridiculous—"

"DIETRICH!" someone screamed across the room.

They all turned and watched Mrs. Appell storming toward them.

"Yes, Mrs. Appell?" Dietrich called back.

"What is going on here?" She looked around at Hector, then Lenny, then Patricia. "Why are you talking to these people? You should have been watching Carly and Robert. They're tearing up the place."

"Sorry, Mrs. Appell," Dietrich said, "but we're having an important conversation."

"You're what?" she demanded.

"We're talking about the . . . experiment. And don't say you weren't in on it. I know you were. Right, Hector?"

Hector thought about all the times in the past two weeks that Mrs. Appell had punished him for no reason, and he concurred. "Right."

Mrs. Appell realized that her cover was blown, but she suddenly felt afraid of the consequences. What if Hector's parents sued her . . .

"I don't know what you're talking about, young man, but it's time for all of us to get back on the bus." Turning to Patricia, she said, "And you are . . . ?"

"Call me Patricia. I'm in on the experiment, too. My job was to treat Lenny Fahrer with kindness and with respect, things that everyone is entitled to, to see if it would cure his autism."

Mrs. Appell looked skeptically at Lenny. "And did it?" she asked.

Everyone looked toward Lenny for an answer. He thought for a moment, then said, "No. it did not. I'm still the same person."

"But I'm not," said Hector quietly, looking down at his feet.

# Chapter 28

*April 8, 2010—7 p.m.*
*The Fahrer Residence*

Patricia Nottingham was now faced with a dilemma. She had lived with Lenny for two weeks, but the experiment could no longer continue. Did that mean she could no longer homeschool Lenny? Would she have to give the money back?

On the train home, Lenny was in shock. He didn't know why the adults around him were so determined to change him. What was wrong with autism? What was autism anyway?

He was terrified that now he would have to return to his horrible life and that he was a failure because he hadn't magically turned into a normal boy like Hector, who got pleasure from hurting other people. Or he used to.

When they got home, Patricia knew it was time to call Lenny's parents. And so she did.

After she had explained to Christine, Lenny's mother, that another boy had spilled the beans about the experiment, Christine cried, "Another boy? What other boy? Wasn't this experiment supposed to be confidential?"

"Apparently not," Patricia said. "It turns out that Dr. Wikedda arranged to have another part to the experiment. She chose a normal bully and attempted to turn him into an autistic child by treating that boy the way everyone treats Lenny."

"What are you talking about?"

"Think about how you treat Lenny, and how many times you confused him, reprimanded him for everything he did, made him feel as if everything he did was wrong, told him—"

"Okay, enough. I get it. But you say that there was another boy in this experiment who was mistreated?"

"Yes, according to Lenny, he was a normal boy, you know, a bully."

"But how did his parents allow this?"

"Search me. Maybe they were bullies, too, when they were in school."

"I think it's time for all of us to confront Dr. Wikedda."

*April 9, 2010— 1 p.m.*
*Buffett Elementary School, Dr. Wikedda's Office*

Patricia couldn't sleep that night, wondering what was going to happen to both Lenny and Hector. The next morning she got a call from the Buffett School asking her to attend a meeting with the principal. She was told she could bring Lenny along.

When they arrived at the school that afternoon, she learned the Lenny's parents, Hector's parents, Hector, and Dr. Griffiths were also attending the meeting. When they walked into the conference room, Lenny saw his parents for the first time.

"Hi, Mom!" he said cheerfully.

"Oh, my goodness," his mother exclaimed. "You said hi to me without being reminded. How wonderful!" Then she walked up to her son and hugged him.

He did not flinch.

"What's going to happen now?" he asked.

"We're coming back home," she said. "And you don't seem terrified anymore. That's wonderful!"

"Well, an experiment is an experiment," Patricia remarked.

"This positive outcome can only be the result of the homeschooling," Dr. Griffiths observed.

Just then Dr. Wikedda walked into the room.

Everyone turned to her with hostile expressions on their faces. Trying to deflect their anger, she said, "Well, I see that everyone is here."

"Yes, and I think we all want to know the whole story about this *experiment*," Christine Fahrer said.

"Patricia?" Dr. Wikedda said. "Could you tell us how Lenny has been doing for the past two weeks?"

"Well, Lenny has gotten a lot better. When I first met him, he was withdrawn and unhappy. He was shutting down and doing what he called 'playing frozen.' But he gradually started coming out of his shell, and now he is willing to interact with me."

"Lenny?" Dr. Wikedda asked gently. "Do you feel better?"

Lenny looked down in his lap, afraid that if he gave the wrong answer, he might be sent back to school. If he said yes, that might mean the end of homeschooling because its mission was accomplished, but if he said no, then that might also mean the end of homeschooling because its mission was *not* accomplished.

Finally, he said, "Yes, I feel better, but does that mean I have to go back to school?"

Dr. Griffiths said, "Well, I'm not your parent, but I would say that if homeschooling has reduced your stress, then you should continue to learn at home."

Lenny smiled, something he rarely did.

"Does this mean," Christine began, "that my son is not a hopeless case after all?"

"Your son was never a hopeless case."

"Do you mean that he isn't autistic?"

Dr. Griffiths continued, "I didn't say that. I think your experiment showed that Lenny does indeed have autism, and in fact, I believe your experiment proves that autism exists. However, what you and much of the world's population call autism is not a disorder, but a logical reaction to stress and a mismatch with one's environment. What did Gandhi teach his fellow Indians to do in response to their oppressors? Freeze. Become motionless as a way to resist. Autistic children have taught us that if you threaten or hurt someone, they will act in a predictable way. Threaten or hurt a normal child, and if he cannot run away or fight you, he will react as Lenny did, by shutting down. Although an autistic person may not be able to build a building, he has the ability to feel pain and to be hurt. But take away the fear and the hurt, and the autistic response to the environment will lessen."

"You're right, Doctor," said Christine. "Maybe . . . it's not so bad that he has autism after all."

"Actually, Christine," said Dr. Griffiths, "last week a girl came into my office. She said she was your son's friend. And her mother asked me to evaluate her for autism, and I diagnosed her with it using the standards I told you about diagnosing girls differently. I ended up diagnosing her with autism, too. She has sensory issues with her clothing, struggles with taking notes in school, and was even set up by one of her classmates whom she thought was her friend. If there's any proof your son Lenny has autism, it's that his best friend ended up getting diagnosed with autism as well. Kids with autism can become the best of friends . . . and autistic kids often find that they get along better with the opposite gender."

"What about my son?" Lydia Fairfield demanded. "He was living a wonderful life before you tampered with it. How can I get him back?"

*I don't want to go back to the way I was*, Hector thought, then quickly clamped his mouth shut. If he expressed an opinion, he was certain the adults would jump on him.

Turning to Dr. Wikedda, Dr. Griffiths warned, "Stop doing what you're doing. You're engaging in a dangerous psychological experiment involving children."

"It's over as of this moment," she reassured him, although inside she was feeling utter disappointment at losing the Nobel Prize.

"Will my Hector ever be the same?" Mrs. Fairfield wailed.

*I hope not*, Lenny thought to himself.

"Only time will tell," said Dr. Griffiths. "But all of you learned how quickly a child can deteriorate when treated abusively. How many days did it take for Hector to make a complete personality change?"

Mrs. Fairfield thought for a moment, then said, "Only a few days. And after two weeks, he ran away from school and hid in the forest preserve."

"Now you have a better understanding of why Lenny might have been hiding himself away from all of you."

"And what about Lenny? Will he go back to withdrawing from every-one?" asked Lenny's mother.

"If he goes back to school, perhaps yes," Dr. Griffiths said. "But if he stays at home, he might—"

Dr. Wikedda interrupted, "Don't listen to him. Lenny belongs in school."

"You saw how he changed, Patricia," Dr. Griffiths argued.

"Yes, I did," Patricia agreed.

"I guess I'll have to do it," said Lenny's mother. "The truth is, he's been in speech therapy in school for four years, but until today he never said hi to me without prompting. He's made more progress in the last two weeks than he had in those four years. But I can't teach him myself. He's always been so difficult."

"I'll be starting a charter school next year," Patricia said. "Lenny can be my first student."

Lenny didn't say anything, but inside he was smiling. Even though he would have to go back to school until June, at least he wouldn't have to return after the summer. The time would pass quickly.

# Epilogue

And the truth was, time did go by quickly. Lenny left school in June as happy as any other child. Over the summer he spent a lot of time with Patricia, telling her what he wanted to study, and visiting the old woman downstairs, who finally got around to telling him about the 1950s.

Of course, Alice and Lenny remained friends and would have frequent playdates, understanding each other because of their shared experiences as autistic children. Lenny's autism did not change, but the experiment proved that his life could change for the better in spite of his basic nature. Claire remained Alice and Lenny's friends, and did not abandon her friends even after Alice was diagnosed as autistic. Tammy did not get rejected by Wendy and Lisa—they stayed friends and remained a tight-knit group of friends that later on, in middle and high school, became a feared clique of popular, but mean girls.

Hector's life after the experiment became happy once more. Everyone who bullied him apologized and said they would never treat him like that again. They returned to their normal behavior. Hector, however, did not return to his previous behavior. For he, like Lenny, was permanently changed. Ever since he'd started school, he had teased and hurt other children. No one questioned it, and he assumed that it was normal, acceptable behavior. He himself had not found anything wrong with it. No one told him to think about what his victims felt like, and so he never had.

Until the experiment. Now he knew what it was like to be one of those children. He started feeling sorry for the outcasts and the weirdos of the world. He started feeling sorry for Lenny—or at least the Lenny that he once knew. After the experiment was finished, Hector never bullied another child again. He even stopped being friends with bullies.

Though Lenny did not return to school, he and Hector talked to each other—over the phone and when they would happen to meet in a store or on the playground. Hector apologized to Lenny, and Lenny forgave him. They did not become friends, but they were always civil to each other.

The years flew by for Hector, Alice, and Lenny. As teenagers, Lenny and Alice helped each other cope with the physical changes they were going through without giving a second thought about appropriateness or awkwardness because of their differing genders. Alice graduated from high school, went to college for one year, then got a job as a one-on-one aide for a high-functioning autistic girl whose social struggles were similar to what Alice had endured in school. Hector graduated from high school, went to college to study biology, and got a job working for the Cook County Forest Preserve, having never forgotten his one magical night with the plants and animals in the woods. Lenny spent the rest of his educational career at Patricia's charter school—since she did not return Dr. Wikedda's money and had her start-up capital—and he became one of her best students. He learned how to advocate for his disability, how to speak out about things that bothered him, and he finally started giving presentations about autism. He eventually became a well-known advocate and speaker on autism, traveling around the country regularly, and gaining the respect of parents, teachers, and health professionals.

None of them remembered much of what they learned in grade school, but Lenny and Hector would never forget what they had learned when trading their lives. Meanwhile, Alice felt proud that she, too, had autism, and could use her personal knowledge of this disability to help other girls like her.

Claire, after graduating from high school, went to college and became an elementary school social worker. Having not forgotten what happened to her and Alice, she used her experiences to help other students struggling with social difficulties. As for Tammy, after graduating from high school with her two friends, she started a painting business and became a successful painter in Lake Forest, having not forgotten skills from her paint peeling days.

Dr. Wikedda remained principal of Buffett Elementary School and eventually retired, coming to terms with the fact that she never would become famous. She never did publish the results of the H.A.L. Experiment. Too risky. But had her three subjects been changed for the better? She liked to think so. In their hearts, they knew that they'd been changed for good.